Jimmy Reardon had to take a break. Too much was going down too fast.

One girl had taken him for the money he needed to go to college.

Another girl was going to destroy his bond with his best friend if he ever found out what she and Jimmy were doing together every Saturday afternoon.

Still another was going to drain him of every ounce of his energy if she didn't let up on her inventive fun and games.

And his own girl friend was going to rob him of his sanity if she didn't stop blowing hot and cold.

Jimmy Reardon had made up his mind. He definitely had to take some time off—if he ever found the time . . .

JIMMY REARDON

(Originally titled
Aren't You Even Gonna
Kiss Me Good-by?)

William Richert

A SIGNET BOOK
NEW AMERICAN LIBRARY

PUBLISHER'S NOTE

This book is a work of fiction. Names, characters, places, and incidents either are the product of the author's imagination or are used fictitiously, and any resemblance to actual persons, living or dead, events, or locales is entirely coincidental.

NAL BOOKS ARE AVAILABLE AT QUANTITY DISCOUNTS WHEN USED TO PROMOTE PRODUCTS OR SERVICES. FOR INFORMATION PLEASE WRITE TO PREMIUM MARKETING DIVISION, NEW AMERICAN LIBRARY, 1633 BROADWAY, NEW YORK, NEW YORK 10019.

This book originally appeared as *Aren't You Even Gonna Kiss Me Good-by?*

SIGNET TRADEMARK REG. U.S. PAT. OFF. AND FOREIGN COUNTRIES
REGISTERED TRADEMARK—MARCA REGISTRADA
HECHO EN CHICAGO, U.S.A.

SIGNET, SIGNET CLASSIC, MENTOR, ONYX, PLUME, MERIDIAN and NAL BOOKS are published by NAL PENGUIN INC., 1633 Broadway, New York, New York 10019

First Signet Printing, July, 1987

1 2 3 4 5 6 7 8 9

PRINTED IN THE UNITED STATES OF AMERICA

To Leonard Kantor

FRIDAY night in early September. Outside, the rain was exploding on the streets, but it was warm and dry in the Hub, where the sound of the downpour was overcome by the wild sounds of a juke box.

Nervously crippling his straw in three places, Jimmy glanced at the empty booths. The long, narrow restaurant, which had proved so fruitful on other nights, was an empty church pew tonight. Of all nights!

Across from him, Fred bit the end off a dill pickle. "I say screw it. It's a bust."

Jimmy looked at him in disgust. There were still twenty minutes left.

"The deal was, we wait till two o'clock," he said.

Fred sighed. "I'm getting tired of sitting around. My ass is even getting numb."

"Do you want to give up? Is that what you're trying to tell me?"

"For the past two hours," acknowledged Fred, pushing his glasses up on his short, stumpy nose. "Ever since we left the Dead Pigeon, in fact."

"All right," said Jimmy, pissed off. "Be the only Harvard freshman who's still got a full-bloomed cherry! But how're you going to feel when they ask you how many times you've scored, for crissakes? Those Ivy league schools send out questionnaires on that stuff, y'know."

"I'll lie," said Fred.

"If that's your attitude, we'll forget the whole thing," Jimmy bluffed, starting to leave the booth. But Fred rose to follow him, so Jimmy sat back down.

"I really don't know what to say to you, Fred,"

Jimmy began again solemnly. "All the hours I spent teaching you everything I knew—"

"Shit, you made most of it up," interrupted Fred.

Jimmy ignored that. "—helping you win back Denise—" He usually avoided any discussion of Denise Hunter, Fred's girl friend, because of things Fred didn't know about. But this was an emergency.

"It's not the same thing," said Fred.

"What's the difference! It's friendship, isn't it?"

"A hundred and ten dollars," said Fred. "That's the difference. I might have loaned it to you as a friend, but you didn't ask me as a friend. It was your idea to ask me as a pimp."

Ask Frederick Bowles Roberts as a friend. As if Jimmy hadn't tried. . . .

Fred was standing in the doorway in response to Jimmy's ring, wearing white socks, tan pants, a button-down shirt, and a glass of Ovaltine, and he said accusingly: "You've caught another venereal disease!" Like he was from Rome and wore a skullcap and had Roman numerals after his name.

"Something else," Jimmy said. "I'm desperate. Can we talk inside?"

They glided over thick carpets to the game room of Fred's house which had the biggest damn lawn and guest-house garage in Weston, Illinois, and then Jimmy was leaning against a billiard table surrounded by seascapes Fred's mother painted-by-the-numbers. He put out a cigarette in the ashtray that Fred's father called pre-Columbian art and started to speak, but Fred stopped him with one more stab: "You're going through another abortion!"

Jimmy almost wished it were another abortion, just to make Fred happy, but it was worse than that, much worse. "It isn't a new abortion," said Jimmy. "It's that when I got home tonight, my old man let me know he found out about the *old* one!"

"I told you something like that would happen," Fred said loftily.

Jimmy refrained from hitting the bastard right in the goddamn eyeglasses and went on: "And now he won't give me the tuition to the University of Northern Illinois—unless I get the hundred-ten back by noon tomorrow!"

"So you want me to give it to you, the money you spent on some girl's abortion—that's what you came here for," said Fred.

Jimmy bowed his head and had to admit it.

Whereupon Fred clasped his hands behind his back and looked towards heaven, which his relatives were probably leasing for tax purposes. "I see. You thought of me because I've loaned you money before, under other circumstances; like the time I gave you seventeen dollars and thirteen cents for the music box you gave your beloved Lisa on her birthday. Like the time I generously advanced you eight dollars and six cents because you wanted to take Lisa to the London House after the prom. You came to me, dear schmuck, because all this summer long I've driven you and your beloved Lisa to the beach and never once asked you to contribute gas money."

Jimmy had had to sit through an accounting of every time Fred put his hand in his pocket to buy him some popcorn, and in the end be turned down anyway.

And that's why Jimmy had been forced to come up with a brilliant scheme. At least, it was brilliant when he first thought of it, because it capitalized on Fred's condition, which was chronic virginity.

Jimmy knew that deep down Fred was ashamed of his handicap, and had desperately but unsuccessfully tried to change it. Even a wide-open Vassar freshman, home on Christmas vacation, had pulled down her mistletoe when she saw him coming. Jimmy, on the other hand, had laid seven distinct and separate girls—a few of them more than once—so tonight, when he'd offered to employ this uncanny ability in Fred's behalf, in return for one hundred and ten dollars, it was like doing them both a favor.

At first Fred had balked at the scheme. Why should he give Jimmy that much money when he could get a working whore for ten? To this, Jimmy had very sanely pointed out that Fred didn't know where to find one, and even if he did, he'd be too scared to approach her.

Not to mention that tonight was Friday, and Fred was leaving this Sunday; not much time to stall. Could he really leave Illinois, go all the way to Massachusetts, or wherever the hell Harvard was, in his condition? Might Fred's fears not worsen in a new environment? Jesus, four more years of celibacy could render him incapable of any future action!

Finally, Fred agreed to the proposition, providing, naturally, Fred being Fred, the hundred-ten was considered a loan. So they stormed every likely spot in Weston, from the White Castle to the Dead Pigeon expresso house. But because of the rain, every place was dead. The only probable score they found turned out to have a nine-hundred pound boyfriend and a "killer's instinct," in Fred's own words.

Now here they were, sitting across each other in a pink booth at the Hub, Weston's last unstormed citadel; empty, at twenty minutes till two o'clock, except for one lousy, pregnant, Oriental waitress. Jimmy's whole future was ebbing away minute by minute while Fred grappled with corned beef sandwich, complained of a numb ass, and spouted off about pimps!

"It was your idea to make this a strictly cash proposition," said Fred. "I was perfectly willing to go along. Is it my fault that as a pimp, you're nowhere?"

"Quit calling me a pimp!" glowered Jimmy.

He was about to sacrifice everything by telling the smug sonofabitch to go fuck off when he caught sight of possible salvation coming through the restaurant door wearing a ponytail and a fuzzy gray coat. He watched over Fred's shoulder as she neared their booth.

"Wait a minute," said Jimmy. "I've still got twenty minutes, right?"

He watched the girl circle the place and light in a booth directly across from them. Oblivious to Jimmy's attention, she took off a rain-drenched scarf and wiped her freckled face with a paper napkin before patting her damp red hair into place. It was all accomplished with mathematical precision, and now she dove into an oversized pouch to come up with a thick paperback book, which she bent open on the table.

With affected uncaring, Fred glanced in her direction. "You've got fifteen minutes."

"If I can slice it for you, you'll lend me the hundred-ten?" Jimmy was making sure.

Fred rubbed his ass. "Go."

Jimmy waited until the pregnant Chinese waitress took the girl's order before leaning into the aisle with the smile that conquers.

"Hi," he said. "What're you reading?"

She was the natural type, with a shiny nose and no lipstick, and the smile made no impression on her.

"Kierkegaard," she said, barely glancing up.

"Looks interesting, the way you're reading it," said Jimmy.

"He's a gas." She said it like other people say shut up. He sat back in his booth.

"Fourteen minutes," said Fred.

"Give me a chance, will you!" said Jimmy, studying the girl as her reddish-brown eyes licked the print in quick, thirsty rolls. When she looked up to sweeten her coffee, he tried again.

"Sure isn't very swingin' in here tonight."

Using her finger as a bookmark, she glanced around the restaurant to verify the statement, then nodded.

"Summer vacation," explained Jimmy. "Really moves here during the winter, though."

"You go to Northwestern?" she asked, stirring her coffee.

"University of Chicago," Jimmy lied. "Me and my friend. Juniors."

"Good school," she said, looking over to include Fred, who grinned and dropped his eyes.

"You go to Northwestern?" said Jimmy.

"Sophomore." She threw it away.

"What's your major?" he persisted.

"Political science, and don't ask me why," she said.

"You could always go into the Foreign Service," said Fred, without looking up from his dill pickle. She laughed, and Jimmy seized the opportunity to press onward: "I'd like you to meet Fred Roberts," he said quickly.

"Elaine," she said in a way that promised no further

intimacy. "You don't know a George Stilton, do you? He goes to Chicago. A senior, I think." She spoke to Jimmy.

"George Stilton. . . ." Jimmy pretended to examine his memory. "Sounds familiar. Say Fred, you know a George Stilton?" Fred shook his head.

"Can't know them all," Jimmy said lamely.

At that, she slipped back to Kierkegaard. With a triumphant grin, Fred leaned across the table to Jimmy.

"Just because a girl's got a pulse rate doesn't mean she's in heat!"

Jimmy glared at him, but said nothing. There was nothing to say. He'd just have to face Father and tell him he couldn't make it. In a way, the old man was right. Jimmy had no one to blame for his predicament but himself.

It had all started in the Dead Pigeon on a Wednesday night three weeks after graduation. Jimmy had just finished reading one of his greatest poems, "I Was Talking to God Last Night but God Wasn't Talking to Me," when he noticed two chicks in the corner of the room. They were drinking hot cider under a painting of a Negro dancer with yellow eyes.

Since there were only seven people in the whole place, counting two waitresses and a cook, Jimmy capitulated after a sparse round of applause, turned off the microphone, and weaved among the wooden tables to approach the prettiest of the two girls. Hidden behind thick, purple, glow-in-the-dark lipstick, and mascara that crawled an inch sideways out of each eye, she laughed softly with her girl friend, who was topped like shortcake with whipped pink hair.

"Hello, ladies," said Jimmy, straddling the chair in the hippest way. But the girls went right on talking about a red Corvette and its owner, who apparently had been arrested because he wore straight pipes, or something. Neither of them exactly acknowledged Jimmy's presence, but the pretty one flicked the ash of her purple-tipped cigarette on his shoe, which she didn't *have* to do, so that was an indication of something.

"Jimmy Reardon's the name," he announced loudly.

"I read original poetry here. You may have seen my name on the program."

The pretty one returned the purple-tipped cigarette to her purple, glow-in-the-dark lips and told him with the ultimate in last words that if he didn't go away, she'd call the manager.

Two days later, Jimmy screwed her on the Oriental rug in the living room at her grandmother's house. Even then, while he was doing it, he thought about how he might catch something from her or maybe even get her pregnant. He thought about it, but that didn't stop him. It didn't stop him three times that night.

Some weeks after that, she telephoned and said she'd been knocked up and needed to get married or have an abortion, so Jimmy gave her one hundred and ten dollars out of the money he'd saved for college by working part-time at Mr. Spaulding's photography studio, and considered himself pretty goddamn lucky.

Until he found out about three other guys who'd paid for the same abortion. When he tried to locate the pretty one, she'd moved on. What happened was Jimmy had been swindled by a sixteen-year-old con woman.

"Eleven minutes," said Fred, with all the charm of Poe's raven. His wide mouth was crunching ice.

Jimmy stared pensively at the black-framed copy of *Stars and Stripes,* Paris edition, announcing the death of President Roosevelt, which hung over the delicatessen counter. Eleven minutes. What the hell. Abruptly, he leaned into the aisle once again.

"Say, Fred just came up with a great idea."

Elaine looked up questioningly; Fred swallowed the ice whole.

Jimmy talked fast. "This place is closing in a few minutes, and Fred thought it might be fun if we all went out for coffee. Fred's got a car, so there's no problem about transportation."

"I have one too," said Elaine.

"There's no use taking two cars, right Fred?" Jimmy laughed nervously. Fred giggled.

"Where's there to go?" said Elaine.

"Fred thinks the Dead Pigeon might be fun."

"The what?"

"An expresso place. You know, poetry reading, folk singers. We were there before it started to swing, but it ought to be moving fine now."

Elaine looked speculatively from one to the other. Now Fred was counting matches.

"It's only six blocks from here," urged Jimmy, sounding more desperate than he'd intended. "Just to relieve the monotony," he added to cool it off.

"Okay." She decided all at once, and dropping Kierkegaard into the pouch and whisking her tab off the table, she slid out of the booth to the accompaniment of Jimmy's bubbling stomach.

"Don't worry about the tab," he said, snatching it from her. "Fred'll charge it to one of his old man's department stores." He delivered the girl's check, along with a victor's smile, to old pale-faced Frederick Bowles Roberts. "See you in the car," he said airily, leading his hundred-ten dollars out the restaurant door into the rain.

They had to make a run for it. When they got to Fred's car, Jimmy opened the rear door for Elaine to enter, but she demurred. "I like to sit up front," she said, choosing her own door to open. This put her in the front seat alongside the driver, screwing up the plan to get her in the back seat to wait for Fred. Jimmy now had no course but to slide in under the steering wheel beside her.

As Elaine proceeded to undo the barrette on her ponytail, releasing the girl-smell of her hair, Jimmy, fogging the windows with his breath, anxiously watched for Fred.

Moments passed in silence while the rain pelted the roof and streams coursed down the windshield, making the car a cozy little island. To break the spell, Jimmy turned on the radio and got a thousand violins shimmering love music. Frantically, he switched the dial to the final brass sounds of "The Star Spangled Banner" and felt his teeth shake from the volume.

"I guess that station's off the air," shouted Elaine above the din.

"Guess so," answered Jimmy.

She shut off the radio. "What did you say?"

"I said it must be."

"What?"

"Going off the air. The station."

"Oh. Yeah."

They lapsed into silence. He ran his hands around the slick steering wheel while she bent her head down, struggling to put her barrette in place. Out of the corner of his reluctant eye, Jimmy saw a little bone appear at the base of her neck, below the rising tufts of hair. Looking more frankly now, he saw that her nose was straight, kind of right for her face, and that a small drop of water clinging to her chin glistened when she turned.

"Could you put your finger here?" said Elaine, wiggling her ponytail. "Just pinch it."

That's what really started it. If it was undecided before, it jumped to a quick decision now as he obediently pinched her ponytail and she clasped the barrette over it.

"Thanks," she said.

Returning his hand to the wheel he said, "Fred must've gotten lost in the rain."

"My brother's name is Fred," she said meaninglessly. "He's in the Army."

"Fred's in the R.O.T.C.," said Jimmy, not missing a bet. "Officer material."

It wasn't clear whether he'd moved closer to her, or she'd moved closer to him, but there they were, and he could feel the pressure all the way up to his earlobes. Jesus, what the hell was keeping Fred?

"Wish I had Fred's brains," said Jimmy. "The guy barely cracks a book—straight A's every time."

His hands were growing tired from their tight grip on the wheel, so he placed his arm on top of the seat. Elaine rested her head on his sleeve and stared thoughtfully at the ceiling. It was the wrong thing for her to do, but he couldn't just rudely take his arm away. Instead, he'd have to look at the soft curve of her neck, follow the white arc with his eyes until it disappeared into the darkness of her coat.

Elaine sighed. "Rain—I love it—don't you?"

"Me? I don't know. But *Fred* does—a lot."

"I like the sound of it," she said. "Makes me melt, kind of."

Jimmy couldn't keep diverting his basic instincts forever; it was unnatural and it hurt besides. Maybe he should give Elaine a bit of a once-over. Sort of classify her availability. After all, it would be cruel to put her alongside a shy kid like Fred if she was the frigid type. Hell, if she screamed or slapped him or anything, it might keep Fred from women the rest of his life! It was practically a moral responsibility to find out. . . . Gently, he raised his arm, and, lo 'n behold, she slid right down until her head rested on his cheek.

Then the strangest thing happened. Her tongue was suddenly halfway down his throat. And if that wasn't the most curious thing, what happened next was positively astounding because he certainly had no intention of allowing his hand to explore her breasts. And how her body got into the cove of his legs, he'd never know! Nor could he ever explain how his fingers found the little bristles of hair tickling his palm, and found willingness there. How easy it was to roll into position in spite of the steering wheel! Just a little further down and the two nations would be united into one single—

Holy shit!

The door sprang open and Jimmy was looking straight into Fred's eyes. The round face was suspended in the rain for a second, then suddenly, it was gone.

Jimmy ran after it, zipping his fly.

"Fred!" he shouted, rain streaming down his cheeks and dripping off his chin.

Fred ran very fast, but Jimmy managed to grab his arm and hold it.

"What're you getting so pissed off about?"

"Let go!" Fred said, struggling. But Jimmy held tight.

"Jesus, I was only priming her up for you!"

"Like hell! You couldn't control yourself! Your goddamn pecker leads you around like a mule chasing a carrot!"

"But I didn't even get it in! We were waiting for you!"

"Balls!" Fred broke free, but Jimmy got him in another grip.

"I swear, Fred!"

"Bullshit!"

"Let's go back to the car, I'll prove it!"

"I hope like hell you get another venereal disease," Fred shouted as Jimmy dragged him back to the car.

"I'm telling you, she's crazy about you! I was only a temporary substitute," Jimmy said, breathless from the struggle.

But when they reached the car it was clear that Jimmy's argument had deserted him. Elaine was gone.

Moments later, Jimmy found himself in the rain with the six pack he'd stowed away in the back seat of Fred's car. Without another word of explanation or apology, the sonofabitch was making him walk home in all this downpour. Jimmy began his trek up the street even as the motor started and he saw, out of the corner of his eye, the car pull away with Fred at the wheel.

Oh, well. There was something noble about trudging home in a storm, like Napoleon on the way back from Russia, except that was snow. Jimmy adopted a military gait. Snow or rain—it's not much different. In the end, it's all water.

He'd advanced a block and a half when, in the middle of an embarrassing struggle for his dignity, which is to say, the struggle to keep the cans of beer from dropping out of the rain-soaked container, Fred's car appeared alongside him.

"Come on, let's go," said Fred.

It was Jimmy's turn to say balls.

"You don't want a lift?" Fred got no answer. "Okay," he said matter-of-factly. "I'll pick you up in the morning if it stops raining."

It was beyond human comprehension, what Fred did then! With an amiable wink, a smile even, the guy rolled up the window and pulled away, leaving Jimmy where he was before! For the second time!

Spraying water from its wheels, Fred's car disappeared up the street.

Jimmy walked on, clamping the slippery cans to his

chest, blinking away a fat raindrop which landed smack in his left eye. For some reason he didn't feel much like Napoleon anymore; he felt closer to the Little Match Girl.

He stepped into a doorway and carefully set his beer cans on the concrete. One of the cans went pop as he pulled the pin. A goddamn hand grenade! His mouth filled with the bubbling liquid, and in three seconds, exactly, it was gone. Practically nobody in the whole United States could drain a half-quart can of Schlitz in three seconds. He was getting that Napoleon feeling again. One marvelous burp later, clutching the five full and one empty to him, he moved on to continue his wet, miserable journey.

When you thought about it, who the hell remembers the names of all the rich, stingy, heartless people who fucked up the Little Match Girl? And who would herald the name of Frederick Bowles Roberts? Nobody, and you could be sure that when Jimmy got famous, he'd see it was dropped from all *his* biographies. But not the old man. He'd give Father an entire chapter, two maybe, so future generations could see for themselves the sort of adversities James A. Reardon was made to overcome in his youth. . . .

Another doorway, another pop, six seconds this time because he was tired from walking so much.

In the chapter entitled "The Tragic Years," in the *Collected Reardon Papers: New, Revised Edition,* Columbia University Press, 997 pps., 1983, the entire goddamn mess would be spelled out. The whole truth about how when Mr. James A. Reardon was almost eighteen and had just graduated from high school three months before, was still, in fact, dependent on the good graces of his bastard father, he was ruthlessly and for no actual reason whatever threatened with imprisonment in the snobbish suburb of Weston, where he lived in utter misery with his two parents, sister, and brother in a six-room apartment with almost no furniture, which was of great embarrassment to young James when he wished to invite his young friends over. The chapter, of great interest to Reardon buffs the world over, would list unexpurgatedly the story about how the sonofabitch old man tried to deprive the world of Mr. Reardon's talent forever because of one night on an Oriental rug. . . .

Another doorway. Took a bit more concentration to get the can to pop properly this time, but soon there were two more empty cans in Jimmy's little nest, and that made his load easier to carry. It also made the rain seem warm and not nearly as wet.

And so anyhow, Jesus dammit, Mr. Reardon Senior did willfully tell his oldest son, after unmercifully confronting him with a lot of hollering and screaming, that because Mr. Reardon had caused this girl an abortion, which wasn't even true, and even if it was, shit, he was young and never had an abortion before, doesn't that count for something? So now young Reardon found himself deprived of the one thing he wanted most in the world: to take his rightful place in the academic circles of the University of Northern Illinois, a former state teachers institution which boasted a boy-girl ratio of four-to-one, though that wasn't the reason James wished to go there. . . .

To lighten his load still further, Jimmy knelt down on the sidewalk and unpopped one of his two remaining cans. Since he hadn't timed the last two, and to keep his records in order, he counted eight seconds for this one, a bit over the limit, but what the hell.

Anyway, Mr. Reardon's sonofabitch father told his son he wouldn't send him to college if the young lad couldn't raise a hundred and ten lousy dollars! Crime against humanity. And none of young Reardon's trusted companions, whose names are omitted here, would lend him the money, even though Mr. Reardon had helped them out, especially in affairs concerning Denise Hunter, details of which are also omitted. Besides which, if Mr. Reardon couldn't join the academic circles of the University of Northern Illinois, that meant he'd have to get a job in Weston while almost all the kids of the rich-race cartwheeled to Harvard and Yale and other eastern places. . . .

A brick wall somewhere allowed Jimmy to lean against it while he popped the last can and finished it on the spot. Getting crocked absolutely, and it was beautiful.

Moreover, Mr. Reardon Senior did this to his son after all that bullshit he spouted about opportunity. Senior was the get-out-and-find-opportunity type because he was born poor, and still was, when Jimmy thought about it. And what the hell did the old man know about recognizing opportunity? He wouldn't know it if it kicked him in the ass. The only reason the sonofabitch was still working at the plant was because the company couldn't afford another Xerox machine. . . .

One of his little baby beer cans fell from his arms and clattered into the street. He stumbled after it, but as he bent over, two more dropped into the flooded gutter, giving him the desperate problem of saving three of his kin from the raging river. Wasn't easy, but now he set them on the curb, artfully piling them into a pyramid: three on the bottom, two next, and one on top. As he surveyed his newly-created aluminum empire, he noticed a familiar building across the street, and found himself under the El, looking into the candle-lit windows of the Dead Pigeon. What he should do was get up from the curb and zoom across the street and read some of his poems to meet another broad, because he really didn't get it in the last time, which Fred didn't believe because the guy was a virgin and didn't believe anything, didn't even know what "in" was, for crissakes. Except the chairs were piled on the Pigeon's wooden tables. The place was closed. Wow, after three-thirty; Saturday already. And Jimmy had to go to the beach in the morning if it ever stopped raining.

Suddenly his beautiful pyramid toppled, and the six cans scattered on the sidewalk. He realized it was caused by the vibrations of a racketing train approaching overhead, could see its lights flickering through the tracks, and it pissed him off, it really pissed him off.

He grabbed a can and let it fly at the train, but it missed and soared through the tiers to make a distant clatter up the street. The second one scored smack on the tracks but it wasn't enough, so Jimmy waded into the gutter for the rest of his ammunition, throwing can after can with increasing fury at the monster flying overhead, drowning out all the sounds of the night.

Then suddenly he was standing there exhausted, one foot on the curb and the other in the water and the train was gone.

But something else was taking the monster's place. Like giant moons they raced toward him from the darkness, coming from all directions at once. He ran fast and found a shadow somewhere and ducked into it, kneeling down to make himself small. It didn't help; a piercing-bright light in his face. Then:

"All right, buddy." A cop. His companion remained seated in the squad car parked a few feet from Jimmy's hiding place.

"Pardon me, officer?" Jimmy blinked in the light.

"Get up, kid," said the cop.

"Do I have to?"

The cop took Jimmy's arm, raised him to his feet.

"What's your name?" he said. "Where'd you get the liquor?"

The cop was holding his arm tightly, police-brutality style. Best not to mention that, though. "What beer?" said Jimmy.

"Let's see some I.D."

While Jimmy searched all the wrong pockets for his wallet, the other cop left the patrol car. "Hey, look at that," he said, pointing to the blood staining Jimmy's pants at the knee.

"Better get him to emergency," one of the cops said. "Before he puts a dent in the blood bank."

"That's all right, I can walk," Jimmy said, limping pitifully. One of the cops picked up a broken whiskey bottle with a single glistening spire.

"Jesus," said Jimmy, staring at it. "Maybe I'm mortally wounded. Do you think they'll amputate or something?" He himself didn't know whether he was kidding or not.

"You'll be okay, kid," said the cop, leading him to the car. "Let's go," he told the driver.

Jimmy leaned back in the seat of the patrol car, and the beer dizziness flooded him. Sound, objects, and movement merged to make everything far away. . . .

Later, he remembered speeding toward the hospital and hearing himself say something which made the driver laugh. After a while, some doors opened, lots of doors, and a shiny counter seemed to slide by as the cold whiteness of the hospital surrounded him. He remembered particularly an intern with a bland face and blinking eyes and a steel bed rolling out from somewhere, which Jimmy was stretched out on while someone was telling him that the hole in his leg was not serious at all and could be closed up with some simple embroidery. He didn't mind the humor. He'd foxed them; the cut would keep him out of jail. Then Jimmy saw a patrolman talking to his mother. She wore her cotton nightgown under her coat and didn't seem very happy about how Jimmy foxed the cops. She couldn't imagine where her son obtained the beer, he'd heard her say, and she began to cry while a two-hundred-and-fifty pound nurse looked soulfully into Jimmy's eyes. He bet himself she never got laid in her life, though he didn't say anything. Meanwhile his parent was on again, saying dumb things like her son will never get into trouble like this again, officer, and she'll keep him in line in the future and thank you officer for your kindness. As he walked down the hall beside his tight lipped, interior-suffering mother, a young woman came running towards them with a baby in her arms crying, "It's all right, it's all right," and was led away. He remembered to let his mother out of the hospital door first, the way she was always reminding him to do, then followed her into the car while she said mother things about what a disappointment he was, and what would his father say. It all became a part of a too familiar tune he could whistle in his dreams. But soon he was climbing the stairway to the apartment and limping into his room while Mother drank milk of magnesia in the kitchen. He peeled off his clothes, letting them fall where they might, and finally he was in bed, and sleep, all too-welcome sleep, was pulling him inside out. . . .

"Hey, Jimmy!" A shrill voice called. It was attached to Rosie, his ten-year-old sister, a small girl with nervous eyebrows and long black hair.

Jimmy shut his eyes. If he were asleep, maybe she'd commit suicide or go to the bathroom or something. She was always going to the bathroom.

"Jimmeee, wake up!" said Rosie, now halfway in the room.

"Uuumph," said Jimmy, with all the anger he could muster.

"I have to tell you something," she said urgently, stamping her foot and slapping her arms against her skirt like an excited penguin.

"Go 'way," Jimmy said. "Beat it!"

"Okay," she agreed like the snot she was, "if you don't want the money. . . ."

He sat up. "What?"

" 'Course, it's not a hundred-ten dollars."

"What do you know about a hundred-ten dollars?" said Jimmy.

"I heard all about how you've got to have it to go away to school. And I know how you can get some of it, anyhow."

"How?" Jimmy said, in spite of himself.

Raising her arms high in the air, then crashing them down on her head: "I've got Toby and Jack and Mike, all of them are going out this morning as soon as Toby finishes his breakfast, if he ever does, but I need one more because this lady just called who needs a hedge job. You don't have to know anything about a hedge job because it's very easy actually. I could teach you in a minute if you want to."

"What the hell are you talking about!" interrupted Jimmy.

"I'm telling you! This lady called me up this morning and wanted to know if I have a kid who'll do a hedge job this morning. You can still work for Mister Spaulding later like you have to, and she'll pay you a dollar an hour; 'course I get fifteen cents so you only get eighty-five cents, but that's only because I do all the real work about getting the jobs. It's two hours work so that means you can get almost two dollars!"

Jesus, had it come to this? Exploited by a ten-year-old capitalist!

"Get out!" he shouted.

Rosie clicked her tongue the way Mother did sometimes. "Just like Father says, you'll never 'mount to a pile of you-know-what! "

Jimmy made a threatening move toward her.

"Lazy bum," she said, and slammed the door.

JIMMY'S bedroom, about twice the size of a small bathroom, was located off the kitchen in the rear of the apartment. Its windows looked down across an alley to the dingy backyards and gray wooden landings of a row of identical private houses. But even if it wasn't mountain greenery, the view outside was a hell of a lot better than the scenery inside. The room had been a nursery once, and no doubt the children who had occupied it then had long since died of old age. The wallpaper, yellowing and peeling near the floor and ceiling, depicted thousands of look-alike cowboys, each eternally frozen in his attempt to lasso a fiery-eyed longhorn steer. In case that wasn't enough, etched on the light fixture hugging the ceiling was some Indian's profile complete with feathered headdress to remind someone of his American heritage, or something.

Whatever its hideous decor, the room was at least Jimmy's own room, and getting it was about the best thing that happened to him since Father led his helpless brood to exclusive Weston. Two years ago they occupied spacious, less expensive, and far more comfortable rooms on Chicago's North Side, where none of the neighbors complained if dust mops were shaken out the windows. Only there, Jimmy had to share his room with Toby, who was a goddamn raving maniac in his sleep. Not only did the kid snort and rattle his dishes in the middle of the night, but once Jimmy woke up to find himself nailed to a pair of wild, staring eyes, under which a weird voice was threatening to kill him with a bicycle pump. So having Toby sleep on the living room couch and not in Jimmy's room was half an inch of paradise right there.

The room had other benefits, too. It was first to catch the morning light coming off Lake Michigan, and first to grow dark in the evening. That was good because when it got to be night, the cowboys and Indians went somewhere else to play, and the improvements were more prominent. Like the fishing net Jimmy swiped from a junk shop on downtown Maxwell Street; like the candles in Black Label Jim Beam bottles which, unfortunately, had only been lit once officially. That was a disaster.

It happened shortly after Jimmy and Fred Roberts became friends, which was before he knew Lisa. He and Fred met this girl at the Cock Robin dance sponsored by the Weston Y.W.C.A. Jimmy suggested the three of them make it to his room and maybe listen to records and read poetry. So Fred supplied the phonograph, along with assorted records, and Father embarrassed Jimmy by saying how pretty the girl was, like a dirty old man, in front of everybody, and by asking Fred how Jimmy was doing in school, as if he cared. But Jimmy lit the candles anyway, making the room seem moody and faraway. The girl was pretty neat-looking, too, and no virgin, and Jimmy felt there was definitely a mutual attraction. But then Mother wouldn't let him shut the door, saying "What would Fred's mother think?" She said it partly because she was still new in Weston and didn't want to offend anybody's old lady—which was ridiculous because she couldn't guess what took place in some of those mansions—and partly because she imagined it was what a mother was expected to say, the only way of explaining her sometimes. Anyway, it was embarrassing as hell with the door open, because even at full volume Thelonius Monk couldn't compete with the blasting television set and the fights she and Father were having in the living room. It all added up to a goddamn bust, and Fred giggled about it for months. Jimmy never had another party in his room.

Besides the fishing net and candles there were special decorations like the beautiful beer can, rusted and eaten away in spots by the waters of Lake Michigan, and the ostrich skin case for cuff links, initialed, except one initial was missing. The case held a picture of Lisa. Not that Jimmy was the picture collecting type. The only other picture he had was one that had been forced on him, and *it* lay buried in the bottom of the Sears Roebuck dresser with the sticky drawers, a picture of himself the old man passed out last Christmas like he was a goddamn movie star or something, which Jimmy had to keep just on the chance that Father would pull an inspection.

Most of all, Jimmy was proud of his library. In the corner of the room under the fishing net was a very impressive stack of paperback books, already measuring three feet four inches tall and still growing. Between brick bookends at the foot of his bed was the hardbound library, acquired from the collection of Weston High School through no generosity of theirs.

He glanced at the two-dollar clock on the unpainted chest of drawers. Subtracting the ten minutes he'd added to keep from being late for work during the week, the clock said 9:22. Fred Brutus Roberts promised to pick him and the girls up for the beach by ten, but even if Fred showed, Jimmy couldn't wait that long. He had to be dressed and out before the old man got in the room and trapped him without his clothes on. On guerrilla tactics, Father could give the Red Chinese a few pointers.

As he was lifting himself out of bed, someone knocked on the door. He pulled the covers back up to his neck for protection.

"Jimmy, are you covered?"

He relaxed. "Yes, Mother," he said patiently.

Mother quickly shut the door behind her and advanced to the edge of the bed. A plain white scarf covered the huge curlers in her hair; her face was still shiny from the cream stuff she plastered on it before she went to bed at night. She wore a new turquoise satin robe which trailed to the floor; the wide sash pulled tight to a show a slight, youthful figure. But her face was drawn, her hands excited.

"How do you feel? Is your leg all right? Let me see."

He flinched away. "It's fine."

"Let me look at it," she said.

"Can't I have any privacy?"

"Jimmy, I am your mother," she said, pulling rank. The man from Murder Inc. was lurking in the hallway, and she had to play Florence Nightingale. Reluctantly, he pulled back the sheet to his knee, expecting to find a mass of gauze and bandages. But there was nothing but a plain Band-aid, and beneath that, a tiny threaded sore spot with almost no swelling.

"Look at that," said Mother. "You'd think it was cut off, the way you carried on last night."

What the hell did she want to look at it for, if she wasn't going to show some pity. "I practically bled to death!" said Jimmy.

"You should have. Might've taught you a lesson."

Removing the wound from merciless eyes, he said, "Most mothers would be a little concerned about their kids."

"Most mothers don't have you for a son. Now get up and get dressed."

"I suppose Father's waiting out there with his machete?" Jimmy said, like he wasn't scared stiff at all.

"He just drove down for milk, and I want you gone before he gets back. My nerves won't stand another fight."

Jimmy felt safer, now, courageous, even. "It's my bedroom, isn't? Why should I have to live my life according to that dictator?"

"You've caused enough trouble already. Do as I say."

"I don't see why you're so scared. He can't hurt you."

"Put on your pants. And if you intend to come home for lunch, you'd better shave first. You know how your father feels about that."

"Who cares? I may even grow a beard now that I'm not going to college. A long Vandyke or something."

"What do you mean, you're not going to college!"

"I changed my mind. Mr. Spaulding says I'm probably the most talented potential photographer he's ever seen. An artist. And artists don't need college."

"Artist or no artist, you're going to college!"

"With what? Foreign aid?"

"Then you still didn't get the money to show Father."

He didn't answer.

She sighed. "Well, I can't afford to have a nervous breakdown over it. There's a clean shirt in the closet; the cuffs are a little scorched so roll up the sleeves. And for God's sake, hurry up," she said, and left the room.

As soon as the door was closed he lost his bravado and leaped out of bed, grabbing a pair of khaki pants and the scorched shirt from the closet. He wasn't really frightened of the old man, at least not like Mother, but he wasn't dumb enough to sit around and wait for the bloodshed, either.

To save time, he carried shirt, shoes, and socks into the bathroom with him so if Father arrived before he was finished he wouldn't have to go back to his room to dress.

Studying himself tenderly in the mirror over the sink, he took his daily inventory of the changes in the man, Jimmy Reardon. His beard was advancing pretty damn fast. Fred had some fuzz on his cheek, below the sideburns, but not on his chin like Jimmy. Shit, Jimmy was even beginning to get hair on his chest; a great long one was there the other day, up near his shoulder. He'd cut it off to make it grow back with two more, but the damn thing never did. Jesus, he sure as hell didn't want to have body hair like the old man, just a few straggly ones right in the middle of his concave chest.

Jimmy looked deep into the clear blue eyes of his mirror image. No matter how much he drank, the damn things never got bloodshot. He could never even swing a headache in the morning, and it would probably take ten years before he could achieve a proper hangover. But his hair looked all right; black and matted; not careless, more animal. It was exciting that way; he might just leave it natural.

No time to shower, so he wet a towel and wiped his back and underarms, taking a quick glance at his nipples. He never thought much about his nipples—he never even heard the term used to describe men's things—until Denise made that crack about one of his being lower than the other. He must've been leaning to one side or something when she said it, because they sure as hell looked even to him. And Lisa saw them a lot at the beach, and she never mentioned it; she even said he had a great build. Shit, he was president of the weightlifting club at school. It was true that there were only four guys in the entire group, and he only got elected because the coach asked him to take the roll at the first meeting, but he was president nonetheless; it was in the graduation program. The sonofabitch Fred was vice-president, but that was because Jimmy nominated him. Still, it was too bad Denise hadn't kept her mouth shut, because it was enervating at times, having to worry about whether one nipple was lower than the other.

Someone banged on the door, Jimmy jumped, ramming his elbow into the sink.

"Hey, Jimmy!" shouted Toby.

"What the hell are you screaming about, dammit!" Jimmy said, soothing his crazy bone.

"If you're gonna holler, forget it," said Toby.

"Forget what!" said Jimmy.

"Fred's here."

So the bastard showed up after all. "Tell him to wait downstairs."

"Tell him yourself, violent."

"I can't! I'm shaving!"

"Big deal. I'm not your servant, y'know."

Foul blood ran in Jimmy's family. "Will you *please* tell him to wait for me in the car?" Sometimes dignity had to be sacrificed for expediency. Fred couldn't be around when the old man got back with the milk.

"I'll think about it," said the obscene kid, his footsteps sounding up the narrow hallway.

Grappling with a tangled shoelace, Jimmy sat on the edge of the tub. Soon he would be with Lisa, on their last day together before she left for Hawaii. What would he say to her? Guess what, I'm not going to college because I knocked up this girl a couple months ago and there was a problem about her abortion?"

"Jimmy, open the door," said Mother. "I want to talk to you."

"Is Father coming?"

"Not yet."

He rushed into the shirt and let her into the bathroom.

"Listen to me," she said, with seldom heard determination, "you're going to college whether you like it or not."

"It's not exactly my choice," said Jimmy.

"You just come home for lunch before you go to work; I'll take care of the rest," she said.

For a moment he stared at her in disbelief. He knew she had money for new housecoats and stuff, but it never occurred to him that she might act in defiance of the old man and give it to him. And he never figured she had a hundred and ten dollars, either, even though she worked part-time in a stationery store and had a bank account which she didn't tell Father about.

Awkwardly, he kissed her on the cheek. Just like Father said, she was an aristocrat. The old man didn't give a damn if Jimmy was starved for an education, but Mother did. Breeding sure as hell showed. Mother's mother had been the cream of Philadelphia's crop, part of a famous streetcar family with a hyphenated name. She had run away with a milk distributor from Chicago, who left her destitute with a daughter two years after the elopment. So Mother's mother worked in a bookstore until she died, and Mother worked in Woolworth's until she married Father. And though she worked in a Western stationery store, Mother was still an aristocrat, and every spring she bought *Town and Country* to see if the Philadelphia branch of the family was still breeding.

Now she was furthering the noble traditions of her family by giving Jimmy, in spite of her lower-class husband, the means to gain his rightful place in life. It was too bad Jimmy didn't know she had the money last night, before he had to humiliate himself with Fred.

Softly, with deep gratitude, "I'll write you every week, I promise," he said, knowing how she loved to answer letters on the fancy letter paper she bought wholesale from the stationery store.

"Jimmy," said Mother, "I know your father very well. Psychologically, he's a very complicated man, and sometimes I don't think even *he* knows why he does things. But I do, at least I try to, and I've figured out why he's been so strange about making you come up with that money. It wasn't just how you spent it, it was more than that."

"Now what'd I do!" He sounded shocked.

"I think you wounded him deeply when you chose your college," Mother said, with her goddamn aristocratic tone.

"What're you talking about?" He knew he was losing something, but he didn't know what.

"College," she said. "He wanted you, his oldest son, to follow in his footsteps."

Jimmy was aghast. "You mean he wanted me to go to *his* school? Mother, are you kidding?"

"I should think you'd be proud of your father's alma mater. Most sons would want to go to the same school."

"Yeah, but *McKinley College?* Who the hell ever heard of *McKinley College!*"

"It happens to be a very respected business school," admonished Mother.

"But I'm an English major—English!"

"It has an English department."

"But it's a monastery, an all-boys' school!" shouted Jimmy.

"I thought what you wanted was an education," Mother said coolly.

"Who can get an education right in the middle of downtown Chicago! In a skyscraper! Besides, that would mean living at home. How could you expect me to study with Rosie and Toby around all the time and you and Father in the ring every night?"

"Your father managed. He didn't get his degree until after Rosie was born. You, you've got your own room to study in, which is more privacy than he had."

"I am not going to McKinley College!"

"Jimmy, let's face the facts. It's the only way I can get your father to send you to school. You know his alternative: a full-time job, and none of this dollar-an-hour potential artist nonsense. A real job so you can contribute your share to the house. It's either that or McKinley, that's what it comes down to."

Actually, when he came to think of it, McKinley College might not be so bad after all. Although the school occupied the top three floors of the old Industrial Liability and Trust Corporation Building, it was right across the street from the Sarah Gomberg College for Women in the DeKalb Insurance Tower, and it was an oft-quoted saying that those S.G. girls screw like bunnies. Besides, considering how the guys at McKinley shaped up looks-wise, he could have the whole damn S.G. student body to himself.

Jimmy's silence encouraged Mother.

"I'll have everything arranged by the time you come home for lunch. Just be on your best behavior," she said, affectionately fixing his collar before opening the bathroom door. "And don't be late," she added like the fairy godmother.

Shiny and clean, Jimmy, to avoid running into the old man, which would be disastrous before Mother softened him up, went down the hallway through the kitchen, only to be confronted by Rosie.

"Where are you going all prettied up?" she said, closing the refrigerator door. Her mouth was full of grapes.

Even as she spoke, the living room door slammed shut and milk containers dropped on the dining room table. "Faye?" It was the old man. "Where the hell are you?"

Rosie smiled. "Father's back."

"Quiet," said Jimmy, opening the back door.

"Should I tell him you're leaving?" Rosie said innocently.

"Keep your mouth shut about this or you'll get Mother in trouble."

"How can I get Mother in trouble?"

"Faye!" shouted Father.

"Just keep your mouth shut," said Jimmy, moving out on the landing.

"Wait!" said Rosie. "Can I have your Frostie?"

"What?" Jesus, he was almost free!

"Frostie, you know, your Frostie!"

"All right," he said. She knew he was helpless to refuse.

He fled down the stairs and ran around to the street, where Fred Roberts was waiting in the car, a wide guilty grin on his face.

"Told you I'd come," he said.

IT seemed a very ordinary Saturday morning. The sun was out, pedestrians were on the sidewalk, all the traffic lights worked fine, and the breeze, washed clean and velvety by last night's rainfall, rushed in cool against Jimmy's face through the open windows of the car as it hummed smoothly along Magnolia Street. Suzie Middleburg sat in the front seat with Fred among the little things she brought along because, who knows, somebody may need them. There were, to mention only the bulkier items, two bright orange blankets, a stack of movie magazines, a jug of lemonade, several books including *The Night of the Rape and Other Tales,* a larger-than-life straw picnic basket, and, in the back seat with Jimmy, an inflatable mattress plus a red-and-yellow beach ball. They were only going to spend a couple of hours at the beach, but try to tell her.

Suzie had blond hair and blue eyes, and might have squeaked by, as far as looks went, if she were composed of average proportions of chins and things, but unfortunately, she was mostly excess, and the blue checkerboard muumuu she wore today didn't exactly improve her image, either. But her voice was as lean, lively, and long-playing as ever as she rattled on tirelessly about the sex lives of several movie stars, cut down the woman her father married, and mimicked her former botany teacher, who talked with a lisp. Then, for a switch, she editorialized on the danger of infection from the waste dumped by certain industries into Lake Michigan, which she somehow equated with the possibility of earthquakes in California.

Jimmy was used to it. They used to sit next to each

other in Mr. Hendersen's first period English IV class, where no subject was too complicated for her to grasp. She knew instinctively, for instance, that Hamlet must have done something with his mother, probably a lot, because the rooms were so drafty in a castle that keeping warm was more basic than morality. Besides, it was an old tune before Hamlet whistled it. How about Oedipus Rex? It was even draftier in those Greek tragedies than it was in Shakespeare. It was always fun to watch the way Mr. Hendersen's lips quivered whenever Suzie raised her hand.

Suzie and Jimmy frequently shared lunch hours, too, especially when he was a bit short. She'd not only stand him a lunch without wanting the money back, like, say Fred, but she was always good for a rundown on which girl put out, just how much and how often. If Suzie Middleburg wasn't the best loved girl in school, she was at least the most feared, and not because she was vicious, but because she knew too much. An observer, she lived vicariously, wearing anyone's hat but her own.

The more the rich-race of Weston High School disliked her, the more Jimmy Reardon respected her, and the fact that her father was Arthur A. Middleburg, Chief Justice of the Illinois State Supreme Court, which put her up there amongst the top-drawer social set, added to her charm. But their friendship was more than mere camaraderie. The truth was, Jimmy might have packed Fred in and just had Suzie for a best buddy, if she hadn't asked him to her house one day last winter.

She needed help, she said, on her term paper.

It was in December, and the roofs and streets were white with snow. He arrived at her house to find Suzie in the sunken den, which was all wood and leather and gleaming brass. He saw that cushions had been placed strategically before the pine-spitting fire, and a crystal decanter full of burnt gold liquid, along with two brandy snifters, stood impatiently nearby. And everywhere the elusive, furniture-polish smell of wealth.

"I'm glad you could make it," Suzie told him as he lingered awkwardly near the doorway. "Here, sit down.

The fire's nice. It crackles almost like rain. How about a drink?" She straightened a lock of hair and crossed to the fireplace.

For the first time since he'd known Suzie, Jimmy felt strange with her. Maybe it was the room lit by flickering firelight, or the painting over the mantel, a pink, fleshy nude with a light over it and metal plate below with the name A. Renoir on it, or maybe it was Suzie herself. Her hair usually hung from her forehead in ropes, but now it was combed and pinned, her eyes lined and mascaraed, and her mouth wore a fresh coat of lipstick. It was one of the few times he'd seen her wear make-up.

"Have a seat, swinger," Suzie said as she poured some brandy into the goblets. "When Daddy finds out someone's been at this juice he'll have a fit of habeas corpus or something. This is his company best—twenty years old. But we might as well finish it before it's old enough to vote. Be prepared," she warned, handing him a snifter, "tastes awful. It's these big brandy glasses I dig, really."

"Hey, don't sit there," Suzie called as he carried his drink to a deep, tapestry covered armchair. "That belongs to Daddy, which makes it holy. Here," she said, padding a cushion, "lie down by the fire. Warmer."

Jimmy took a good slug of brandy. "Won't these sparks cause trouble?" he said anxiously.

"That's what sparks are for," she said as Jimmy lowered himself.

"Well," he said, lightly, sort of, "all we need now is a barge and a couple of bare-breasted slaves waving those feather things."

"Drink up, Julius Caesar." She smiled.

He thought of the empty house and drained the glass while she stared into the fire. When she spoke again, her tone was serious.

"I'm glad you came, Jim." She had never called him *Jim* before.

"I guess we ought to get down to business," he said. "Where's the term paper you need me for."

"Right now it's Britannica, 100 proof. A little 'you' will louse it up nicely." She started to rise, thought a moment, then said, "Why don't we have another short one first. Sort of brace us for the run."

He watched the fire flicker shadows on her face as she poured the brandy. She really wasn't bad, not what anybody would call out and out ugly. Suddenly he got the feeling that, more than anything, he wanted to be able to hold her and watch her grow beautiful the way girls do when they're held, and to hear her laugh the way girls laugh when they're not afraid. He wanted to be able to tell her how pretty her eyes were, and maybe explore her boobs a little, and even get it to come up so she could feel it against her. But then he glimpsed the sexless dimples in her elbows, and all he could say was, "You really have a nice pad here. What kind of furniture do you call it? I mean, does it have a period or something?"

"Early Confusion," she said with forced animation.

They laughed at that, and she knelt before the fire, studying him, while immediately he drained half his second glass of brandy.

"You know," she said, "you really are quite handsome when half your face is in a shadow."

"Maybe I should wear half a mask all the time," Jimmy said uneasily. He felt her move closer. He could hear her breath loud and uneven. Ever since he'd entered the room he'd known it would come to this. What he should have done was gotten sick, or remembered an appointment, or even volunteered to go upstairs and get her damn paper himself! But now it was too late. He saw and felt her lips part almost at the same time. He tried to respond; he found himself smothering in her beefy softness and nearly overcome by her expensive perfume.

Then somehow he was standing above her and trying to explain: "I'm sorry, it's my stomach. I—I don't feel so good!"

The house seemed ten times its size as he ran through it, out the door and into the snow.

On the Monday morning after, he came to school to rumors that Suzie Middleburg had been found walking barefoot through the snow in the pre-dawn darkness of Sunday morning. They found her along Sheridan

Road, stumbling about senselessly and crying, the mascara she seldom wore screaming down her face. Lisa said it was because Suzie's mother had left Weston with a Palm Springs resort owner just a few days before, which Jimmy had heard Suzie laugh about, but anyway, she was sent to a rest home by her father to recuperate from a nervous breakdown. Jimmy always wondered if she would have taken that walk in the snow if he had stayed.

Anyhow, this Saturday, a few months after Suzie returned home from the sanitarium hale and heartier than ever, she was on her way to the beach at Jimmy's invitation, which came in a kind of a backhand way.

It seemed she had refused him a loan of a hundred-ten dollars when he called yesterday because her father didn't trust her with cash or a checking account. Instead of thanking her very much anyway, Jimmy allowed himself to be drawn into answering questions like what did he need the money for anyway, the "clap" again? And stuff like that. Which somehow got to, as usual, his plans for the next day, swimming with Lisa and Fred, etc., which opened up the can of peas that Fred wasn't going to bring Denise Hunter, in fact was going dateless.

And now Fred, black-rimmed glasses, Indian Madras shorts, desert boots and all, was at the wheel of his car and heading for Lisa's house, his Jimmy-arranged date beside him.

Suzie had long since passed over the possibility of California earthquakes, and after a quick skip through the British parliamentary system, she settled on Sarah Bentwright, Lisa's mother and, it seemed, a rather close friend of Suzie's father, Judge Middleburg.

". . . And after the next two dry vermouths on the rocks, Sweet Sarah was hominy-gritting all over the Judge," Suzie was saying. "And then, after all the guests had gone home, they both got very southernly in the den."

"Are you sure it was Mrs. Bentwright?" Jimmy said from his perch on the inflatable mattress in the back seat.

"Yeah," said Fred, who was usually apt to put down gossip, "how do you know?"

"Dum-te-dum," said Suzie, leaning back against the car door to better view her audience. "The party was at my house, wasn't it? And it's part of the record that before the Judge elected Little Miss Muffet, Mrs. Bentwright was entering all the primaries. . . ."

Suzie always called her father "the Judge," as did everyone else in Weston, except the *Tribune,* which called him "Pink" and said he was against the Constitution, the American Way of Life, Free Enterprise, and the Founding Fathers and was also advancing the Communist Conspiracy because of his stand on baseball—he thought chess should be given equal time. But the citizens of Weston were quite willing to forgive the Judge his liberalism because he was very, very rich—and sanguine, in the poetic sense, and unattached, in the marital sense. That is, until he joined Miss Moffet, his twenty-six-year-old secretary, in holy wedlock. Among those who felt the greatest loss at that was Sarah Bentwright, according to Suzie.

"She called every night for two weeks after the engagement was announced in the papers."

"I think you make that stuff up," growled Fred.

"That's because you're new here," Suzie said snippily.

"I was born here!" Fred bellowed.

"But your grandfather wasn't," said Suzie, "and it takes at least three generations before you can follow the trends."

"Trends, hell!" shouted Fred, somewhat illogically.

"Par example. You've been dating Denise Hunter for six months and three weeks now, what do you know of her parents?"

"He's chairman of the Illinois Central, and she plays tennis!" Fred screamed. She sure had him going.

Suzie sighed her condolences to Fred, then rolled her gaze back to Jimmy, staring at him for a moment with spooky, Siamese-cat eyes. "I don't suppose you might know something of Denise Hunter's parents?" she said coyly.

"Hello, no!" Jimmy over-protested.

"I didn't think you would," she told Jimmy with a

knowing (or was it? Jesus, he hoped not) smile before going on briskly. "Suppose I give you both a quick survey course. Her father is George Hunter III, Chairman of the Illinois Central, who summered in the same sea as Virginia Reade—that was on the Italian Riviera, right after he graduated from Yale and she left Vassar—but he had to give her up because Virginia was already engaged to Rawson Pyne Hollinder, and that's how she got to be the mother of Matthew Hollinder, but she's in California now, married to a high school principal in Glendale. . . ." Here she paused and glanced significantly from Fred to Jimmy. "You both know who Matthew Hollinder is, don't you?"

"He's a football player, isn't he?" said Fred.

"Among other things," Suzie said mysteriously. "Anyway, after George Hunter III missed out on Virginia, while he was in New York on a business trip in the late thirties he got a call from one H. Bayard Oakes, who was married to Louise Balies, the daughter of George Latham Balies, who started the corn syrup family with my grandfather Farley. So—H. Bayard said that his daughter, Esme Balies Oakes, was expecting and would he please see what he could do about it, which meant marry her, and George did, even though I personally don't think it was his mistake because Gregory Bentwright, whose father was Alexander Augustus Bentwright from Kansas City, used to wrestle with her on the hammock in her terrace. But poor Georgie wasn't sure his father's will was going to probate in his favor, so he decided to get his social security with Esme. They had Denise three months after the wedding in the St. Johns Lutheran Church."

"But Denise's mother is not named Esme," Fred said triumphantly.

"Not her present mother, no," said Suzie. "Because at Judy Bright's coming-out party, Esme met a Count Hugo Mosing, who was from an old family in Austria or Japan or someplace like that, and she divorced Denise's father, who then married Lilly Schmidt, and she's the one who plays tennis—and is having a bit of hanky-panky with Arthur Wyatt, in case anyone's interested."

"No one is," Jimmy said wearily.

"Well then," said Suzie, never at a loss, "shall we talk about last night? Did you guys find the girl you were looking for?"

There was a moment of silence while Fred looked at Jimmy through the rearview mirror, and Jimmy tried to sink deep into the mattress. How the hell did Suzie find out about that!

"She's iust testing, she doesn't know a thing!" he said.

"Dum-te-dum," said Suzie.

And from then on to Lisa's, it was quiet in the car.

Lisa Bentwright lived with her mother in a Spanish house at the crest of a low hill. The driveway was guarded by dogwood trees; there were windows in odd places, and it looked as if the shingles on the roof were made of orange clay pipes which had been split in two. The doorbell chimed and kept chiming until the maid finally answered.

She escorted Jimmy through a dark hallway into a blinding, sun-filled room. It was all white walls, white rugs, and white furnishings, including a bleached white driftwood log. One end of the room was a sliding glass door opening onto a swimming pool with white Spanish-style dressing rooms beyond the diving board. Jimmy had never been invited to swim in that pool, not that he ever wanted to; Mrs. Bentwright would probably sit underwater in a diving bell to see that nothing went on between him and her precious little ol' daughter.

As soon as he was sunk uncomfortably in a modern chair with no arms and a deep seat like the pit of a wheelbarrow, the maid, with mechanical efficiency, began fluffing up cushions on the white sofa and, as Jimmy lit a cigarette, she stuck an ashtray in his hand before he could blow out the match. A white ashtray with a daisy painted in its cup, for which he thanked her, and she left, leaving him alone.

When he thought about it, this was the first time he'd ever been alone in Lisa's house. Usually Lisa met him at the door, with Sarah rum-tum-tumming right behind, making sure Lisa's ranks were closed to this Yankee bum. Holding his cigarette high he looked out at the pool with a baronial squint in his eye. Some day he'd have a pad like this, but he wouldn't furnish it in modern Better Homes and Gardens; his house would be authentic Spanish Revolution, and this room would be his study. But there'd be no more than two maids, because Lisa would manage the more ordinary household tasks, though naturally, as the wife of a famous author, poet, and musician—or whatever he was going to be when it came right down to it—she'd be called upon a lot to speak at women's clubs, Rotary luncheons, the Royal Academy of Arts and Sciences, and McKinley College, his alma mater . . . Jesus.

But mostly she would be there for his own personal pleasure, dressed in something filmy like a nightgown, so once in a while he could glance up from his work to be reassured by the familiar nipples peeking out at him. Then, when she got up to get him a drink, he would note with satisfaction that she was naked at the rear end.

"Why, Mr. Reardon, how marvelous to see you!" Mrs. Bentwright was charging at him from behind, her syrupy voice chiming every note on the scale and—holy shit! Jimmy snapped into consciousness, crossed his legs, and rushed the ashtray to his lap in the sudden, horrible awareness that it, having taken that dream of Lisa in the negligee seriously, was up!

"You certainly have been scarce these past few days, or have I just been missing you?"

Mrs. Bentwright, a small, square-shouldered woman in a white dress and sparkling brooch, was standing in front of him now, her arm outstretched.

"Lisa should be out in a jiffy, she's just a little beaver in there, packing for school. . . ."

In what seemed to take longer than the life and death cycle, he put the cigarette on the daisy, slipped the ashtray onto the seat, plunged his left hand into his pocket, and rose to his feet, awkwardly hunched over, to meet the firm, quick grip of Mrs. Bentwright.

". . . It's those last-minute things," she went on in the Alabama gush carefully nurtured and preserved during her twenty-five years in Weston, Illinois. "You know, female necessities? So now you just sit down and make yourself to home. And you, are you all packed away for school, Mr. Reardon?"

She turned toward the sliding glass pool doors before he could answer, "Almost." Her legs were thin, and she wore open-toed shoes showing coral toe nails. Jimmy took the ashtray off the seat and made himself uncomfortable again in the wheelbarrow chair.

He didn't notice the catastrophe until after Mrs. Bentwright began to talk again, and then he saw it ten-thousand times its size: The white ashtray where he set his lit cigarette was empty! The goddamn daisy was bare!

Keeping one eye on Mrs. Bentwright, he frantically searched the base of his chair for the missing cigarette as the lady chirrped on, not needing a partner to her conversation, Southern style.

Just as he spotted his cigarette on the rug, she spun back to him. He couldn't move toward it; she'd see! He watched in agony while she sniffed and tested like she smelled something burning, oh no. . . . But then she was off and gushing again.

When she turned away to fix some white flowers on an end table, he seized the opportunity to lean over quickly and recover the butt, only, shit! Under it was a big black hole! Burned into the white rug!

Suddenly she was facing him. He stuck out his foot to cover the crime. Was her expression telling him she'd asked something that demanded an answer?

"Excuse me?" he said politely.

"Matthew Hollinder," she said.

"Oh, yeah sure," he tried to finesse as she soared on.

"A scholarship to Yale University, isn't that the most wonderful thing? Not that Matthew needs it, of course, his daddy's got oodles of money. . . ."

She was in gear once more. Jimmy's leg began to ache. He could actually feel the burnt spot under his arch. When he stood up she'd see it anyway—maybe he should tell her, say it right out. Another question.

"Excuse me?" said Jimmy.

"I said what school are you going to, Mr. Reardon?"

"Oh, University of Northern Illinois." Somehow, he couldn't say McKinley to Mrs. Bentwright.

"You mean that little school way up at the tip of the state? Why, I know that place! Teacher's college, isn't that right? Why you don't mean you are going to be a teacher, do you? Of course, that's a very noble profession, very nice."

Then Lisa was beside him in a blue backless bathing suit, a beach towel embroidered with drinking slogans in seven languages draped on her arm, and wearing a yellow, straw coolie hat. "Here I am," she said, and the simple words cleared everything else from Jimmy's mind. "Here I am!" And he saw her breasts rising over the top edge of her suit, and her lean brown legs, and he wanted to scream and recite poetry from the tallest building in the world.

"I hope you intend to wear a jacket with that outfit," Mrs. Bentwright was saying.

His foot still covered the hole, and Mrs. Bentwright was hovering over Lisa, who said good-by, her hand attached to his, urging him gently toward the hallway. He still didn't move.

"Come on, Jimmy—is something wrong?" The voice was Lisa's.

Well, here goes: forward steps to the hallway, not looking back. Any minute now Mrs. Bentwright was going to start wailing.

He didn't want to look back, but he couldn't help it. As Lisa opened the door he turned to see Mrs. Bentwright, standing exactly on the spot, her coral tipped toes covering the damage!

"And don't you forget to bring her home early, hear? She's got to get ready. . . ."

He shut the door behind him and it was over. Now it was Jimmy pulling Lisa, galloping with her to the car, feeling the greenness of the morning and the promise of it, and screw the mark on Mrs. Bentwright's rug!

At the end of Horizon Lane (KEEP OUT), a private road winding along a cliff between the great mansions overlooking the lake, they left the car. From so high up they could look out to sailboats catching the wind, to where the blue lake spread into the sky. Jimmy and Lisa followed pack-horse Fred and wobbly Suzie down the old wooden steps, passing oak and cedar trees to the sandy beach below.

Suzie spread her blanket at the bottom of the cliff, placed the air mattress on top of it, and arranged her magazines, lemonade, and picnic basket, which Fred had simply dumped.

"If you were a gentleman, you'd help me with this," she told him.

"Yes, ma'am," Fred answered wearily as Lisa dropped her towel on the sand and raced to the water. She plunged in waist-deep beside a long, rusty steel pier.

"You're going to freeze!" Jimmy shouted after her.

"It's great," Lisa shouted back. "Come on in!"

"I can't, I didn't bring a bathing suit," said Jimmy.

"Roll up your pants. Don't tell me you're shy," Lisa laughed.

"But I cut my leg, there's a bandage on it."

"Poor baby," mocked Lisa. "Anything for an excuse."

Jimmy walked to the edge and stuck his hand in the water. "Jesus, it's like ice!"

Behind him, Suzie sprawled out on the mattress, holding a movie magazine. "I'm going to read about current affairs," she said.

Jimmy called to Lisa. "Let's walk up the beach!"

"I can't, it's colder outside than it is in,'" she shivered back.

Fred stared at the straw basket. "Watcha got to eat?" he asked Suzie.

"You name it," said Suzie, dropping the magazine to hand Fred a sandwich.

"I hope it isn't mayonnaise," he said, eating it anyway.

"Dammit Lisa!" Jimmy said impatiently. "I have to be home by lunch time!"

"Hey, Jimmy," said Fred, "you ought to try one of Suzie's sandwiches. They're great." He sounded a little desperate.

"She thinks she's a goddamn mermaid or something," was Jimmy's answer.

Lisa pressed her cheeks and shot a stream of water from her mouth. "I'm a dolphin."

"Hell," said Jimmy, "I'm going to walk up the beach by myself."

"Wait up, I'll go with you," Fred called anxiously.

"You'll stay here or toss up my sandwich," Suzie ordered without looking up from the magazine.

Jimmy turned away and headed up the beach. Except for a random breeze skittering along the surface to cause an occasional whitecap, the lake was calm. On the other side of him the cliff rose nearly thirty feet, and he followed its curve to an isolated stretch of sand, stopping finally to lean against the grizzled stump of an oak tree which had been torn from above during some spring rain, landing there wounded but refusing to die. Green shoots rose from its branches. By day it endured the humiliations of the scores of land and sea creatures that explored it, and at night it was a great place to make out.

He kicked up a cloud of sand. Shit, there were times when he couldn't figure Lisa out. They came all the way out here, and she decides to take a swim! With a whole private lake in her own backyard, why did she have to waste their day together? Their last morning!

Suddenly he was knocked off his feet by a bundle of wet hair and giggles.

"Dammit, you're all wet!" he said, lifting his face from the sand.

"Mmmm," answered Lisa, kissing his cheek and face, "mermaid bring water to white trader. Heap nice mermaid."

He turned away, unintentionally brushing her cheek with his mouth. The cool water felt good. She touched his ear with her lips and wiggled her hand on his stomach, trying to make him laugh. But no matter what, he was going to hold out.

"Why don't you run down the beach and play by yourself, little girl." He thought he sounded cool and uninterested. But Lisa knew better and pressed herself tight on his back.

"Oh, because," she said matter-of-factly, playing ticktacktoe on his neck, "I'd rather stay here with you. You're much more fun when you're mad."

"Who the hell's mad? I just think you'll fit into the landscape better by yourself."

Digging her fingers into his shoulders and tightening her knees against his armpits, she straddled him like a horse. "Giddyap," she said, whipping his buttocks and bouncing up and down.

Jimmy pushed up quickly, slamming her against the tree stump.

"Hey! My head!" She winced, holding on to it and making a hurt face.

"I'm sorry. Does it hurt?"

"You didn't have to do that."

"I don't mean to do it, and I wouldn't have if you didn't act like such a kid."

"Well, you'd better apologize," she pouted.

"I did."

"No you didn't!"

"Dammit! What the hell do you want me to do? Build an altar!"

"Why are you so mad?"

"Who said I was mad? I didn't mention anything about being mad, didn't say a word about it."

"Jimmy, if you don't tell me what's the matter, I'm going home."

"Go ahead."

"Come on, Jimmy!"

"Look, every time we go someplace you have to start running around like your ass is on fire. Why the hell can't you stay with me just one time? Huh? Are you embarrassed to be with me or something?"

"You know I'm not."

"Then why the hell do you do such stupid things?"

"All I did was go swimming. Isn't that what we came here for?"

"Don't give me that. Almost every time we're alone you have to make some excuse to stay away from me."

"Every time we're alone you find some reason to, well, to start things."

"I don't start anything. You're so goddamn scared. Sometimes I think you're frigid or something!"

"You just expect every girl you see to plop into bed with you the first time you look at them. Oh, I hear things, I hear about you and those girls you go out with. And I heard about your venereal disease too! I heard all about that!"

"That goddamn Suzie!" He glared in Suzie's direction.

"It wasn't Suzie; it was all over school! How do you think I felt, walking down the halls with a boy who bragged about things like that in the lunch room."

"I didn't brag about it. I only told Fred."

"Fred and ten other boys at the table."

"The doctor cured it with one shot, so what the hell difference does it make!"

"It makes a difference to me. I wouldn't want to catch anything like that!"

"You couldn't catch that by kissing! And don't tell me you don't make out with other guys, because I know different. Every time I cross that goddamn Southern threshold of yours I have to be reminded of your gentlemen callers."

"If I didn't go out with other boys, I couldn't go out with you," said Lisa. "Mommy wouldn't let me go out with just one boy, you know that."

"I suppose she gives you a thorough examination when you come home to make sure no one has crossed the Mason-Dixon line!"

"The only one she worries about is you. Mommy has no illusions about you, and neither do I!"

"I'm no different than those other guys she approves of: the sonofabitches you go out with have cars with back seats to screw on, that's the only difference!"

"It's not the only difference! Mommy's right. You're always in trouble, and if you're not in it, you're looking for it!"

"And by the way, what the hell did your mother mean by telling me to get you home early so you can get ready? Ready for what?"

"I had to tell Mommy you were taking me to the dance. I always have to tell her something before I can go out with you."

"The country club dance?"

"Yes."

"I wouldn't go near the place!"

"You would if you could."

She struck home. "You're crazy. Plain nuts," he answered. It was weak, they both knew it. He broke a twig off the stump and drew a face in the sand with it. "The only reason your grand-lady mother doesn't like me is because my parents don't happen to have been born with silver hominy grits in their mouths," he said. "And you know it."

Lisa became awfully busy with her hair, too busy to respond, so he went on: "Well, you can tell *Mommy* that we're going to the Dead Pigeon tonight and drink thirty-five cent coffee, ten cents extra for refills, and not to the goddamn snobby country club dance!"

She was suddenly quiet in a hurt way, and he felt guilty for having yelled at her. Now he threw the twig away and made nervous marks in the sand with his foot.

After too long, Lisa said in a quiet voice, "I'm sorry if my mother made you uncomfortable today, but the thing is, she had an accident."

He was immediately contrite. "What happened?"

"Did you see it?"

"See what?"

"The hole she burned in the rug this morning," explained Lisa. "She was standing on it, trying to cover it up as we were leaving. She takes those things very seriously."

Jimmy burst out laughing.

Lisa frowned. "What's so funny?"

But he could only laugh louder, confusing her more, until she tried to run away. Then he took her arm, pulling her down so that she lay on him while he tried to control himself and explain what had set him off like that. But the explanation got lost somewhere, and the laughter too. He crossed his legs over her and held her tight, feeling the softness of her boobs spread out on his chest, and, as she joined her mouth with his, he thought how warm she must be inside. He rocked her gently and enjoyed the rush of blood to his middle and the growing hardness as she probed between his lips with her tongue and began to move her hips in response to his.

"Don't Jimmy, please . . . please . . ." she said. "Don't—" But she held him even nearer as he travelled up the furrow of her back with his fingertips. He knotted his hands in her hair, their bodies tight together, their intermingling mouths warm and wet, their lips tingling, sending each other into shivers and gasps.

He know it would go no further, that she would break away as always when her breathing reached a pitch. But he thought if he could hold her just a little longer, drown out whatever warned and frightened her. . . .

Then, unexpectedly, he heard her say: "Jimmy?"

"Huh?" His eyes were shut so hard they almost hurt.

"Jimmy. . . ." She slipped from him and lay her hot cheek on his bare stomach. It took time for her to go on. "Jimmy, can I see you?"

At first he wasn't sure what she meant. Then he opened his eyes and saw where she was looking. She had never acknowledged it before, not with a touch or even by a glance, as far as he knew. A thrill of anticipation shot through him.

He reached for the zipper without talking, afraid that spoken sounds might come between them. But she stopped his hand with hers. He waited, but she didn't move. Then he heard the zipper separating. Hesitation again. Now she reached inside. He spread his legs without thinking and ached at her touch.

He watched her study him, embracing it with her fingers.

"Will anything happen?" she said.

"Not if I don't want it to."

Silence again. Then: "It looks funny."

"You're going to hurt its feelings."

"I apologize. It's just that—well, I mean—I never saw one before." She took her hand off it.

"Please, don't stop."

"Is it big?" she said, as though she hadn't heard him. "I mean, bigger than others?"

"I don't know," he answered, embarrassed by the question, but adding quickly, "I've been told it's not exactly small."

She took it in hand again, watching fascinated as it responded to her touch. Keep going, he thought. But he was afraid to talk or move.

"It isn't always this hot, is it?"

"Only when it likes someone."

"Does it like me?"

"Don't you know?"

"It looks funny. It's so red."

"It's supposed to be."

She turned away to look at him wide-eyed. "It's funny and it makes me feel funny." He brought her up gently, and turned her over to try to put himself between her legs. But she fought him. "No. Please, Jimmy. . . ." She pulled away and stood up, her hair blowing wild.

"Please!" And then she was gone.

Jimmy adjusted himself, rose, and tried to run after her, but the bandage on his leg had become unstuck, and by the time he'd finished replacing it, Lisa was a blue pebble far up the beach.

When he finally caught up with her she was sitting in a white-flaking summer house halfway up the cliff, staring at the lake. Silently he took a place beside her to look out at the sailboats on the water.

"After tonight, I won't see you till Christmas, when you come home for vacation," he said.

"You'll probably forget all about me by then, with all those girls at U.N.I."

"I probably could—except I'm not going there," he said.

"How come? Yesterday you couldn't wait to go!"

He kissed her cheek. "I found me a better deal. A really good school, McKinley College."

She broke away. "McKinley College?" she repeated in a weak voice.

"The family has always gone to McKinley," he said, giving it the rich-race sound.

"But, I mean, isn't it a business school?"

"Jesus, you sure don't know much. Sure, it's a business college, but it happens to have one of the best English departments around. Hell, everybody studies English at the University of Northern Illinois, but you know how many English majors there are at McKinley?"

"No . . ." she said doubtfully, not knowing whether to sympathize with him or believe him.

"Practically none! So you get individual instruction, right? Like a private tutor, and not only that, but it's right in the middle of the Loop. Hell, I can practically walk to the Art Institute, and concerts—they don't have that at U.N.I.!"

"Well, it certainly sounds nice," she said without conviction. "Only I thought you didn't want to live at home."

"Look, what's more important, personal comfort or a good education? Do you think I'd be able to study with all those kids running around the campus, drinking beer and everything? Hell, I'll have ten times as much privacy in my own room at home. Besides, it practically killed my father when I decided not to go to his alma mater. It's the least I can do to make the old man happy."

"You're doing this for your father? Is that why?"

He nodded slowly, for effect, and she put her head on his shoulder.

"Oh, Jimmy," she said, "I think that's wonderful."

"What really bothers me," he said, "is that you'll be so far away, it'll be months till I see you."

"It's hard to believe I could lose you that easily," she said dreamily. "I just know one morning I'll open one eye and there you'll be, all tan and wet because you just went swimming. And I won't ask you what you're doing in Hawaii or how you got there or anything. It'll be just like we never stopped seeing each other. And we'll run along the beach and climb coconut trees and go to a big luau every single night, except Wednesdays, of course."

"Why except Wednesdays?" asked Jimmy.

"Because on Wednesdays we make love, silly," she explained.

"Just on Wednesdays?"

"Well . . ." She considered it thoughtfully. "Maybe Saturdays, too. That way it'll be spaced out. Wednesdays and Saturdays. And we'll have a huge white yacht named LISA—that's because you wanted to name it after me—and it'll be parked in Akacusi Cove or something that sounds like that, and when the water gets cold we'll take off for Haiti, and when it's warm we'll dive for oysters and hang pearls from our chandeliers. And you'll find a black one and wear it in your left ear. That's what I pull when we make love."

"You sure have become liberal since we've been in the Islands," said Jimmy.

They laughed at that, and he put his arm around her, and they melted close. For the moment, somehow, it all seemed real: he could almost smell the red blossoms as round as a man's head and hear the throaty rumble of Island volcanoes and feel the warm sand and the warm Lisa and see the oversized petals and the pink-breasted girls. But then the moment was gone. Hawaii was for Lisa; he'd be left behind in that goddamn skyscraper with English teachers who no doubt signed their names with X's and those girls at S.G. who screwed like bunnies and probably looked like bunnies too.

"Of course," he went on in a dour voice, "there are the practical things to be considered before we actually get set to plant pineapples in our own backyard."

"Practical?"

"I'm referring to what some people call money."

"Oh, that". . . ." She dismissed it with a flick of her wrist.

"Oh, that!" he repeated glumly.

"There's always Mommy," said Lisa.

Jimmy thought about that for a second. Mommy.

"Don't move, Jimmy," Lisa said suddenly.

"What?"

She blotted an eyelash from his cheek with her finger. "Now blow it off and make a wish."

He smiled at her and blew away the lash.

"What'd you wish for?" she asked.

"You," he said, and kissed her hard.

"Hey!" she shouted, pushing him away.

"Lisa," he said struggling with her, "listen! Listen to me. Do you remember how much your ticket cost, I mean the plane fare to Hawaii?"

"A hundred and eighty-nine dollars and twenty-seven cents. Why? What's the matter with you? You look funny."

Since he spent that hundred-ten on that girl, Jim had saved another seventy dollars from what he earned at Mr. Spaulding's. And today he would get thirty-two dollars more from his boss, which meant he was still eighty-eight dollars short.

He turned to Lisa, bright-eyed. "Lisa, I need eighty-eight dollars," he said, trying to conceal his excitement. "Eighty-eight dollars."

"Are you asking me for it? Where would I get that much money?"

"Mommy?"

"Jimmy, you're kidding, aren't you? You know how Mommy feels about you."

But Jimmy wasn't to be put off. The hell with Mommy. He nearly got a hundred and ten dollars last night, didn't he? Eighty-eight would be a snap. That practically accomplished, he dreamed aloud.

"Once I was there I could get a job! It'd be easy as hell to earn more than the lousy dollar an hour I get now from Mr. Spaulding, and my old man wouldn't have to give me a cent! I could work during the day and go to the University of Hawaii at night!"

"How do you know you could find a job?"

"I've worked for a photographer, and that's like a profession. And I've sold clothes; I could always work in a men's store. And if I don't find a job right away, I could stay with you!"

"With me?"

"Sure! You're not living on campus."

"But where would you sleep?"

"In a bed, where do you think?"

"*Whose* bed?"

"We'll talk about that when I get there."

"Jimmy you can't! You just, you just can't! You're dreaming!"

"Lisa I'm not dreaming—it'll work, it has to work!"

HAWAII was no dream. For Jimmy, Hawaii was waking up. As they drove home from the beach he saw clearly what the dream had really been.

The dream had to do with Fred, and Fred's house, and his game room, and his father's yacht. Jimmy would have strangled in the ivy of Weston High if it hadn't been for Fred, who was the first to befriend him, who helped him with his homework, got him invited to a few parties, and even introduced him to a few intelligent girls who weren't virgins, not to mention Denise Hunter, who Jimmy didn't even want to think about. They played pool in the basement game room of Fred's mansion, and Jimmy went for his first real boat ride, outside of Lincoln Park, on the yacht that belonged to Fred's father. He also ate sandwiches served by Fred's maid, and got invited to outdoors brunch by Fred's parents, and it was Fred who took him to a reading by e. e. cummings just before the poet's death. Somehow it all seemed true—the game room, the rich-race parties, the restaurants with Fred paying—it all seemed available to Jimmy, and sometimes he even felt part of it. Yet always, when it was over, he went back to the cowboys and Indians of his own room.

Suzie Middleburg was in the dream too. She knew all about which girls put out and which didn't, but what did that have to do with Jimmy? Even if they'd been genuine nymphomaniacs he couldn't have hacked it with most of those rich broads, especially not unless he had a car, which he didn't. And Suzie's father, the Judge. Jimmy could listen to Suzie for a long time about how her old man was always eating the olives out of some strange woman's martini, and he could understand how Suzie got all upset when her mother ran away with some resort owner, and when the Judge finally married his young secretary. They were problems, but they were rich-race problems. Jimmy's old man didn't even have a secretary; he got his typing done by some woman from a pool, who probably had volleyball boobs, giggled, and wore contact lenses. And Mother worked in a stationery store for fifty-seven fifty a week take-home. And if Jimmy ever had a nervous breakdown, he could be goddamn sure nobody would send him to some Connecticut rest home—he'd have to get cured on his own!

And Lisa. Even Lisa hadn't exactly been reality. She thought it was cute that Jimmy always took her to the Dead Pigeon instead of downtown to Kelly's or the London House or the Camelia Room or the Palmer House or wherever the rich-race went. She thought it was romantic when they talked about someday getting married, and how at first they would only be able to afford hot dogs and oatmeal instead of lobster and steak. Lisa never understood that it was neither cute nor romantic: it was poverty. She thought just because Jimmy looked like everybody else, wore the same clothes, lived nearby and spoke English, that they were the same. But they weren't. Her mother was really loaded, Alabama accent and all, while Jimmy's mother only had a few aristocratic corpuscles bluing her veins.

But Hawaii would be real. He and Lisa would be equal there, both strangers, pioneers together. Weston and Mommy would be thousands of miles away, and so would Jimmy's cowboys and Indians. The two of them could build something together, something private.

The problem was getting there. All he needed was eighty-eight dollars to be on the jet tomorrow with Lisa, beautiful Lisa, and by tomorrow night they'd be swinging in the same hammock, or whatever they swung in down in the Islands.

Jesus, would Mother be surprised. She'd probably

cry a little when he first told her, but in time she'd learn to accept it.

But not the old man.

Jimmy didn't remember the urgent thing until they were already pulling up in front of Lisa's house. Lunch! He was supposed to be home for lunch because Mother was going to tell the old man about McKinley. Only Jimmy wasn't going to McKinley now—he had to get home before it was too late!

It was.

Resting his elbows on the dining room table, Jimmy stared thoughtfully at the two soggy hot dogs on the serving plate. A moment ago, when he arrived home for lunch—late, dammit—the hot dogs looked good because he was hungry, but he had since lost his appetite.

The hideous sound of Father's chewing stopped as the old man pushed the serving plate nearer to Jimmy. "Here, take the big one. Go ahead," he urged with shattering generosity.

That was the trouble. Ever since Jimmy came home, the old man had been polite. Now he was—Jesus, it was unbelievable!—now he was putting the biggest of the two hot dogs on Jimmy's plate!

"Thanks," said Jimmy.

"Toby, pass the buns to your big brother," said Father.

Toby passed the hot dog buns to Jimmy, who took one and opened it with a dazed expression on his face. He'd been all girded to fight for Hawaii and his eighty-eight dollars until the old man had squelched him with his brand new human characteristics. If only he had been able to talk to Mother before they started to eat and told her about his change of plans.

Although the rest of the family used buns, Mother ate her hot dogs daintily, with a knife and fork. Now she set the fork down on her plate, took the napkin off her lap, and, wiping the corners of her mouth, said, "Rosie, why don't you go out after lunch and play with little Alice across the street?"

"Because Alice doesn't *live* across the street," Rosie

said by way of tired explanation, and she turned to look a dagger at Toby, who was industriously stripping the skin off his last remaining hot dog. "Is he going to sit around all afternoon?" she asked.

"Can't I even finish my lunch?" shouted Toby.

"You can take a break after the banisters are done," said Rosie. "You don't have to be at the Hollinders' until three o'clock."

"Big deal! Do the pukey banisters yourself!" said Toby.

"Father," said Rosie with poisonous sweetness, "Toby is using bad language at the dinner table."

"Toby, shut up," Father said, but without venom.

"She gets away with everything," said Toby, pushing himself away from the table.

"Don't forget to turn over the tip to me this time," Rosie shouted after him.

Incredible. Lunch was almost over, and the old man had not raised his voice, slammed a single glass on the table, or told Mother to use your goddamn head, Faye, like he usually did. Even Rosie and Toby were able to argue in peace.

On a normal Saturday afternoon Father was like a goddamn hurricane. He could be heard two blocks away, bellowing about how much overtime he put in at the office, about how his wife didn't know how to raise her kids, and about her aristocratic ways.

Jimmy glanced furtively at Father to catch him chomping on his hot dog, his stern, heavy-jowled face set in sweet contemplation. He wore the usual gray pants, white shirt with open collar, loose tie, and sleeves rolled up to show his anchor tattoo, which he got in the Navy and which read "U.S.N." in a little box and below that, "December, 1942." Father always said he was sorry he got it, that he was going to have it removed. But still he displayed it every chance he got, even though he spent the war in Miami, Florida.

Mother and nearsighted strangers always said that Jimmy looked like the old man, and though Father did have black hair and fierce blue eyes, all resemblance ended there. Jimmy was tall and sort of classic looking when he thought about it, while the old man was all peasant, with big hands and worker's shoulders. And while Jimmy's voice was deep and well modulated, Father's was husky and always loud, except when company came.

Company was the Pearsons. Mr. Pearson was a wispy, balding man who was always washing his hands. Jimmy hated to greet him because the guy had a handshake like wet liver. His wife, Sally, had a nose like the Pontiac Indian. She powdered her face thick right down to the middle of her neck, and from there on she was greasy white as far as the eye could see. And you could frequently see down the front of her dress and up her skirt, which was always climbing above her knees.

On Pearson night, before they arrived, Father made everybody miserable. Mother's dress was creased, Rosie's dress was too short or too long. Toby didn't wash his face clean enough, the cheese dip wasn't oniony enough, and Jimmy had damn well better behave himself and get in there and shave, for crissakes. It was like Mr. Pearson was the French Ambassador, instead of a fellow accountant at the Great Lakes Tool and Die Company.

Then, as soon as Mr. Pearson stuck his liver hand in the front door, Father would change. His husky voice would grow meek, and after a few drinks he'd start to giggle at almost everything Mr. Pearson said, and suddenly he'd begin to love his family, start to brag about how Mother's ancestor's were so wealthy and social, and how everybody was getting on so well in Weston, and about the new car he bought. Jesus, once he even made Jimmy read a poem of his called "Heredity Take Your Hands Off Me," which was really a protest against parents, but no one got it anyway, so it was all right.

Jimmy often wondered if Father's work made him such a bastard. Work seemed to be the old man's real life, and he spent long hours at the office, poring over production costs on machines that made screwdriver blades and curtain rings. Often he stayed far into the night. But instead of making him happy, his job only served to make him more anxious, and when he came home from a hard day he was meaner than ever. Nothing seemed to satisfy him.

Yet he was where he wanted to be; he did damn well for himself, he always said. And maybe he had. After all, the old man did grow up in Cicero with a lot of poor immigrants, tough, ignorant people—even gangsters. And maybe it was true, as he was always saying, that as a kid he worked during the day and went to high school at night, giving all his salary to his mother and keeping just a quarter for the movies on Saturday night. (Movies were sure cheap then.) Even Mother repeated his tales about how he worked his way through McKinley College while Jimmy was growing up. Trouble was, the old man was still working like that even though he could go no higher at his job. Maybe he thought if he could go on long enough he might win something, some kind of gold watch, maybe. Or maybe he just couldn't help himself, like one of those old junkman's mules that keep making the same rounds after the cart is on the heap. Or maybe that's how you get when you've had a hard climb: suspicious and stubborn. Even his anger gave him no relief. He would shout and scream and hit everybody—once he even broke his belt buckle on Jimmy—but it didn't do any good, because what made Father angry was still locked up inside. Jimmy was sure that the old man looked the same way when he made love as when he spanked Toby; it was only a matter of pivoting the crusted hulk in a different direction.

Jimmy caught a quick glimpse of the baldness spreading in the back of the old man's head. He wasn't extremely old, but moving on now at forty-six. Seeing that bald spot made Jimmy feel funny for a second, like maybe Father wasn't so bad after all. He wondered if the old man had ever slept with some little girl in the basement of a Cicero tenement, or met some secretary from the plant in a motel after work. But he couldn't imagine Father really doing it—he'd probably start to giggle if anyone ever really touched him. Still, you never knew.

Rosie drained her glass of milk and, licking her lips clean, said, "I guess I'd better take off now."

"Use your napkin," said Mother.

Rose re-licked her lips. "All right now?"

"You haven't finished your potato salad," said Mother.

"Can't waste the time." She slid her chair back. "I've got an intuition that lazy Toby is skipping all the corners again."

"Now don't you start any fights with your brother this afternoon," Mother said as Rosie neared the doorway.

"He'll be all right if he just sweeps the corners." Rosie closed the door behind her.

The old man pointed to Jimmy's limp hot dog. "What's the matter? Too watery for you?" He turned to Mother. "How do you expect the kid to eat a watery hot dog like that? I told you the damn things are all water when you leave them in too long."

"All it needs is mustard," Jimmy said, reaching for the jar. "Except there isn't any more."

"There's more in the kitchen," Mother said, getting up.

"I'll get it," Jimmy said quickly.

"Your mother doesn't mind," said Father.

It was getting worse every second! "That's okay. I want a glass of water anyhow," said Jimmy, rushing out before the old man could do him a courtesy or something!

He heard the wooden floor crackle underneath the linoleum as he walked across to the kitchen sink. He turned on the water loud, so they could hear, though he really didn't want a drink.

If only he and the old man could reach the same point at the same time! But it was always like this. Wasn't the summer well on its way before Father finally agreed that if Jimmy could save two hundred dollars, he would give him the rest for the University of Northern Illinois? By then Jimmy had already spent most of the money on the abortion. And now, today, even as it seemed that McKinley was his answer, Lisa got on the Hawaii kick again and something snapped in him and McKinley was out-of-it forever. So there was Father, on a different wavelength altogether, expecting something that was true this morning to be true this afternoon! Life just didn't work that way!

It was like when Jimmy was ten, when they lived in a Jewish neighborhood and every kid on the block, including Jimmy's best friend, Mickey Robbins, went away to summer camp at the total cost of thirty dollars for the entire two weeks, including the handicraft supplies. Jimmy begged like crazy, but the old man wouldn't let him go, because when Father was a kid he never had to ask his parents to buy things for him to do—kids found their own games, free. So Jimmy spent the time practically alone, selling Kool Aid on the sidewalk, and going just once to Lincoln Park. Worst of all, Mickey Robbins came back from camp with a case of genuine poison oak and a real rawhide belt. Jimmy was miserable through the whole sixth grade.

And what was the clincher? When Jimmy was fifteen and a sophomore in high school, and they lived in the Catholic part of the North Side, where practically nobody went away to camp, guess what the old man decided to give Jimmy as a birthday present, and guess who took Jimmy's movie money away when he found out that his goddamn kid didn't want to spend two weeks at camp!

After turning off the water and slamming an empty glass down to make it sound as though he'd finished drinking, Jimmy creaked across the floor to the refrigerator. But there wasn't anything of interest in it, except creamed spinach in a covered dish and some of Wednesday's meat loaf wrapped in tin foil. No Frosties left either, thanks to Rosie; about the only edible thing was an orange. As he was biting into it, something started in the living room.

"What? When?" shouted Father.

"I invited her for four-thirty," said Mother.

"Not while this is still my house!" said Father.

"Al, will you please lower your voice," Mother said. "The neighbors know enough about us already."

Father raised his voice. "Goddamn it, Faye, use your head! You can't bring that kind of woman into a house with children."

This was beginning to sound pretty neat, so Jimmy moved a bit closer to the hallway.

"She is not 'that kind of woman,' " said Mother. "She is intelligent and I like her."

"And I told you I didn't want her in my house! That's final!" said Father.

Mother used her cool, omnipotent voice. "You certainly didn't seem to mind her at the Mariner's Club. I saw the way you watched her!"

"Who didn't watch her? She was dressed like a burlesque cutie, sticking herself in everyone's face."

"Joyce is a very successful woman in real estate. Half her business comes from being friendly to people. We ought to be thankful she invited us to the club. God knows when we'd get out otherwise."

"She was selling at that party, all right—but it wasn't real estate!"

"If she chooses to use her womanly qualities in business, that's her concern," said Mother.

"All right, all right," Father said with finality, "but if Joyce Fickett is here when I get back from the office I'm going to be damned sore. Now I'm warning you Faye—"

"Please, Al, the children!"

"You use your goddamn head, that's all I'm telling you!"

"All right, Al, all right. . . ."

Then a chair scraped, and footsteps came toward the kitchen. Jimmy hurried back to the sink and pretended to be cleaning up the orange peelings. But it was okay; it was only Mother.

"Go in and talk to him. This is your chance," she said in a muffled, urgent voice.

"Mother, there's something you ought to . . ." Jimmy began.

"Don't worry. I told him how much you want to go to McKinley and he's pleased as punch."

"Yeah, but—"

"Faye," shouted Father from the dining room. "Where the hell are the Fig Newtons?"

Mother reached into a pantry shelf. "I'll go to the

bedroom so you two can talk in private," she said as Jimmy tried to get a word in.

"Faye!" Father demanded from inside again. Jesus, if the world were being blown up like a cherry bomb, the old man would still be screaming for his goddamn Fig Newtons.

Mother thrust the box into Jimmy's hands. "Here, you give him his Fig Newtons and for heaven's sake, use your goddamn head." With that, she was gone.

Jimmy found Father at the table, casually thumbing through *Life* magazine, looking at the pictures. At his elbow a chrome and brown plastic electric coffee pot perked rhythmically. Barely any furniture in the house, everybody always complained about how little money there was, yet right there on the dining room table was a thirty-four dollar electric coffee pot with extension cord and push-button thermostatic control.

"Here's your Fig Newtons," said Jimmy, handing Father the box.

Father looked up. "Thanks," he said, adding, ". . . coffee's ready."

"Thanks," said Jimmy, awkwardly taking his place at the table. He found a clean cup and filled it with the steaming coffee while the old man went back to *Life*.

After a while Father said, "Cream?"

"Pardon?"

Father held out the pitcher.

"No thanks."

"Like it black now, huh?" Father's tone implied Jimmy was a regular little man now. Hell, he'd been drinking black coffee for a year.

Magazine pages began to flip again. So the old man was following the usual court procedure: not a word until Jimmy approached the bench and said he was heartily sorry for all his sins.

At a loud slurp from Father's end of the table, Jimmy looked up from noting in the reflection how big his nose got when it almost touched the black liquid in his cup to see how the skin on the old man's throat moved as his coffee went down. Then a bite of Fig Newton and the sound of chewing. In the small dining room it sounded to Jimmy like gravel falling off a truck. He couldn't stand to watch television with Father because he ate peanuts. But what he could do with a Fig Newton was beyond belief!

Father smiled, Jimmy smiled back and averted his gaze, which accidentally landed on a photograph of some Danish princess in a bikini. The picture filled an entire page of *Life*, opposite the editorials, and for an instant it seemed that he could see down between her boobs, but it was just the way the light hit the page or something, because he couldn't.

But all at once Jimmy was overcome by the sensation that it was reacting to the princess's boobs like even if *he* couldn't see between them, *it* could! He set his spoon soundlessly on the saucer and tried to stop it before it got out of control.

Suddenly a chair moved away from the table. The old man stood up, and it was no longer a problem.

"You aren't leaving for the office already, are you?" Jimmy said anxiously.

"Sure, what'd you think?" Father raised the knot on his tie.

"That's what I thought."

Lifting his suit coat from the back of his chair, "Got to bone up on the old cost-accounting procedure," Father said cheerfully.

"You sure work hard," Jimmy said lamely. The office bit was a dead end. He needed something stronger, and fast!

The old man beat him on it. "Just remembered," he began with a broad, embarrassed grin, "I found something you might be interested in." He reached in his pocket and pulled out a folded newspaper clipping. "Here, look at it."

Grateful for the extra moment, Jimmy took the clipping and opened it up.

It was from the *Daily News*.

"In the corner, to your right," prodded Father.

There was a small box with the headline: "Johnston's Markets buys Smythe Chain."

"See it?" said Father.

"The market one?" said Jimmy, as though he couldn't wait.

"Near the bottom. Look near the bottom," said Father.

". . . This brings the number of its units to 22 with over 500 employees and sales of $30 million per year," said the article. ". . . Chief in the negotiations for Johnston was Gene Sherwood of Kennilworth, Illinois."

"Where it mentions Gene Sherwood," said Father.

"I see it now." Jimmy held the clipping tenderly, like it was old parchment.

"Gene went to McKinley too," Father said proudly. "We were pals through school. Buddies, me and Gene."

"No kidding!" Jimmy was practically beside himself with enthusiasm before he realized he might be overdoing it.

"Show what you can accomplish if you put your mind to it. Of course, a young man has oats to sow," Father added philosophically.

"I guess I overdo it though. I'm the first to admit it," Jimmy said with controlled sincerity.

Father agreed, dammit. But at least he wasn't leaving. "I wouldn't have given two shits and damn for you after last night."

"I wouldn't blame you."

"But you came round in the end, that's what counts." Folding the coat over his arm he added warmly, "You'll like McKinley. Well, see you later."

"Y'know," Jimmy said loudly, stopping him, "I was talking to this guy yesterday who said he was going to Hawaii. His father's a bank president and could easily afford to send him to Yale except this kid wants to work his way up from the bottom, and he's taking off and getting himself a job." Jimmy went on desperately, "Isn't that admirable? I mean, his father's probably proud."

"Don't be impressed by that crap. Hawaii's a lot of beach bums like Miami, same thing."

"You were in Miami, weren't you? During the war?" Jimmy said it quickly. "That's where you got your tattoo."

"I have to get that taken off," Father said on cue.

"What's it like? Miami, I mean?"

Father grinned mysteriously. "Wait a few years and I'll tell you."

He was probably thinking of the time he kissed some leftover girl at a U.S.O. dance, but Jimmy didn't call him. Instead he joked like an all-around good kid. "I guess it's lucky for us you came back!"

"War had to end sometime," said Father, like it was some game. "We all have to come to our senses and get back to reality."

"But it isn't fair somehow," Jimmy said, following the old man to the door.

Father dusted his hat off with his sleeve. "What's that?" He bit.

"The way you had to work your way through McKinley and everything. Fifty hours a week, besides raising us kids. And I get it all for free."

"Since when are you worried about getting something for nothing?" said Father. Not what he was supposed to say, but at least he wasn't opening the door.

"I was thinking in terms of character development." Father winced and Jimmy realized he was sounding ridiculous. The old man would never swallow that from him. "I mean, I might get to be a lot richer if I had to learn to do things for myself instead of counting on you and Mother for everything." That was much better.

"You've milked us for almost eighteen years; four more won't make much difference. Besides, both your mother and I want you to go to college.

"And I appreciate that," Jimmy said, almost too anxiously. "Except, did you ever think how all this might be ruining me?"

"What the hell are you talking about?"

"Well, I've been pretty selfish. . . "

"Mmmm," Father said warily.

"I mean, I've got to admit that spending so much money on that girl because of my stupid mistake, when you and Mother need so many things, was a selfish thing to do."

"What are you getting at?" Father was all-out suspicious now.

Jimmy had to talk fast. "It's like when we moved away from the old place. It cost you a lot of money to come to Weston. And we still don't have much furniture. I mean, Mother does the best she can, but the apartment still seems like someone's just moving in or moving out. Here you're struggling so hard and trying to get ahead, and I went out and blew over a hundred dollars."

"If you mean you don't know your ass from your elbow, you're right," said Father, "but that's all under the bridge. Just start thinking about your studies, and let me worry about the finances."

"But I'm worried about your finances too! I mean, sending me to college is going to cost you." Jimmy's coolness was gone now.

"I know what it's going to cost me, dammit!" And Father's fuse was beginning to sputter.

Jimmy lowered his voice. "Do you really think it's worth it, Father?"

The old man's eyes narrowed. "What are you up to, you little sonofabitch?"

"I was just thinking of your brand new car." Bull's eye!

Father's expression changed. No longer a simple man on his way to a few hours at the office, he was now a prince of the Church barring a hoard of infidels from the Holy Sepulcher; a frail Hindu saving his sacred cow from butchers; a lone Arab, holding back the River Jordan from the thirst of Israel. Question the old man's patriotism; doubt his love of family; call him lousy in his profession; threaten his life hereafter. But say a goddamn word against either bucket seat in that shiny new automobile and he'd chop off your head before your mouth could close.

"What about my car?" Father said.

Facts and figures, Jimmy needed a few facts and figures—the old man was crazy about them. "Well, it's going to cost two seventy-five a semester to send me to McKinley, right?"

"Go on," said Father.

"And let's see. . . ." Jimmy couldn't add very well. "That comes out to about six hundred a year, right?"

"Fifty-five."

"And that means . . . let's see, twelve goes into five, I mean fifty-five, about four times; four times twelve is. . . ."

"It comes out to forty-five eighty-three a month," said Father.

"Thanks. Now how much do you pay for the car every month, not counting the down payment, I mean."

"Get to the point," Father said impatiently.

"About a hundred-fifteen, right?"

"So what?"

"So forty-five dollars is about a fourth of your monthly payment," said Jimmy.

"A third," corrected Father.

"See! You could pay off the car one third quicker!"

Father pointed to the table. "Get over there and sit down."

"But I haven't finished."

"Sit down!"

Jimmy sat down.

"Now goddamn it you tell me what this is all about and quick! What's your new scheme? What'd you dream up this time?"

This was it. Jimmy was conscious of squaring his shoulders, but when he spoke there was kind of a squeak in his voice. "I want to go to Hawaii," he said.

Father had trouble believing his own ears. "Hawaii!"

"Like this kid I told you about."

"Hawaii!" Father bellowed loudly.

"I've already saved seventy dollars, and Mr. Spaulding's giving me thirty-two this afternoon, that only leaves eighty-eight bucks!" Jimmy said urgently.

"You little sonofabitch! I wouldn't give you one goddamn cent for Hawaii, understand? Not one goddamn cent!"

"But think of the money you could save!"

"I'll save money all right! You either go to McKinley College or you get out Monday morning and find yourself a job that pays so you can start kicking in around here. You'll pay your share or get the hell out!"

A cheery voice rushed in from the bedroom. "There's

some cold meat loaf in the refrigerator if anybody's still hungry," said Mother.

Father spun around angrily to greet her. "You!" he shouted. "You and your goddamn aristocratic son!"

Mother paled. "Al, what's wrong?"

He turned back to Jimmy. "Not one goddamn cent, understand?"

The old man thundered across the room. As he opened the front door he shouted back to Mother, "And if that goddamn woman is in my house when I get back from the office there's going to be hell to pay!" The door slammed hard behind him.

Even after the old man had gone, Mother stood watching the doorway, shock and bewilderment on her face.

Jimmy was a bit shaken himself, when he thought about it, but he couldn't let one of the old man's temper tantrums throw him off course. He turned to look pleadingly at his mother. There was another way of getting on that plane tomorrow morning, and he knew she had money stashed away. Besides, she was a sympathetic ally and she knew what a sonofabitch the old man was.

But before he could speak, Mother turned to face him.

"What did you do to your father *now?*"

Jesus.

JIMMY left by the front door of the apartment and began the four-story walk down the stairs to the street. The windowless stairway was lit by yellow light bulbs pretending to be the flame of the cardboard candlesticks affixed to the wall at each landing, and the dirty brown rug beneath his feet was nearly worn through to the reverse side. It was depressing.

Having been renounced by his father and—when it came right down to it—abandoned by his mother, he now had to rely on his own cunning. If they'd read a little Freud they might know what they were forcing him into. He wondered how much he could get for the old man's typewriter at the pawn shop.

Taking the steps two at a time, he raced back up to the apartment. He was almost at the door when he remembered that the backspacer on Father's typewriter was broken. Too bad, because he had a false I.D. now, which you needed to hock something. He'd found that out when he was fourteen and took Mother's gold watch out of her jewelry box and tried to pawn it on South State Street. They said he had to be twenty-one and the watch wasn't gold anyway. When Mother learned what he'd done she practically got hysterical. What bothered her wasn't so much that Jimmy had tried to pawn it; it was finding out that the watch the old man gave her on her birthday wasn't real gold. She accidentally dropped it down the kitchen sink a few days after that.

If the typewriter wouldn't work, something had to. It was already two o'clock, and he had to be downtown to work for Mr. Spaulding by two-thirty. Even if he hurried, he wouldn't be finished there until four, and it was Saturday afternoon and that meant Denise. Jesus, the day was passing quickly.

When he reached the second landing he looked down between the banisters to see Toby on the ground floor near the doorway. He was polishing the intercom next to the brass mailboxes. The thing hadn't worked since the day the building was constructed, probably, but Toby was polishing it anyway, and the corners had been swept clean. Rosie sure scared the hell out of him.

Toby looked up when Jimmy reached the tiled entrance hall. The kid was really well integrated into Weston. He wore a Weston Y.M.C.A. T-shirt, tan pants with smudges, white socks and desert boots.

"Hi," Jimmy said as he passed through. He had to say something; the kid was his brother, after all.

"Boy," Toby said sarcastically. And after shaking his head, he went back to polishing.

"What the hell's wrong with you?" Jimmy was sorry now that he'd said hi.

Toby ignored him to continue polishing.

Jimmy was willing to forget it. "Keep your mouth shut," he said, opening the heavy front door.

Then Toby said, "You're really a big deal."

"You want to get hit?" Jimmy said, going back.

But Toby seemed to know that Jimmy wouldn't hit him. The reason Jimmy wouldn't hit him was that the kid hit back, and it was embarrassing to be caught fighting with your thirteen-year-old brother.

Toby turned defiantly. "You really had to get Father mad, didn't you? Every time you see him, you make Father mad."

"What're you talking about?"

"I heard him hollering at you. Can't leave him alone, can you?"

Toby was the only one in the family who was stupid enough to like the old man. At his age he probably needed a father image or something.

"You're too young to understand. Wait a few years, then maybe you'll figure it out."

"Think you're so superior," said Toby.

"I know a lot more than you do, you little shit." He was late for work and he was losing patience. "Get back to your polishing before I tell Rosie on you."

"I'd rather polish than work for a pukey photographer," said Toby.

"It's more suited to your station in life."

"Bet I make more than you do!"

"Ha, ha."

"Rosie gives me two bucks for doing the banisters and sweeping, and when I go to Mrs. Hollinder's at three o'clock I'll get two-fifty more, not counting the tip Mrs. Hollinder gives me. Half a buck, usually."

Jimmy laughed.

"Go ahead and laugh, big noise; me and Rosie made over two hundred dollars this summer."

Jimmy stopped laughing. "You did?"

"And we've got it to show," added Toby. "Do you?"

Two hundred dollars. . . . Jimmy felt the blood leave his cheeks. "I don't believe you."

"Ask Rosie."

"I will," said Jimmy, and he left the building to his kid brother's horselaugh.

Near the apartment house was the Weston-South shopping center, consisting of a small supermarket, a women's dress shop which had been in a closeout sale ever since anyone could remember, Vivi's Beauty Salon, and a small pharmacy with overcrowded shelves and cluttered counters. It was in the pharmacy that Jimmy found his little sister.

Rosie was surrounded by a group of small girls. In one hand she held a fistful of Tootsie Rolls, and in the other a coin which she was handing the druggist. Although the other girls mostly wore colored T-shirts and cordoroy pants with sneakers, Rosie remained apart in a navy blue jumper with a lace-collared blouse. She smiled benignly as she passed out the candy.

"Hi," said Rosie when she saw Jimmy.

"I want to talk to you, Rosie," he said, making it sound important.

"This is my brother." Rosie introduced him to the girls, producing a chorus of whispers.

One girl giggled loudly, and the one beside her in a sailor cap said, "I don't think he's so handsome."

"They're learning to be window washers," Rosie said of the girls.

"I've got a brother, too," said the one in a sailor cap. "He's in the Marines."

"That's great," said Jimmy, who wasn't sure whether he had to be nice to all of them or not.

"So what do you want?" Rosie got down to brass tacks.

"I thought you and I might be able to talk in private," Jimmy said.

Rosie unwrapped her own Tootsie Roll. "These are my friends," she said.

"But it's kind of important."

"To what?"

"To you. . . . It's a business proposition."

Rosie looked from Jimmy to her girls. Then, like a protective madam, she told them, "Wait here, I'll be right back."

Rosie led Jimmy out of the drugstore. They stopped by a dime-operated fire engine in front of the market. "Now what's the proposition?" she said.

Jimmy kneeled down before her so their sizes would match up. It was less humiliating that way. "Look," he began gently, "I've never asked you for anything before, have I?"

She seemed suspicious, but didn't say anything.

"And I'm not going to ask you for something now. I'm going to give you a chance to earn a lot of money."

She broke off another segment of her Tootsie Roll and brushed away a wisp of hair that she'd also been chewing. Her wide brown eyes grew more wary.

"Well," said Jimmy, who was getting nervous, "what do you think?"

"About what?"

"About making some money!"

"You haven't said how yet."

Jimmy's legs were getting cramped, so he propped himself against the fire engine. "If I tell you, promise to keep it a secret? You can't tell anyone, not even Toby."

"I never tell Toby anything," she said with something like contempt.

"All right, I'll trust you."

"Will you please stand up? You're beginning to make me nervous," said Rosie.

Jimmy stood up and leaned over. "Rosie," he said in a voice guaranteed to capture a little girl, "tomorrow morning at eleven forty-five a plane is going to leave from O'Hare Airport. Where do you think it's going?" His voice oozed mystery.

She shrugged.

"Hawaii!"

No reaction.

"You have heard of Hawaii?"

"Sure, everybody has."

The kid wasn't normal. "Well, don't you think it's great? Your brother is going to be on that plane tomorrow. Bound for Hawaii!"

Suddenly her eyes shone with life. "You're nutty."

"It's the truth!"

"Did Father say you could go?"

"Father doesn't know. I told you, it's a secret."

"What's the proposition?"

"You can stake me."

"I can, huh?"

"You see, there's a lot of new stuff going on there because of the population explosion. . . ." He paused. She was only a kid after all. Better take it easy. "You know about the population explosion, don't you?"

"I think so," she wrinkled her brow.

"Well, with all those new people being born there, I'll be able to get in on the first wave, so to speak, and grow with them, raise pineapples and coconuts—and sea shells, and—natural pearls—"

"But what about the snakes and headhunters?"

"I'll take my chances," Jimmy said grimly.

"Wow!"

"So you see, Rosie. . . ."

"Sure, I see," Rosie said. "You mean you want me to give you some money."

"Not *give* me money—*invest* it with me," Jimmy pleaded.

"Look," Rosie said levelly, "when I give those kids Tootsie Rolls it makes them work for me. That's an investment." She stopped for a breath and went on. "But you—no one ever got anything out of you, so if I laid some bread on you it wouldn't be *investing,* it would be *giving.*"

They were interrupted by a messenger from Rosie's new window washers, the one in the sailor cap.

"Hey, Rosie, hurry up!"

"Just a minute," said Rosie. "I'm talking investments."

"We're going home if you aren't going to hurry up" said the sailor cap.

"She'll be right there. Shut up and wait!" said Jimmy.

The sailor cap stuck out her tongue at him and rejoined the group.

Jimmy turned back to Rosie. "Okay, so it's a long-term investment, let's put it that way. But I'm desperate, Rosie. I'm at your mercy."

"How much do you want?"

"Eighty-eight dollars is all I need," he said, trying to conceal his rising hopes.

"That much?" Rosie considered hard.

"You'll get it back, I promise."

She drew a quick breath and got down to business. "Okay, what have you got for collateral?"

Jesus, where did she learn that one?

"What do you want?" he asked hesitantly.

"How about your record player," she said calmly.

"But that's not mine; it belongs to Fred Roberts!"

She shrugged and started to walk away; he grabbed her shoulder strap.

"Okay, the record player," he conceded.

"I thought you said it belonged to Fred," she said coyly.

"Well, yeah, but—it's mine too, in a way. I mean he practically gave it to me."

"The records, too?"

Jimmy nodded. "The records, too."

"Then I'll lend you twenty dollars on it," said Rosie.

"Twenty dollars!"

"What do you expect for stolen property? Take it or leave it."

"Please, Rosie, I'm begging you. Look, you can keep the record player and I'll send you twice as much as you lend me as soon as I get to Hawaii. Please?"

"Will you throw in your cuff link case?"

"Anything."

"Okay, then, twenty-four. That's as high as I'm going."

"Thirty," said Jimmy.

"Since you're my brother, I might be willing to go up to twenty-eight, but that's the best I can do."

"I'll take it."

They shook hands.

A SHIVER of electricity shot through the train and it began to hum. Then, with a shudder, it started to leave the station. Inside the last car on the El, Jimmy settled himself by a window near the center doors to watch it push free of the long wooden platform. Soon it was clattering above streets, rolling past gray roof tops, brick chimneys, and "100 ROOMS 100 BATHS" painted on the backsides of old hotels. Jimmy tried to see beyond dirty windows, through lace curtains, but it didn't work, so he looked down at the people in the streets playing their endless game of staying around another day: slow-moving housewives with paper bags; children hop-skipping-jumping; old men spitting their diseases on the side-walks; twitching teenagers full of resentments, ideals, and sex. He looked up to the faces in the car. They were the same as the ones below. Jesus, he hated to ride the El. He didn't know when it all began, but the fear was there far back in his memory, way back when he could walk under the turnstiles. He was afraid of being trapped in the train while it carried him into the hole under the city, right down to the center of the earth where he would suffocate. When he thought about it, it was a stupid fear, and Freudian as hell. He should have gotten over it long ago, but he never quite did.

Still, it wasn't as bad today as other times. Even when they rounded a curve and the cars swayed and banged, and the wheels let out awful screeches, it didn't bother him too much.

And when the El neared the Loop, and with a rush descended underground, the sudden fear didn't grip him as it usually did. Other times, when the train went into its tunnel he would have to look away from the windows and read the advertisements above his head, quickly, as though they were salvation words from the Bible.

But it wasn't like that today. He was less than twenty-four hours away from total freedom. Rosie said she would put the money in his top drawer, where he could find it when he got back from Mr. Spaulding's. (Shit, only twenty-eight dollars for a stereo and a stack of records. Except Jimmy neglected to tell Rosie that the record changer got stuck all the time. Too bad he wouldn't be around to see how that grabbed her.) But he was still short of his economy fare to the Islands.

The ticket was, roundly, a hundred-ninety dollars. He'd already saved seventy, Rosie contributed twenty-eight, and in a few minutes he'd be collecting the week's salary from Mr. Spaulding: thirty-two dollars after taxes. That left sixty bucks still to go. A pittance, really, if someone had some place to get it.

Of course, he might ask Mr. Spaulding for an advance on his salary. After all, Jimmy had been a faithful employee, and with Mr. Spaulding giving him all that apprentice bullshit, he had been underpaid. Not that that was altogether the photographer's fault. When Jimmy applied for the job at the beginning of the summer Mr. Spaulding had asked him whether he wanted a summer job or a career, and Jimmy'd lied and said "career" to please him. But it didn't so much please him as make him forget all about the minimum wage law.

Since Mr. Spaulding never knew Jimmy was planning to quit for college in the first place, there would be no reason for him to know that he was going to Hawaii tomorrow, either. Especially if Jimmy could wrangle an advance in salary, which was really money Mr. Spaulding owed him out of the career swindle, anyway. All Jimmy needed was a clever but simple excuse for putting in his request.

It had to be a good one, though, because Mr. Spaulding would make even Fred Roberts look like the Ford Foundation. Not that Mr. Spaulding was stingy with himself, just with other people. Like when he gave his renowned Saturday-night parties in his lush "upstairs" over-the-studio living quarters where everything was real Louis and antique birdcages full of birds and original oil paintings with lights over them like at Suzie's. He invited only his special artsy friends from the "chic" race and made them bring a bottle. As it worked out, there was always too much liquor, so every Monday morning Jimmy was sent down to the package store to cash in the extras, which was embarrassing as hell for Jimmy, but that's how Mr. Spaulding was.

The train was coming into the station when Jimmy got the inspiration—it had to do with Mr. Spaulding being chic; which was more important to him than being Catholic. His top-floor skylight was chic; his birds, especially his macaw, were chic; his cigarettes, licorice-smelling and imported from New York, and which he never smoked, were chic; the music he had piped into the studio, mostly Broadway shows of the thirties, was chic; and most of all his mother, who was very rich and lived on Lake Shore Drive and refused to sign her will and wet her pants every chance she got (the old woman blamed it on bad kidneys but Mr. Spaulding blamed it on sheer meanness) was chic.

The only thing Mr. Spaulding had around him that wasn't chic was Jimmy Reardon, because Jimmy came to work in old khakis and rolled-up shirt sleeves. Mr. Spaulding was really appalled before he got used to it. He said Jimmy represented the studio when he went on errands, and should wear a chic suit. But Jimmy was damned if he'd wear his only suit to work, although it was more diplomatic to tell Mr. Spaulding he didn't have one. It was one of the rare times he'd ever seen the guy moved to generosity. Well, not generosity exactly. He'd offered to advance Jimmy the money from his salary to buy a suit, only Jimmy had refused then. Hell, he needed that money for school—even if it turned out that wasn't how the money was spent. That was a month ago, now it was altogether different. If he could just get Mr. Spaulding to be generous again. . . .

Nearly three P.M. when Jimmy walked by the chic red garbage cans and turned down the steps to the entrance of Mr. Spaulding's brownstone. Pushing open the black door with the lion's-head knocker he went into the cool, damp studio.

Voices were coming from the living quarters upstairs, so Jimmy waited a moment before announcing his arrival.

"I won't have you prying into my personal affairs," Mr. Spaulding was saying. "I've told you I intend to spend the evening alone."

"Then why are you so set against having dinner with me?" It was the baritone voice of Mr. Spaulding's mother.

"Because I'm exhausted!" Mr. Spaulding shouted. "I spent the entire day getting the Sally Victor hats proofed. God, Mother, do you have to be so annoying?"

"I've a perfect right to look after my interests. Don't forget who put up the money for this little hobby of yours. If it weren't for me you'd still be dressing windows at Goldblatt's."

"I was very happy there," said Mr. Spaulding.

"I'm sure, and you'll be happy there again if you don't tell me who's coming tonight!"

"No one, I told you! No one!"

So that was it. All summer long Jimmy had come to the studio on Saturday afternoons to clean it up for Mr. Spaulding's parties, and all summer long they'd argued.

Pretending he'd just arrived, Jimmy opened the door again and slammed it hard. "Mr. Spaulding, I'm here," he called up the stairs. When there was no response, he decided to go ahead and begin work anyway.

The studio, a long, narrow, no-nonsense room, had floors of white painted tiles. An antique desk dominated one wall; above it were shelves for cameras, props, and small equipment. And lots of lights, on and off tripods, stood around impatiently like people waiting in line to get into a movie or something. Hiding the rear wall was the no-seam paper, suspended from the ceiling like a giant roll of paper towels, which was used as a no-background background for pictures. In a corner, closed off by a black velvet curtain, was the darkroom, and across from that, a mirror and vanity table for the models, and a door leading out to Mr. Spaulding's garden.

The walls of the studio were covered in burlap and hung with photographs Mr. Spaulding had taken over the years, mostly portraits and fashion pictures, except for one prominently-placed shot of a nude bathing—back view. That nude was the first thing Jimmy had seen while he was being interviewed for the job at the start of summer. Jesus, the Weston High Placement Service had finally come up with something worthwhile, he'd thought. But the only things Mr. Spaulding photographed since, at least while Jimmy was around, were women's hats and shoes for the Marshall Field's ads in the *Daily News.* Still lifes, he called them, Jimmy never gave up hope, though, of someday finding a picture of that nude from the front.

Tackling the darkroom first, he began sweeping in the eerie red glow. The floor was littered with crumpled paper still wet from the developing solution, and discarded negatives. He was careful to sweep in the corners. Mr. Spaulding would be more easily disposed to give him an advance if he did a good job.

The upstairs voices sounded even louder in the darkroom, and he could hear footsteps directly overhead.

". . . That awful Caroline Mengers will be here, too, I suppose," Mrs. Spaulding was saying.

"What do you know about Caroline Mengers! Have you had me tailed again?" demanded Mr. Spaulding.

"How dare you accuse your own mother of such a thing!"

"Mamma, for three weeks I could look out of my window and see the same man parked across the street in a tan Chevrolet. When I joined some of my friends for cocktails at Poopie's Pub, there would be a tan Chevrolet parked outside the door. When I slipped out for a little bridge at Arnie's, a tan Chevrolet. A late date at the Tempest Bar, a tan Chevrolet. Even when I come out of mass at St. Michael's! Well, I've never been married, I pay all my bills, I'm not trying to work for Civil Service—so why on earth, dear

Mamma, why on God's earth should I be followed around by a tan Chevrolet!"

"How the hell should I know!" snapped Mrs. Spaulding.

"You know all right; who the hell was having me followed around by a private detective?"

"Well, I'm your mother. I have my rights," the baritone said. "Besides, I fired him weeks ago!"

"Oh God! Protect us from those who love us most!"

"Lose me, and you lose my money," Mama said.

"You won't have any money if you throw it away on private detectives!"

"How sweet of you to be concerned about my money. You needn't be, you know. I only paid Terry two hundred a week."

Jimmy paused in his task. Jesus, two hundred for sitting around in a tan Chevrolet! He would've done it for a hundred. Eighty-five, even!

"Who is Terry?" said Mr. Spaulding.

"The tan Chevrolet."

"You mean you call him *Terry!*"

"That was his name."

"Damm you! I won't be followed by any damn Chevrolet any more, you understand?"

"I suppose you expect me, a woman of my age, to follow you myself!"

"I don't want anyone to follow me!" Mr. Spaulding's voice got higher and weaker as his mother's got deeper and stronger.

"Well, someone's got to watch out for you," Mamma sniffed.

"Mamma, I'm thirty-eight years old!"

"And you still can't look out for yourself. Those dreadful parties—and that awful Caroline Mengers."

"Carry happens to be one of my oldest and dearest friends."

"Then why don't you marry her?"

"Because I don't want to marry her. . . ."

Pushing back the black curtain, Jimmy left the darkroom to empty the dust pan. Now that he thought about it, he'd seen that tan Chevrolet himself—hell, he even bought that Terry guy a sandwich one afternoon because he'd said he had an appointment and couldn't leave the car. It had been worth a fifty-cent tip. But Jimmy had never heard of Caroline Mengers before. That was a surprise because the truth was he always figured Mr. Spaulding was a little queer, judging from the way his men friends called Jimmy "darling" when they mistook him for his boss on the phone. Not that Jimmy cared—that sort of thing had been around for a long time if you believed *Bulfinch's Mythology*. It said Apollo dug this youth Hyacinthus so much that when the kid was accidentally killed by Apollo's own quoit (whatever that was) Apollo, grief stricken, changed him into a flower so he could live forever, which is how the world got hyacinths. (Suzie insisted it was the only authentic queer flower in spite of the fact that the pansy was official.)

When Jimmy returned to the darkroom the voices upstairs were silent, and the only sound was the faint fluttering of birds. Maybe the old woman had kidney trouble again. Mr. Spaulding was complaining last week that he had to have two of his best chairs recovered because of her visits. Maybe she'd just made it three and old Spaulding had seized the occasion to faint dead away. Anyway, Jimmy had to hurry if he wanted to keep the date with Denise Hunter, his Saturday afternoon habit.

With deft hands he took the acrid-smelling trays away from the workbench, and unloading them in the utility sink next to the enlarger, turned on the water. While they were rinsing he moved speedily into the studio to clean Mr. Spaulding's desk. He did this in two main steps: first, by dropping everything into the top drawer; and second, by blowing off the excess dust with his mouth. What was left came off with a judicious wipe of his sleeve.

Not pausing, in continuous motion, Mr. Clean took the camera from the center of the floor, passed it onto the shelf, and slid the lights into their cubbyholes, even as he kicked a stray stool underneath the desk. It was amazing how he had the whole operation timed. Now he directed his attention to a set-up of Sally Victor hats, left over from the morning's shooting, which stood in front of the white paper backdrop. Without crushing them too much, he put them back in their boxes and stacked them near the front door, then, having cleared the floor, he began to sweep. Only three places got really dirty: near the front door at the bottom of the stairway, in the center of the studio where Mr. Spaulding did most of the shooting, and under the desk. No sense sweeping anywhere else.

That accomplished, his eye searched for something undone, something special, some unique deed to impress Mr. Spaulding with how much Jimmy Reardon cared about the goddamn studio. Of course, the props on the shelves above the desk might be set in order, only that would take all afternoon. There was the long radiator under the front window, except that would only draw attention to the thick dust underneath it. But wait! The white paper roll! Its bottom, smudged with black marks from Mr. Spaulding's shoes, could be cut off the giant roll in seconds. And since the paper was almost ten feet wide, Mr. Spaulding couldn't fail to notice that Jimmy had taken care of it. Perfect.

He had a little trouble finding the shears in the top desk drawer because of all the new junk he'd just put in, but soon he was merrily cutting a tear in the huge paper roll suspended from the ceiling. So merrily did he work that he pulled too hard and the roll broke away from the ceiling and thundered to the floor, barely missing Jimmy, who stepped back and watched it unroll itself clear to the other end of the studio.

Afraid to move, he listened for a sound from the stairway.

But no doors opened and no one came. Thank you, God. He'd been granted a reprieve.

He'd need a ladder to put the paper back up. Where had he seen one? Oh yeah! Tearing out the back door to the garden he found the old stepladder lying beyond the hyacinths along the brick wall. He tore some of the burlap on the studio wall bringing the ladder inside, but only a little. Setting it up was easy, except it wobbled pretty bad. Next he had to roll up the fallen paper, only the goddamn giant thing kept swelling lopsidedly; it just wouldn't roll evenly. Shit!

Unbelievably aggravated, Jimmy unrolled it back across the floor, for the third time, to start again. Now he stood on the paper, taking small steps backwards as he rolled it towards himself—noticing too late that he was leaving his footprints on the virgin white stuff.

Calming himself, he took the shears and cut all the goddamn extra paper clean off, leaving a fifteen-foot swath of it in the center of the studio floor. Expensive stuff, he could almost hear Mr. Spaulding's voice reminding him, but what else could he do?

He slipped the ladder into position under the "L" shaped steel hooks attached to the ceiling. The roll was heavy and he had to balance it on his shoulder just right while mounting the ladder, which trembled under the weight. It might've worked, too, except in the midst of the attempt a foreboding sound reached his ears . . . water. Water? Jesus! The darkroom sink was overflowing!

And right at that moment of realization, there came the noise of birds, an old woman's baritone voice, and footsteps. They were coming down!

". . . The last time!" Mamma was saying. "It's the last time I'm coming here!"

"You know I'm not that lucky, Mamma."

"You'll find out how lucky you are when you hear my will."

"I'm sick and tired of hearing about your lousy will!" Mr. Spaulding was straining his voice. Slam! The Spauldings went out without noticing Jimmy. He guessed Mr. Spaulding was walking his mother to her chauffered car; that'd take some time, anyway.

Dropping the roll gently to the floor, he jumped soundlessly off the ladder, rushed into the darkroom, plunged an arm into the overflowing sink, shirt sleeves and all, to pull the stopper out of the drain. Then, quickly, grabbing a thick rubber mat from under the developing bench, he plopped it down on the floor to cover the water.

Now out of the darkroom and into the paper problem again. He could dump the dirty swath in the garden, but what if Mr. Spaulding decided to take the macaw out back for a sun bath? Jimmy'd have to risk it. Breathless from all the activity, he grabbed the sheet of paper by one end and hurled it out the back door just in time to face Mr. Spaulding coming in the front door.

"Hi," said Jimmy, the friendly kid who'd been interrupted at his work. Mr. Spaulding glared at him over the puffy sacks under his eyes. His monk-bald head was shiny red, and his arms hung straight and stiff from his shoulders. In a moment the transformation would be complete: Mr. Spaulding was changing himself into *The Boss,* all five-five and three-quarters of him. (His *staff* included not only Jimmy but his eighty-seven year old maid Elizabeth, who came in once a week for three hours to empty ashtrays and pilfer scotch, and who Mr. Spaulding forced into wearing a white uniform, lace apron and everything, even though she only rolled her stockings up to below her knees. When Mr. Spaulding spoke to his *staff,* he used chic English, like pronouncing the *d* in Wednesday and both of the *o*'s in floor.)

"What are you doing here?" said Boss Spaulding.

Jimmy kept a very straight face. "It's Saturday."

"Saturday, hell!" he snapped. "Why didn't you tell me you'd arrived?"

"Next time, I will," said Jimmy. He had tried, but what the hell.

Mr. Spaulding seemed satisfied that Jimmy hadn't heard his upstairs argument with Mamma.

"From now on when you get to the studio I want you to come upstairs immediately and knock on my door. And that goes for the rest of the staff too," he said. "Is that clear?"

"Yes, sir," said Jimmy.

Mr. Spaulding pointed to the roll of paper at Jimmy's feet.

"What's that?"

"That?" Jimmy looked down. "That's paper."

"I know very well what it is! What is it doing on the floor?"

"Well, I noticed how dusty it was getting along the top of the roll near the hooks, so I figured I'd better take it down and clean it on my own initiative, like you say I should do. Lucky I did, too, because it looks like one of the hooks is loose from the ceiling. If it's all right with you," Jimmy went on quickly as Mr. Spaulding looked up, "I'd like to get in here real-early Monday morning before you start shooting and really give this place a going over. Fix that hook, straighten the shelf, clean up under the radiator. Maybe I should wait and put up the roll then, I mean if you'd like me to do all that."

But the bastard was looking around, like a good boss, to see what his staff had *not* done. "Did you sweep the floor this morning?"

Jimmy nodded. "And cleaned off your desk."

"How about the Dektol tray—thoroughly rinsed I hope?"

Mr. Spaulding's eyes darted toward the darkroom, where a small pool of water spread before the dark curtains. With a sharp glance at Jimmy, he started over to it.

"I wouldn't go in there," Jimmy said quickly.

"Why not?"

"I mean right now. It's still wet from mopping."

"It is?" Mild surprise showed on his face, then he shook it off. "Well, it's about time you did something around here."

Jimmy flashed what he supposed was an all-American clean-cut grin.

"You aren't finished yet, though. I'm having guests tonight, and I'm going to need the vases rinsed . . . some lemon peelings, thin lemon peelings. . . ." Mr Spaulding counted everything on the same finger. "And get some soda up from the basement. Dear God, you'd better get some vermouth, too. Why on earth no one ever remembers to bring vermouth I'll never know. And fill the ice buckets, but for God's sake don't bang them around the way you did last time: they're Mother's."

Having heard it all before, Jimmy hooked his eyes into Mr. Spaulding's, which left his mind free to wander around Hawaii with Lisa. A sixth sense told him when a fresh order was being given, and he turned himself in just in time to get it, then back to Hawaii.

". . . And those portraits on the stairway. Take down Cornelia Jackson, she won't be back from Rome till Christmas, and put up Harry Tooles instead. That should keep him quiet for a while. And while you're at it, you'd best take down Judge Middleburg's new wife and put up Mrs. Hollinder. . . ."

Shortly after four o'clock the ice was in the buckets, the lemons were in peels (mostly thick), vermouth was at the bar alongside the soda, and Jimmy had just finished the last of the picture changes on the stairway, substituting Mrs. Hollinder for Suzie's new mother.

Flushed with satisfaction from a job well-done, Jimmy mounted the stairs to negotiate the advance which would make it possible for Lisa and him to polish their personally owned goldfish in their own private lagoon.

As he reached the top of the stairs the laughter of Mr. Spaulding drowned out the bird cries. He was talking on the phone, apparently, to Maxie, whom Jimmy recognized as the sports editor of *The Tribune*. Though Jimmy never met him, Maxie called often and once offered to treat him, sight unseen, to a White Sox home game just for the company. But Jimmy was no baseball fan.

". . . Are you ready? Are you *ready?*" Mr. Spaulding sounded like he was choking to death. "And Morty's so *Protestant* about things like that. . . " He laughed heartily in response to something, then pulled to a halt with a squeak. "Well now Maxie, it's around eightish. . . . Yes, and bring a friend. . . . Who? Oh, *that* one. Well, if it makes you happy. . . ." Then, ultra-cheery: "Don't forget to bring a bottle!"

Mr. Spaulding hung up and Jimmy knocked on the door.

"Come in."

The room was high ceilings, puffy lace curtains, a fireplace, white bird cages, a small sofa, satin chairs with white legs, an elaborate bar, a delicate gold-painted table where a chipped bust of Venus stood looking down on an Oriental rug which was supposed to tell some kind of story. Actually, it was old and worn and the nap wasn't nearly as thick as it was on the rug where Jimmy screwed the girl swindler.

It all seemed as though it should be surrounded by velvet ropes and put in some museum. There wasn't a comfortable place to sit anywhere, even if the chairs *were* signed by Louis IV's carpenter, or someone.

As Jimmy went in he passed the brillantly colored macaw, who sat on a perch above a sandbox and watched everything sideways while he spat the husks of sunflower seeds. Jimmy had thought the bird was pretty neat when he first saw it, but he soon learned that under the fine feathers lived a killer who loved the taste of human flesh. Privately he nicknamed the bird Bubonic, after the plague.

Mr. Spaulding was sitting on the sofa next to the phone with his shoes off as the staff approached and stopped respectfully in the center of the Oriental rug.

"Well, I guess that's everything," Jimmy said, adding, "Whew."

"Tough day, was it?" Mr. Spaulding seemed in a better mood than before.

"Sure was."

"And now I suppose you're going to rob me again," Mr. Spaulding said good-humoredly, taking a checkbook out of the bureau with the cherubs painted on it.

"Oh," Jimmy said as the photographer reached for his pen, "could I have my salary in cash this week?"

"Cash? My accountant would skin me alive!"

The sonofabitch would pull something like this. "But couldn't I sign something? A receipt?"

"Well . . ." Mr. Spaulding hedged.

"I need the cash, and the banks are closed till Monday," Jimmy said urgently.

Giving in, Mr. Spaulding set the pen down and took out his billfold. Boy, he was sure in a good mood.

Jimmy watched the thick wad being separated into small bills by chubby fingers. The old bastard probably knew every one of the serial numbers by heart. Anyway, here goes:

"Mr. Spaulding, I was wondering. I mean. . . ." He shifted his feet and groped for words. Young and awkward seemed the best way. "That is, do you think I might get a little advance?" The eyes he hooked into

Mr. Spaulding's now were purposeful and large, open to eighty-five percent maximum.

Mr. Spaulding pulled the wallet back to his chest. "A what? What for?"

"For your sake, mostly."

"My sake?"

"I have to take those hats back to Marshall Field's on Monday. . . ."

"So?"

"So I hate to face them looking like I do. You know, representing the Linus Spaulding Studio like you always say."

Now wait and let that work on old "chic" Spaulding's psyche.

"I told you not to come to work in shirt sleeves!" he said.

So far so good. "I know, that's what I'm saying—you're right. But if it gives you any satisfaction, I've learned my lesson. From now on when I represent the Linus Spaulding Studio I go first class. That's why I need the advance, you see?"

"No, I don't see."

He was sure dense. "For a suit. The one I saw today on the way to work. Fits me perfectly, right off the hanger."

"Now wait a minute," interrupted Mr. Spaulding.

"It's on sale," Jimmy added.

The Boss moistened his lips. Was that interest?

Now adding fact to fancy: "Marked down from a hundred thirty-five dollars," said Jimmy.

Mr. Spaulding bit: "To what?"

Now real fast to dazzle him: "Only sixty dollars! Made of genuine mohair plus olive green lining!" Oh shit, he should've said red; Mr. Spaulding liked red better.

"Wait a second! Are you asking me for a sixty-dollar advance? What about the thirty-two dollars I'm paying you now?"

"Oh, but that isn't mine."

"Whose is it?"

"Mother lets me keep four dollars for cigarettes and things like going to the movies on Saturday nights, but the rest goes straight toward paying my share of the rent and food."

Mr. Spaulding fixed him a fishy look. "Jimmy . . ." he began in a flat voice.

"Sir?" It was the staff again, respectful and correct.

". . . I happen to know," Mr. Spaulding went on, "that your father has a good job and your mother works as well. Do you expect me to believe they'd take your salary? Do you think I'd believe you'd give it to them even if they did?"

The cynical sonofabitch!

Taking Jimmy's silence for total surrender, Mr. Spaulding pushed the assault. "Now, is it really a suit you want?"

"No." Jimmy fell back to a prepared position by letting the smile fade slowly from his lips, at the same time sadly enlarging his eyes to ninety-five percent maximum.

"I'm not promising anything, but the truth might help," said Mr. Spaulding.

He was softening. Jimmy thought hard for something with truth in it, finally said simply, with barely a trace of self-pity. "It's my leg."

"What's wrong with your leg?"

"I can't let my parents know about it."

"Why?" Mr. Spaulding said suspiciously.

"I cut in on a whiskey bottle last night and. . . ."

"Dammit!" shouted Mr. Spaulding.

"But it's the truth! Here, I'll show you!"

Jimmy raised his pants to reveal the skinny little bandage below his knee. Why the hell couldn't they have put some gauze on it or something!

"That?" scoffed Mr. Spaulding.

"It's really much worse than it looks." Jimmy uncovered the wound. "See? Stitches!"

Mr. Spaulding turned away quickly. "I can't stand wounds and things," he said in a choked voice.

"It's infected inside, too." Jimmy was on the offensive again. "Been hurting like crazy all day."

"And I suppose you're going to tell me you need an advance for the doctor."

"That's it," Jimmy said gamely. "You guessed it."

"All right," said Mr. Spaulding, "I won't let you down."

Jimmy's heart beat fast. He was falling for it!

"I'll ask Bobby Ditton to have a look at your leg. He's one of the finest doctors in Chicago and a good friend of mine."

Jimmy lost control of his eye percentage.

"What's the matter, Jimmy?" Mr. Spaulding said innocently.

"Thanks a lot. I'll go see him first thing Monday morning." He was beaten and he knew it.

"Better not let it go that long if it's infected inside." Mr. Spaulding was enjoying it now.

"That's okay, I dig pain." Jimmy turned towards the door and the cannibal macaw. "Good-bye, Mr. Spaulding. Have a nice weekend."

As he walked across the chintzy Oriental rug, slowly passing the crappy chairs and all the other expensive junk, Jimmy let his shoulders sag and his head droop. At the doorway his hand caressed the knob in a sorrowful, hopeless way as he paused to stare desolately into space. He hoped he sort of looked like a wilted flower or something because he was giving that dirty sonofabitch behind him one last chance to change his mind and turn human.

But nothing.

It was his own stupid fault, saying he had to kick in for rent and food. What a dumb thing to say! Still, it wasn't like he'd asked for a loan or anything. Hell, an advance would've come out of his own salary, even if he wasn't going to be around to work for it. But shit, Mr. Spaulding didn't know that!

Sixty dollars. Mr. Spaulding would net that much from just cashing in the scotch at his party tonight. His chic party. Serve him right if Mamma cut him out of her will.

Mamma. Something was trying to tell Jimmy something, and it had to do with old lady Spaulding. He concentrated hard.

Poor Mamma. When it came right down to it, all she wanted to do was be included in Mr. Spaulding's parties—it might even be a humane gesture for someone to help her find out what her boy was up to. Besides, what would sixty dollars mean to her? She could take it off her inheritance tax or something.

Only, what if she was a cynic like Mr. Spaulding? And another thing, now that he thought about it, he really didn't know that much about Mr. Spaulding. Still, the old lady was a thought. . . .

He sighed and wiped the whole problem out of his mind for now. First he'd keep his Saturday afternoon habit, then he'd see. One thing was for sure: he'd make that plane tomorrow morning. It'd take all the uncommitted nations plus France and South America to stop him!

As he opened the door to the street, another door opened upstairs. Jimmy turned back to look. Mr. Spaulding was taking his goddam macaw out to the garden for a sun bath.

IT was Denise Hunter's bedroom, and there she was, like every Saturday afternoon, lying on the four-poster bed on her stomach, with one leg swinging in the air. Dressed in her father's old plaid woolen bathrobe, she was nibbling at the top of her little finger and watching an old movie on television.

She didn't look away from the tube when Jimmy quietly settled on the bed beside her, but she did stop swinging the leg for a second in a kind of recognition.

"*Robin Hood?*" asked Jimmy.

"Sure is," she said through her baby finger.

He waited politely until the commercial went on, taking off his shoes as he explained, "Sorry, I'm late, but Mr. Spaulding gets nervous if I don't check everything."

Now some girl was going Psst with a hair spray on a mirror, and Denise watched in severe concentration. During the break between commercials, she took her finger out of her mouth.

"Who is Mr. Spaulding?" she asked distantly.

"My boss," explained Jimmy, like he'd explained a million times before.

The leg began to swing again, and the finger went back to its slot. Jimmy leaned over and put his face against her robe, blowing hot onto her skin. She'll never last till King Richard returns, he smiled to himself. And neither would he, now that he thought about it, because as usual under these circumstances, it was giving him a very rough time.

She thumped her leg on the bed and wiggled her hips.

"That tickles," she said factually, without looking away from Sherwood Forest.

"Good," said Jimmy, resting his head on the small of her back and letting his fingers tingle up and down her leg like a piano player doing exercises. She was wiggling a bit now, one of her preliminary wiggles, but she was still pretending not to notice him, that's how she liked to play. To increase her awareness, he let his warm palm slide up the cool hardness of her ankle, going first to just below the knees, then higher until he was lifting the protection of Dad's robe above what Dad would consider the rape area, or something. He could feel the tiny bristles of auburn hair scrape his palm. It was going out of its mind, but the rest of Jimmy was playing it cool, even after the robe had been inched up to the crest of two soft white domes.

He could feel Denise settle into the pillow to enjoy his advance work, keeping one eye on Robin Hood. They sure had come a long way since Jimmy's mission of mercy had first thrown them together.

It had been early in May, and a freak snow had come one night to prove winter wasn't giving up completely. But by mid-afternoon of the next day the sun had melted all of it except for some sooty icebergs along the curbs and occasional globs clinging to the grass like melted marshmallow.

A frantic phone call had sent Jimmy rushing to Fred Robert's house in rich-row, where he found his friend in the game room sitting on a bar stool surrounded by his mother's hand-painted seascapes and the ashtrays his father called pre-Columbian art. It was clear that Fred had been crying.

"Jesus, Fred, why don't you just say screw it and find some other girl? Nobody's worth all that, especially someone you've only known for a month," Jimmy said earnestly.

But Fred wasn't answering.

Jimmy was worried. Fred had come to him about Denise Hunter when he'd first met her so that Jimmy could advise him on methods of sizing up the basic situation. This included whether she French-kissed or not (Fred was afraid of finding out if she did, even though he was already a senior in high school), how late her mother let her stay out, how long she sat in the car before going inside after a date. Jimmy, who'd not met her up to then, did further research for his friend via Suzie Middleburg. But, aside from a roll of the eyes which meant Denise was not completely untouched by human hands, all he got was an aggravating-as-hell "Dum-te-dum." Yet even without Jimmy's help the romance had flourished—until now.

"Look," Jimmy went on brightly, "why don't we go out tonight, get crocked, find a couple of broads at the Dead Pigeon or someplace, and forget the whole thing. Isn't that better than killing yourself for a girl you never even put it into?"

Without looking up, Fred slid off the stool and walked over to the window above the billiard table. He took off his glasses and stared myopically out at the disappearing snow.

Jesus, if he'd only talk. Fred without words was an utter stranger.

Jimmy followed him and tried again. "Even if Denise doesn't dig you, that doesn't mean there aren't plenty of girls who do!" He hoped he wouldn't have to name one.

Fred didn't answer.

"Will you just tell me what Denise *did* that was so bad, for crissakes!"

"Nothing," Fred said softly.

"Well, God damn it!"

"She just said she couldn't see me for a couple of weeks because she has a lot of homework. That's all she had to say. I got the message."

"Well, don't you recognize the pattern?" Jimmy pretended to be relieved. "First she wanted to see you all the time, right?" Fred shrugged, and Jimmy went on: "Going to the library together and everything? She even wanted to make out, you told me so yourself. But you didn't make any moves, so she probably thinks you're rejecting her. So now she's entered the aloof stage. I'm telling you man, 'homework,' roughly translated, means come over some night when my mother's out. No shit, Fred. . . ."

"Please, I'm not in the mood for your crappy theories."

"Wait a couple of days," Jimmy urged. "When she doesn't hear from you she'll come bouncing back like a goddamn yo-yo."

"No, I'm just inadequate, that's all. I've always known it—this is just the final finger." Then, very seriously, sending a chill up Jimmy's spine: "I'm going to kill myself, Jimmy."

"Then, why'd you call me? So we could make it a duet?" Jimmy tried to laugh it off.

"I had to tell someone. . . ."

Seeing Fred's eyes get wet, Jimmy got tougher. "Yeah, well I'd rather read about it. I can't stand the smell of cowards." He was calling Fred's bluff, figuring that sympathy would do him more harm than good.

"You're a nice guy, Jimmy. Y'know that?" There was hate in Fred's eyes. He felt betrayed.

"Okay, so I'm a bastard. But I just can't believe that a friend of mine would commit suicide over nothing. I just don't have that kind of taste in friends!"

"It's not over nothing. She'll know!"

"All right," Jimmy sighed. "I guess the least I can do is aid and abet you. How are we going to do it?"

"I'll do it *myself!*"

"But how? With a gun? What if the bullet misses and only rips off your jaw or something? It's happened before."

"No gun. I'll do it simply. Just get in the car, close the garage door and carbon monoxide will do the rest."

"But what about your parents? What if they come home and find you blue, but alive?"

"I won't do it here, I'll do it somewhere else! I'll drive to Indiana and find some deserted road!"

Fred was getting pissed off, which seemed like an improvement.

"What are you going to do for a garage door? Carry it in the trunk of your car?" said Jimmy.

"I don't need a door! I'll connect a hose to the exhaust and get the fumes directly!"

"Boy, if she's just playing hard to get, what a waste!" Jimmy sighed.

Fred choked. "She isn't."

"Can you honestly say you know that, Fred? I mean, really know that? Like beyond a reasonable doubt?"

Fred was held by Jimmy's eye.

"Of course you can't!" Jimmy rushed on with more confidence now. "Listen to me, Fred. I'll tell you what, I'll go talk to Denise and tell her what you're about to do."

"No! You can't do that!"

Jim talked through his objection. "And if she doesn't call you within five minutes after I get there and tell you she's really crazy about you, I'll supply the hose personally and you can return to dust."

"No!" Fred screamed, then thought it over as Jimmy stared him down. He modified his stand. "I don't think it'd work. . . ."

"Well I do! Maybe it's only a straw, but you're a drowning man, and a drowning man can't be particular about what he clutches at!"

"I don't know," Fred said, but this time much more weakly. "I don't know, Jimmy. . . ."

Jimmy had pulled up that first time before Denise's house, an old Victorian mansion along Lake Michigan, and got out with the air of a man on a mission, but the truth was, he wasn't quite sure what he was supposed to do. And he was frightened by the giant house, fully expected a scarred old caretaker to appear behind him and kick him off the premises or bury him in the basement or something.

He tried all the doors in front, creepy doors with the shades drawn that made hollow sounds when he knocked. Finally he found life through a screen on the back door.

"Hi," he said to the girl facing him from inside.

She had black stone eyes and was more or less covered by a zebra-striped bathing suit. She went on staring and he realized awkwardly that he'd have to say something more.

"I'm Jimmy Reardon, a friend of Fred Roberts—Denise Hunter?"

The girl nodded and opened the door. "Come in."

"Maybe I should have knocked harder at the front door, but nobody was answering," he said, following her inside, watching as she piled her hair into a billowing auburn helmet.

"We never use that part of the house except for company . . ." she said and went on, "You read poetry at the Dead Pigeon, don't you?"

"How do you know? You go there?"

"Once. Didn't like it much. Tacky."

She led Jimmy to a wicker-furnished, pine-panelled room with special shelves for all the tennis trophies on display.

"You've got a great house here," Jimmy said enthusiastically.

"It's pretty tacky too."

By the way she was looking at him, she thought he was pretty tacky too, it seemed. He started talking: "What I came to see you about was—"

She stood up, interrupting him. "Is the sun getting in your eyes?"

"No."

"Let me pull this thing down. I don't know why, but the sun always gets in people's eyes in this room. Really a hang-up."

She reached up and released the bamboo roll, letting it drop behind the sofa. Jimmy had to look away from noticing her smooth white body in the brief bathing suit. What the hell was she wearing a bathing suit in the middle of the winter for anyhow!

He was beginning to feel uncomfortable, and to develop the standard problem with it.

"Are you graduating this year?" he asked throatily.

She nodded.

"What homeroom are you in?" he persisted.

"Miss Albee's," she said, with a hint of annoyance.

"I have Mr. Stout," Jimmy offered.

She sat across from him and stared hard. "It's okay. You don't have to strain—Fred called. It seems he had a second thought and phoned to warn me you were coming. . . ."

The way she stared with her black, expressionless eyes, Jimmy forgot to be surprised at the information.

". . . I hope you're as bad as he says you are," she continued.

He glanced up from her boobs sharply. "Bad?"

She smiled now. "He said you were coming over to play John Alden but that he suspected the worst so he called to warn me."

"Good old Fred," Jimmy shook his head. "You do a guy a favor, try and save his life. . . ."

Denise was studying him closely. "It's funny," she said, "if I'd seen you without Fred's advance build-up, know what I'd do?"

Jimmy shook his head no.

"I'd look right through you. But now. . . ."

And that's how, without in any way interfering with either of their relationships with Fred, or Fred's virginity, or Jimmy's feelings for Lisa, Denise and Jimmy became a Saturday afternoon habit. . . .

The television set sputtered.

"Must be an airplane," said Denise.

With his ear pressed against her back, Jimmy could feel the deep rumble in her chest when she spoke.

"Yeah," he said, and his voice sounded deep and vibrant too, so he added, "they usually cause interference," so he could hear the sound again.

He didn't mind her watching television. What the hell, it was cool just to run his fingers over the mounds and in between and think of all the jerks in high school who watched baseball on Saturday afternoons, or gleefully awaited a date which would find them making out for hours on some dark road until their tongues ached, then strike out, lucky if they could swing a good wet dream before Sunday morning.

Another chest rumble. "He's real bitchin'," she said admiringly

"Who?"

"Errol Flynn."

"Yeah."

From the sound of her "Errol Flynn" Jimmy knew that it was time to begin seriously. Her robe was off now, and he softly massaged her shoulders, searching with his fingers the warm places under her arms. He knew every pink and white inch of her, he thought warmly, moving his hand around to place it between her stomach and the bed before reaching up to cage her boob with his fingers. He saw her shoulder shiver forward and felt her hard knob in his palm. It was like she was a neighborhood he felt comfortable in, one where he knew all the people, just who would answer when he pressed what doorbell.

This was the last of their Saturdays, he thought, now turning her gently beneath him. He was going to miss her in a way, although they barely ever got to know each other any better than they did that first time.

"You're breaking my arm," she said.

"Sorry."

Her legs parted under him and he felt it hard on her. She put one hand about his waist and pulled his shirt free, then slipped the other between their bodies to tug at his zipper.

"It's stuck," she said.

"I'll do it."

His pants fell away as he took the full length of her body, kissing her neck and shoulders and swallowing the dark tips of her boobs, while his fingers sought out her liquid darkness.

"Watch your nails," she said.

He tore off his shirt completely without leaving her breast, then he was rattling every door in the neighborhood, and finally he was inside, sending hot breath into her ear while she pulled him deeper.

"Jimmy. . . ."

"Huh?"

"Not right away, okay?"

"Jesus."

He felt himself quickening as she flowed with short sighs. Got to put the brakes on. He opened his eyes to the vision of Errol Flynn addressing the motley members of his camp: "All right men, this is it."

Without losing the rhythm, Jimmy kept his eyes glued to the television set. Some woman was in a cave with a friar. She wore a hat with a long feather. Denise bit her lip and gasped and Jimmy pressed harder.

The frair pounded his fist at the end of a long picnic

table. Denise bit Jimmy's neck and tore his back with her nails. She was almost there. Boy, it was really going to be tough, telling this kid he was going to Hawaii. How would she live through Saturday afternoons without him?

The men gathered around Errol Flynn and raised their bows to the wind as Denise wrapped her legs around him and pulled her knees way up. A moan. He felt her insides cramp and tighten around him. "Are you with me?" shouted Errol. Jimmy pushed more deliberately, all the way out, all the way back, then faster. Faster. Faster.

"Ready?" he asked, almost desperately.

His answer was a long assenting gasp ending in a series of little cries which he rode to the crest, lingering there for one time-suspended instant before crashing down with her. Screw over.

"Hand me my robe."

"Here."

He moved his head down to her stomach while she put her arms in the sleeves.

"Please don't," she said.

"I thought you liked it."

"I don't, really."

"Why not?"

"It's dirty."

"Okay." He lay back and looked at the ornate ceiling as she got off the bed and began to tie the woolen sash.

"It's over," she said in a moment.

"What's over?"

"*Robin Hood,*" she said, and went into the john.

After putting his shirt on so she couldn't make another crack about the unevenness of his nipples, Jimmy looked around at the dresses and sweaters popping out of drawers, the old magazines on the floor, the empty perfume bottles on her dressing table. Even if Denise wasn't one of the world's greatest wits, they'd spent some swinging afternoons here, and it was a habit he was going to be sorry to break. He found his socks on the floor next to an oversized teddy bear with one eye missing and the other blinded by a bra.

Naturally he was going to have something better in Hawaii with Lisa. But still, he and Denise could've had a hundred kids by now, when he thought about it. And though she was going away to school soon, she'd be expecting to pick up again with Jimmy when she got back for Christmas and Easter vacation, and she'd probably be pretty upset when she found he wasn't here. He'd have to tell her he was going; he owed her that. But what if she cried? Or started throwing things or—Jesus!—even told Fred! No, she wouldn't do that. What would she do? It was confusing because the truth was, Jimmy didn't know her well enough to anticipate her.

Denise came back from the john, took her bra off the teddy bear's eye and strapped it on. He decided it would be best to wait until she had all her clothes on.

He came back from the bathroom to find her dressed in black slacks and a bra, sitting at the vanity table combing her long hair.

"What's wrong with you?" she asked, hard at work on herself. "What're you staring like that for?"

"Nothing, I was just looking."

Jesus, this wasn't easy.

"Make yourself useful. Get my purse, will you? On the TV." She gestured toward it.

He got it and gave it to her.

"Thanks." She snapped it open.

"What I wanted to tell you is that tomorrow morning I'm going to. . . ." He stopped abruptly to watch the unbelievable thing happening at the vanity table. Among the girl-things Denise was dumping out of her purse to search for bobby pins or something, was money. Money! Crumpled up like used Kleenex!

"I mean," he amended, "I've been thinking about going to Hawaii soon."

"Really?" said Denise, biting open a bobby pin.

Somehow Jimmy expected a more profound reaction. "Yeah," he said.

Dismissing it altogether, Denise said. "The folks' plane got in at four. They should be getting here soon."

Jimmy took the hint. "Well, I guess I'd better be going."

She smiled agreeably as she got up to find a sweater.

He lingered awkwardly next to the bed. "Denise, I was wondering. . . . You don't suppose you could lend me a little bread, do you?"

She looked up sharply.

"I mean, just till Monday. Mr. Spaulding couldn't pay me today because he ran out of checks. All I need is sixty dollars, or any respectable part of it."

But Denise was shaking her head.

"What's wrong? I'll pay you back Monday!"

"I can't lend you any money, I'm sorry."

"Why not?"

She pulled the sweater over her head. "Fred won't let me," came the muffled voice.

"Fred! What the hell has he got to do with it?"

"He told me you're a bad risk. I promised him if you ever asked me for money I'd say no."

"But how could he find out?"

"I'd have to tell him. I can't keep secrets from Fred."

She went back to her purse and filled it up again with her stuff and all his money.

It was unbelievable!

"You certainly managed to keep these Saturday afternoons a secret!"

She looked at him as though he were nuts to bring it up. "That is entirely different. Fred wouldn't understand about that."

It was no use. She actually meant what she was saying. If he thought it'd do any good he'd beg for it, but since he could tell it wouldn't, he'd show a little pride.

"Okay," he said, trying to be cool. "Then I'll see you and Fred tonight. Ten-thirty. At the Dead Pigeon."

"Hey," she said, as he was leaving the room with terrific casualness, "would you turn the channel please? There's nothing but commercials on that one."

By all rights he should have been pissed off at Denise, he thought as he waited for the bus. But he had to consider it objectively. Obviously, she refused him the money not out of choice, but to ease a crippling guilt complex. The truth was, by honoring her stupid promise to Fred she was subsconciously compensating for her habit with Jimmy.

No, he couldn't blame her. It was his friend. Jesus, who the hell did Fred think he was! Telling Denise not to lend him money like that. The dirty sonofabitch! And Mr. Spaulding with his goddamn doctor friends, and his mother. . . . His mother?

"ALICE! Aliiice!"

Mrs. Spaulding stopped bellowing and turned confidentially to Jimmy. "She drinks," she said, then once again craned past the delicate china cabinet with all its glass figurines to shout "Alice, get in here!" in her surprisingly powerful baritone voice.

Jimmy felt like a giant in the little, round, armless chair where he sat with his feet flat on the floor and his knees higher than his waist. Like everything else in the low-ceilinged apartment, the chair was built in scale to the miniature Mrs. Spaulding, who now sat in round-shouldered impatience on the sofa.

Since his arrival, he had been allowed two whole words because Mrs. Spaulding was so glad to see him that she just keep on talking. She was lonely, he guessed, but kind of a bore, too.

Tuning her out while she went on about her maid, Alice, his eye wandered to a corner of the room where, beside a tiny white piano, a small fuzzy dog sat on a pedestal with one paw hesitantly frozen in air. The dog was stuffed, and there was a name plate below it, but too far away to read. There were also dark paintings in gilt frames, lamps with shades of stained glass, chests inlaid with pearl and ivory, a bust of Pallas or someone, fragile tables with curly legs, and a twenty-seven-inch color television set with remote control.

On top of tables and things were photographs in leather frames: Mrs. Spaulding, at eight, standing beside a Shetland pony. A round picture of the old woman in a frilly gown with what looked like the now-stuffed dog in her arms, and one of her shoulders cut off. Next to that was a shot of a tall man with an

Adam's apple, a high collar and no smile, with Mrs. Spaulding's missing shoulder beside him. There was also a big, recent picture of the old lady which was taken at the studio. Half her face was in shadow, and the other half was retouched to take forty years off it.

". . . Aliiice!"

Mrs. Spaulding stopped abruptly, for Alice was in the room.

"Oh," gasped the old lady, now in a suddenly high, sweet voice, "there you are! The young man and I are waiting for our refreshments."

"I been in the kitchen," Alice said dryly, "doing the silver. I only got two hands."

She was one of the tallest girls Jimmy had ever seen, and she had big eyes and a long neck. Alice reminded him of something, but he didn't know what.

Mrs. Spaulding looked anxiously at Jimmy. "Brandy? Scotch? Milk? Coke?"

Alice peered down on Jimmy's awkwardness with majestic boredom. She wore a nurse's uniform and an old sweater, even though the room was warm.

"I'll have a Coke," said Jimmy, who was a little afraid to look straight up at Alice.

"He'll have a Coke, and I'll have a brandy," said Mrs. Spaulding.

"You will not," snapped Alice.

"All right, then, tea!" Mrs. Spaulding said, and added, "Step on it!"

Alice left the room on large, flat feet while, from nowhere it seemed, Mrs. Spaulding produced a black lace fan. Somehow Jimmy expected it to be a live flamingo, and for her to play croquet with it.

"Oh, my," she sighed, the fan fluttering away, "wasn't today a lovely day? After that miserable rain last night I thought it would be sticky outside! I made Alice drive me over to the pier to watch the lake and we just sat there. . . . That's where I was before you called, sitting with the windows open. . . ."

"Excuse me, Mrs. Spaulding," Jimmy ventured. "I'm sorry to interrupt you, but I kind of have a date tonight. . . ."

Mrs. Spaulding got high and sweet again. "Certainly dear, certainly! You want to tell me about Linus, isn't that what you said on the phone?"

"Well, I mean—what I mean is. . . ."

"Don't stammer, dear, speak up!"

Jimmy stammered some more, this time purposely. "About—I mean about the parties. . . ."

Mrs. Spaulding leaned in to him with scary eyes. "*You* don't go to his parties, do you?"

He almost bolted. "Me? No!"

"I should hope not!" she said, her eyes holding his. "What about the parties, then?"

"I thought, that is—I thought you might want to know who goes to Mr. Spaulding's parties."

"Do you know?"

"Every single guest at every—"

"Shhh!" She put a finger to her lips as Alice appeared again to leave a Coke in front of Jimmy and tea in front of Mrs. Spaulding, then plod back to the kitchen. Mrs. Spaulding watched closely until she disappeared, then conducted the rest of the interview in a whisper so that Alice couldn't hear.

"Who did you say was coming to Linus' party tonight?"

"Well—"

She stopped him with another "Shhh!" and nodded toward the door Alice just took. He went on in a whisper. "You see, I sort of consider that classified information, if you now what I mean. . . ."

"You mean you want money for it?"

She forgot to whisper, so he shushed her. "I thought maybe we could think along those lines," he said.

"Well, really," said Mrs. Spaulding, with a lift of her painted-on eyebrows.

"I'm a lot cheaper than your man in the tan Chevrolet," asserted Jimmy.

That grabbed her. "Who told you about that?"

"You mean about Terry?" He threw it away. "I used to have lunch with him, give him information for you, that kind of stuff."

"Hmmm." She was still skeptical.

"He wasn't worth the two hundred you gave him," said Jimmy.

Mrs. Spaulding stopped the fan mid-flutter. "You mean you were the wholesaler?"

He shrugged. "My job is to work closely with Mr. Spaulding."

A quick glance toward the kitchen, then back to Jimmy. "Okay, what've you got? How many are coming tonight?"

"Fifteen, sixteen." Jimmy saw his money flying towards him.

"Name them," she ordered.

"We haven't set a price yet," said Jimmy.

She squinted at him. "How do I know you're not passing bogus information? You don't expect me to buy a pig in a poke."

"Okay," said Jimmy, "we'll start off with Harry Tooles."

Mrs. Spaulding shook her head.

"What's the matter?"

"I wouldn't give you two cents for Harry," she said.

"Why not?"

"Never mind. Give me another."

Jimmy thought, and said, "Mort Weissman."

"No good," said Mrs. Spaulding.

"Him either?"

"Hit me again," she urged.

But Jimmy was getting wise now. "Sorry."

"What?"

"I can't give you any more."

"Why not!"

"Shh," said Jimmy. "Not till we settle our financial agreements."

"You can't expect me to pay for people I already know about!"

"All right then," said Jimmy, "you tell me who you know is coming, and I'll tell you true or false."

Mrs. Spaulding considered that, then said, "All right, you little bastard, you got me."

"Five dollars a head?" Jimmy asked.

She laughed. "You know what? I like you."

River Phoenix stars as Jimmy Reardon, a young man who runs into enough trouble in one night to last a lifetime.

In an attempt to get a girl for his friend Fred (Matthew L. Perry), Jimmy cruises a coffee shop . . .

. . . but Jimmy gets his hands on Elaine (Anastasia Fielding) before Fred has a chance.

Jimmy and his girlfriend Lisa (Meredith Salenger) discuss the future.

A desperate need for quick cash forces Jimmy to plead with his little sister Rosie (Kamie Harper).

As he meets Lisa's new friend Matthew (Jason Court), Jimmy wonders if he's lost his girl to the wealthy snob.

Mrs. Reardon (Jane Hallaren) insists that Jimmy help to entertain her attractive friend, Joyce Fickett (Ann Magnuson).

An innocent drink at Joyce's house becomes a wild seduction.

Getting drunk does little to solve Jimmy's increasing problems.

Lisa is none too happy when Jimmy calls to say he'll be late for a formal dance.

akeview
Countru

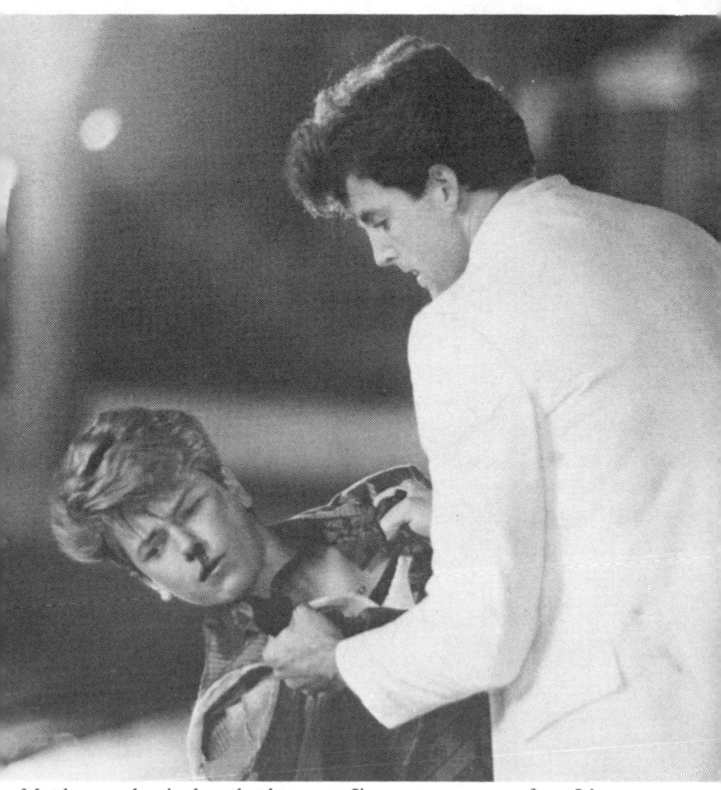

Matthew makes it clear that he wants Jimmy to stay away from Lisa.

◀ *opposite page*

Top: After crashing the dance, Jimmy leaps onstage and spouts spontaneous poetry.

Middle: Wealthy and flamboyant Suzie Middleburg (Louanne) rescues Jimmy and divulges the secrets of their peers.

Bottom: A phony gypsy (Jodie Markell) makes some disturbing predictions during a palm reading.

As if the evening hasn't been disastrous enough, Jimmy wrecks his father's car and realizes that he can't run from trouble anymore.

For the first time, Mr. Reardon and his son come to an understanding of one another.

Jesus, here he was, taking advantage of her, and she liked him!

"Anyway, I don't care to know who's coming tonight. I don't care about anything except. . . ." She broke off to sip her tea noisily, then continued, "Except why *I* can't go. . . . Damn it! It's *her*, isn't it!" She turned to Jimmy, who couldn't for the moment think who "her" might be. "Isn't it!" she demanded loudly.

"Shh!" Jimmy said.

"Isn't it?" she persisted. "Tell me about her. I'll give you all the money you want if you tell me about her."

"All I need is sixty dollars," Jimmy said hopefully. "I'll sell you the whole guess list for sixty—"

"Shit on the guest list!" she rumbled. "Her—tell me about *her*. . . ."

Then he remembered. "You mean Caroline Mengers."

". . . They're always together, or smooching over the phone. An old woman could be dying and she couldn't get past the busy signal. And she's no spring chicken, either!" She probed his eyes. "That bitch! She hates me because he loves me, doesn't she?"

"That's right," said Jimmy, who had no idea.

"She wants to cut me out of my son's life!"

"Cut you out," echoed Jimmy.

"She's poisoning him against me. Weening him away. Not inviting me to his parties is only one step."

"Only one step," Jimmy confirmed it.

"What next?" The old lady asked, horrified. "What next, Mr. Reardon?"

Jesus. But he was saved from answering as she went on: "Soon he'll stop coming on Sunday!"

"That's the next step," he said.

"And then he'll forget Mother's Day, and my birthday, and—and even Christmas!"

Jimmy leaned in confidentially. "I happen to know she's working on Christmas right now."

At that Mrs. Spaulding let out a loud bellow before Jimmy could shush her. Alice must have deemed it a signal, because she ambled in to inquire indiscreetly, "Time for the potty again?"

Jimmy was embarrassed, not Mrs. Spaulding.

"Get out of here, you goddamn bladder-watcher!" she shrieked.

Alice curled her lip and replanted a bobby pin in her frizzy, colorless hair. "Okay by me," she said. "Only next time you wet the sofa, I quit."

Jimmy drank his Coke wishing like hell he could beat some kind of hasty retreat, even without his money. Too embarrassed to look at Mrs. Spaulding or anyone, he dwelt on how big his nose looked reflected in the top of his Coke. Then she was talking again and this time, oddly enough, she sounded almost conversational.

"Thanks," she said. "Thanks for telling me about her. That's worth sixty dollars." Jimmy's heart jumped. "I'll write you a check."

"Oh please," he began, "I need cash. I don't have anyplace to cash a check and I have to buy an airline ticket."

"But I don't keep cash in the house." She pointed toward the kitchen. "She steals, too."

"Well. . . ." He was telling himself it was poetic justice or something. Anyway, Jesus, the poor old woman. "Well, that's okay. I was glad to be of service."

She studied him with sympathy. "I didn't mean to cheat you."

He smiled at her. "Sure, I know."

"How old are you, Mr. Reardon?"

"Seventeen."

She smiled, but her eyes got wet. "Oh my, seventeen. Seventeen, can you imagine that? Seventeen. . . ."

He didn't know why, but all of a sudden it was like someone threw a rock at a flock of birds and they all went flying away, taking the landscape with them. That's how she made him feel for the minute, he didn't know why.

And then she said, "Wait, I may have something put away. . . ."

What was she talking about now? She rocked herself off the sofa with an effort and crossed to a Victorian chest, pulled out a drawer and shoved her arm into the cavity to feel around, frowning. But the frown turned to a smile when she pulled her arm out to display some money between her fingers—two two-dollar bills. It was a beginning.

Before she was through looking it was one whole hour later. She'd dug up an artificial palm tree to find eight silver dollars; eleven bucks were stuck between Lebanon and "I was a 98-pound weakling" in a 1938 copy of *National Geographic* which, for some reason, was pushed up behind the oval mirror that hung over the stuffed dog. He, too, was good for several bills which were, Jimmy blushed to see, removed from up his back door.

Anyhow, altogether, in about a dozen banks, there was forty-eight dollars which Mrs. Spaulding pressed on Jimmy, apologizing for not having his full price.

He felt like a real prick taking the money, and told her so in milder terms.

Her eyes sparkled. "Want to match me double or nothing?" she said.

NEARLY seven o'clock. Carefully treading around the garbage cans on the landing, Jimmy stole into the apartment through the back door—for the last time. Never again would he have to worry about bumping into Father, or feel like an exile in his own goddamn house. Thanks to Mrs. Spaulding, only twelve dollars stood between the old him and the new him.

Twelve bucks. It put Mother back in the picture again. She could swing that, without Father. He might even tell her he needed the money for a going-away present for Lisa. She'd believe that, she was corny that way.

The place was quiet except for two voices coming from the living room, the loudest being Mother's. The other, a strange voice, probably belonged to the woman his parents had argued about at lunch, Joyce, or something.

Only a half hour now, until he was to meet Lisa. He better get dressed, maybe by then this Joyce would have left. Mother'd have to be rid of her by the time the old man got back from the office or there'd be hell to pay. Twelve bucks, she couldn't refuse him. Then he'd have the whole hundred-ninety dollars to show Lisa at the Dead Pigeon; and later, when Fred and Denise showed up, they'd all get crocked out of their minds in one last glorious blast. Jesus, Fred will absolutely shit.

In his bedroom he unfolded a note from Rosie written in a large, little-girl scrawl. It said:

"Dear Jimmy. The changer thing on Fred's record player is broke so that means I can only give you $24.00 not $28.00 like we said. Love Rosie.

P.S. Don't forget you have to pay me back twice as much."

The little . . . !

Well, just chalk that one up as another example of the far reaching corruption of innocents in a materialistic society or something. Now he'd have to tell Mother he needed a going-away present for Fred Roberts besides Lisa.

But he couldn't stay pissed off for too long. Mrs. Spaulding's eight silver dollars felt good and heavy in his pocket, and his seventy dollars unfolded just like new after being squashed under his mattress so long. Added to the rest of the gorgeous loot, it made him feel like a charter member of the rich-race.

He got out of his clothes to take a shower, but then decided to pack first.

When he'd finished filling the black suitcase of pressed cardboard, a remnant of his father's Cicero days, he felt kind of depressed. Practically all he could list among his belongings was a maroon Sears Roebuck sportcoat, which he hated, a few pairs of tan pants, two sweaters, a dirty old white Army ski parka, some of the old man's discarded undershorts, assorted socks and shirts, and one hideous shiny black suit, the only complete suit he owned. There wasn't really a hell of a lot to show for almost eighteen years of living.

Sadly, he kicked the old suitcase under the bed and turned his attention to the typewriter, the broken one belonging to the old man. It reminded him that he owed the family some kind of explanation. They'd be pretty damned upset tomorrow when they found him gone.

"To whom it may concern," he began, but deciding the salutation was a little distant, he changed it to: "Dear Parents."

"Call it the psychosis of my generation," he wrote, "the moral crisis of our times. Attach to it all of society's platitudes. And when you've finished with all that, try to understand, if you can, the truth attending my decision to leave you. . . ."

Not sure of the proper spelling of *psychosis,* he substituted *bane.*

". . . There seems to be a growing distance between what I am and what you determine me to be," he continued. "For this reason I now must sever my life from yours."

And he signed it: "J.," adding below that, "I am going to Hawaii. I'll write you when I get there."

Pretty neat. Maybe he should keep a copy for posterity.

Reading the letter over again, he felt noble and tragic. He looked out the window, across the rutted alley. An old man and his wife played a feeble game of croquet on their soft green lawn. Someday Jimmy's parents would be old like that, and maybe they'd be happier then. Anyway, they wouldn't fight so much.

He wondered what they'd do when they read the letter. Mother would probably cry, sitting in the bathroom so the kids wouldn't see. The old man wouldn't cry, though—just shake his head and say something like "that stupid kid."

Still, it wasn't impossible that Father would cry. Jimmy had seen him cry once before, a long time ago when his mother was in the hospital. Jimmy was in the car and they were returning home from a visit when it happened. Father said she had a woman's disease, a sickness that came from having babies, and that she'd have to have an operation. Then the old man cried. He put his hand on the steering wheel and his shoulders shook. After a long time, when he was quiet, they went home. For weeks he made everyone eat scrambled eggs and baked beans and Jimmy had to do the dishes.

Remembering made Jimmy sad. His father wasn't all that horrible. The old man tried to be a good father, he really did. He just didn't know how. It was as if, when he was a young man, before he got married, Father decided how he was going to live, what he was going to do, and the way he'd raise his children. But the resolution hadn't worked. It was what some people might call a strategic decision, but not a tactical one. Still, the old man stuck to it, because he thought it should be that way.

Like when he made up his mind to have fun with his family.

Father would decide one day: "I think it might be fun to go on a picnic Sunday." And from then on everybody would be miserable.

First of all, the old man would go out and buy a brand-new two gallon thermos jug, which no one but he could touch because they'd damage it. Then Mother would have to make potato salad, which had to be eaten, and sandwiches, which couldn't be wasted. And never enough lemonade.

Then Father would buy a new bat, and a new softball, determined to play ball with his children. Who had to play. And the old ball and the old bat, which Jimmy had been using for months and gotten used to, weren't good enough.

The trip down to the forest preserves near La Grange had to be fun, and everybody had to sing. If they didn't sing, they were pouting and ruining the entire day and it would be the last time any of them would go anyplace, that's it, understand?

So the day would be spent fighting, eating tear-drenched potato salad, and sitting on a hot blanket while everybody else's family was chasing squirrels in the woods or something.

The sedate couple on the lawn across the alley ended their game of croquet, and the old man shook an arthritic fist at the old woman before they went inside.

Lisa and Jimmy sure as hell wouldn't wind up batting a wooden ball around the lawn, Jimmy thought, seeing them. There'd be too many better things.

He thought of Lisa now, and the way she had touched him at the beach. She was afraid, yet she did it, and the feel of her hand set off a barrage of cannon fire in him that made all those Saturdays with Denise seem like a string of quarter-inch firecrackers.

Maybe it was good that Lisa was scared, because then she had more dark premises saved for him to explore while he explained why it was all right that she liked it.

He wondered if Lisa had told her mother about what she'd done at the beach. Not what she actually did, she couldn't tell her that, but about her fears anyway. Lisa confided everything to her mother, she said; they were more like sisters really. When Lisa went on a date, her mother told her how to smile and get the boy to take her to the best restaurants with the most expensive food, and then come home and sit on Mommy's bed for hours and tell all about it: Did Lisa like the boy? And did she kiss him in the car? Not too much, just enough to gain entry next time to an even better restaurant and maybe a play at the Blackstone. Jesus.

Jimmy was the only boy Lisa ever liked that Mommy didn't, so that was something.

"Jimmy, is that you?" Mother's Company Voice blasted through the door. She was inside in her Company Dress before he could answer.

"I didn't hear you come in," she said. "Why didn't you come say hello to our company?" She spotted his note in the typewriter. "Oh, what's that you're writing, a *poem?*"

She said *poem* as though she were shouting over a brass band, obviously for the benefit of the woman in the next room. He took the paper out of the typewriter and said, "That's right."

"Well, when you're finished, come visit for a while. I want you to meet my friend Joyce." Then quietly, urgently, "Hurry before your father gets back. She was late and I just can't tell her to leave."

Jimmy seized the opportunity: "Can I talk to you for a second? Fred and Lisa are leaving for college tomorrow and I—"

"Not now, Jimmy, please!"

"But I won't be able to talk when Father gets back, and it's an emergency. I forgot to get them going-away presents!"

"Later."

"Just sixteen dollars," he persisted.

"I don't have sixteen dollars," she said, starting to close the door.

"What about your bank account?"

"That's my savings!"

He never noticed before how she got that miser look in her eye when she mentioned money. Jesus, that's who Rosie took after! But she did say later: that wasn't saying no—actually, it was a partial commitment.

Jimmy got the suitcase out from under the bed again and took out his suit. Maybe if he made a good impression on Mother's friend. . . .

The trousers kind of reflected light like a mirror, and the cuffs were just a little short, but that made his shirt-sleeve show white, kind of continental style. He told himself if he stayed out of bright lights, the suit was perfect.

They'd never recognize him at the Dead Pigeon, he thought, grinning at himself in the mirror. Too bad the old man had such square taste in ties, though.

"Jimmy?" It was Mother again.

"Don't come in here, I'm getting dressed!"

In a hoarse whisper: "Hurry up, your father'll be back any minute!" She sounded desperate.

"I'll be right out," he said, pocketing his fortune. The way the silver dollars clinked in his pocket was a movement from a symphony.

He took one last glance at his farewell note. This time it didn't seem right. You could interpret it as telling his parents to go to hell, which would look putrid not only to them but for those who would collect him. Best to write another. Simple. True.

> "Dear Mother and Father. When you read this, I'll be in Hawaii. I wanted to tell you personally, but it would only have upset you. I don't want you to think you're responsible for what I'm doing, it's just that I don't want to be a burden any longer. Believe me, I understand how difficult it has been for you both. I'll find a job and go to the University of Hawaii at night and someday you'll be proud of me, I promise. Say good-by to the kids for me. All my love, Jimmy."

Wouldn't be included in Reardon's Collected Letters, but it did sound like the adolescent they think they know.

He found Mother and Joyce seated on the sofa; Mother was a statue holding cup and saucer in her lap.

"This is my oldest boy, Jimmy," Mother said, pleased to find him wearing a suit—that was ten of his sixteen dollars right there. "You've heard me speak of Joyce, haven't you Jimmy?"

"How do you do, Jimmy," said Joyce.

Jimmy turned to see a rather surprisingly good-looking woman with a catlike face and a round figure just this side of plump. He looked into a pair of light blue eyes that were narrow and friendly and crinkly at the corners, and he noticed she had a wide, big-toothed smile and full, full lips. He could smell a nice lemony smell that was perfume but not perfumy perfume, and he liked it so much he almost sniffed hard and made a statement about it, but he decided to play it cool.

"Pleased to meet you," he said. "My mother's talked about you often." Too bad the old man was coming back; Joyce was fun to look at.

"I've heard a lot about you, too," Joyce said, going all crinkle-eyed again. "You're not going to be comfortable on that, are you?" she said as Jimmy reached for a kitchen stool. "Here." She patted the cushion beside her.

"Thanks," said Jimmy, taking her up on it.

"I hear you write poetry," Joyce went on, crossing her legs so Jimmy could hear the smooth scrape of nylon.

Jesus, that's all it needed. He crossed his hands over his lap.

"Jimmy," Mother said, a scold in her voice.

He sat perfectly still. "Pardon me?"

"Joyce wants to know if you write poetry," she said.

"Oh." Jimmy smiled and nodded at Joyce.

"He writes beautifully," Mother chimed in for him. "Read something for us—the one about heredity."

Sure—stand up!

"Don't embarrass him, Faye," Joyce said with unbelievable understanding.

"Joyce is from New York," smiled Mother, changing the subject.

"That's great," said Jimmy.

"Actually Staten Island," said Joyce. "I grew up within sight of the Statue of Liberty."

"That sounds neat," said Jimmy. "What's it look like?"

"How would you look full of tourists?" She spoke with mock seriousness. "Overrun every day and worse on Sundays. We lived in a lighthouse about a quarter of a mile away, and we could see them."

"A real lighthouse?" said Jimmy, nearly forgetting his situation.

"A real one," laughed Joyce.

"You must have had a wonderful childhood," said Mother.

"Well—spent most of it hunting Kleenex. The place was damp in the winter, damp in the summer, and freezing all year round."

"How'd you go to school?" asked Jimmy.

"Ferry," Joyce said.

"I've always wanted to travel," said Mother. "I suppose the farthest I ever got was Kentucky. My family used to have oil wells there before the Depression; I still have a great-aunt who lives there. Her name is Mrs. Lally."

"What's Greenwich Village like?" Jimmy asked Joyce.

"Expensive."

"Maybe someday I'll talk Al into taking a vacation in New York," Mother said, glancing furtively toward the door.

"Don't they have famous writers there?" Jimmy asked.

"The writers I know live off Central Park, on the West Side. The really famous ones live on the East Side, I guess."

"Is that in Greenwich Village?" said Jimmy.

"No, that's uptown, around Central Park."

"I've got two weeks coming in March," said Mother.

"Central Park West," said Jimmy. "Thomas Wolfe wrote about it. The Jewish woman who kept him lived there."

"Jimmy!" Mother barked.

"It's a fact, Faye," said Joyce.

"Mother thinks those things don't happen if you don't talk about them."

"Is March a good time to visit New York?" Mother asked firmly.

"March is pretty unpredictable."

"How long ago did you come here?" Jimmy interrupted.

"About two years. Right after I divorced my husband and got away with the loot, which included a house here."

"Joyce sells real estate," Mother said, proving her friend respectable.

"When I'm lucky," Joyce laughed.

"Well, if you got away with enough loot, you don't have to worry," said Jimmy.

"I'm sure that's none of your business," Mother said, slapping him with a glance.

"I was only kidding. You always take things so seriously," said Jimmy.

"Well, keep your sense of humor to yourself," said Mother.

Without warning, the front door slammed.

"Faye?"

"That's Al," Mother said calmly as her cup slipped soundlessly to the floor.

Father came into the room carrying a worn cowhide attaché case with the faded initials A.R. and a copy of the *Daily News* folded under his arm. Jimmy could hear his own stomach turn over as the old man murmured polite phrases to Joyce. "Good to see you again, Joyce" and "You're looking well" and "How're you enjoying the weather?"

"We've been talking about New York—Joyce lived in a lighthouse there. Isn't that fantastic?" Mother said nervously.

And Father: "Sounds nice." "Wonderful."

With his collar loose and the perspiration lining the edge of his cheeks, the old man seemed like an embarrassed file clerk who'd stumbled by mistake on the president's washroom while the chief executive was taking a leak. The grinning coward didn't even have the guts to admit he didn't like the woman.

And Mother—trying to sew up the Grand Canyon with a needle and thread. Why the hell did he have to be caught in the middle of all this!

"Where are you going all dressed up?" Father glared at Jimmy. If he couldn't be openly shitty to Joyce, he knew where to turn.

"Got a date," said Jimmy.

"Well, you be home early, you hear?"

Mother smiled and you could almost hear the squeak. "He will."

Then the old man asked if he might be excused. Never enough time to finish all the work at the office; still had some letters to get out. Nice to see you again, Joyce, come again soon. You'll have to stop by and visit me, sometime, said Joyce. Love to.

Then Mother was asking if anyone wanted more coffee while Father shouted "Faye!" from the bedroom. And Mother excused herself in a nice way, saying she'd be right back, her husband was calling—probably couldn't find his pencils or something silly, and gave a dry cough. Joyce understood; men were like that.

And Jimmy was left alone with her. He couldn't think of anything clever to say so he lit a cigarette. Then he realized he should have offered one to Joyce. She'd love one. Holding the match to her cigarette he was painfully aware of his sweaty palms.

"I smoke too much," he ventured. He became aware of a murmur, growing louder, coming from the bedroom. Jesus, they're arguing now! Joyce said something, he thought she asked him how long they'd been living in Weston.

"Two years, about," he said—loudly to drown out the hushed anger floating from inside. "Came from the North Side."

"Do you like it better here?" said Joyce.

"A little, but not really. Sort of boring sometimes. You can't drink in Weston, y'know." He had to keep talking till his parents stopped. "Not that I'm old enough anyway, but I have an I.D. I got hold of.

Works greatly, actually—I mean, it works fine if they don't ask me for it until I sit down."

"Why's that?" Was she amused? Could she hear them arguing inside?

Jimmy went on: "It says I'm twenty-four and six foot three. So I have to be sitting down." A glance toward the bedroom. When were they going to stop!

"You can get served at eighteen in New York," Joyce said, as if the conversation held her complete interest.

"That's a long way to go for a drink," Jimmy said, rubbing his hands on his pants.

("Why the hell don't you use your head, Faye!")

" 'Course, some kids shouldn't drink when they're too young. It's really bad for them," he continued loudly. She looked at him oddly, he thought, so he explained, "Sorry, I didn't mean to shout. I always shout when I'm trying to explain something, I'm like that."

("Al!")

Holy shit. He rattled on: "Of course I don't think kids should be allowed to drink until. . . . You know, until they can handle it."

("Lower your voice, Al, *please!*")

"Take a friend of mine as an example," said Jimmy, raising his voice a few more notches. "He drinks sometimes only he doesn't know how to hold it so he gets sloppy and dribbles."

("Please stop it, Al! She'll hear you!")

"And that can be dangerous, you know? Especially when you drive."

("Not another word, Al. . . .")

"It's horrible! I mean, that's why I don't think some kids can drink, because they can't handle it. I mean—Jesus, I don't know what I mean!"

Joyce's cat eyes crinkled, but she wasn't laughing at him; he could tell that. "I'd give anything for a shot now, wouldn't you?" she said.

Jimmy looked at her gratefully. "My father doesn't believe in drinking in his own home, only in other people's. It has something to do with his religion or something."

For some reason Joyce thought that was very funny. She broke up and didn't stop laughing even when Mother blew in, an artificial breeze filling her company sails.

"I see you two have become friends," she said. "Isn't that nice."

Joyce made it easy for her. Glancing at her watch she said, "Oh, I'm having friends for cocktails. I'm afraid I'll have to rush off."

"Oh, what a pity! I wish you could stay longer," tried Mother.

Jimmy could tell she knew that Joyce had heard. Joyce knew that Mother knew. Will rat races never cease!

"Why don't we have lunch next week?" said Joyce.

"That's a fine idea," said Mother. Her relief made her seem human again.

"I'm happy to have met you, Jimmy." Joyce offered her hand.

"I'll see you to your car," Mother said.

"I didn't drive," said Joyce. "I love to walk in this weather."

"Let me call you a cab then."

"No, please. I'd love to walk, really."

"Don't be silly. Jimmy'll be glad to drive you home," Mother persisted.

Jesus, if she wants to walk let her walk!

"I'll go get the keys," said Mother, ignoring Joyce's protests.

"From Father?" asked Jimmy.

"I'll handle your father," Mother said firmly.

"But I've got a date!" said Jimmy.

Mother didn't seem to care. She went after the keys determinedly.

He watched Joyce put her gloves on; both concentrated hard on the task, too embarrassed to speak. Then Mother returned from the bedroom and pressed the keys in Jimmy's hand. There was something else, too. A twenty-dollar bill! The aristocrat had come through!

It was only a short drive to Joyce's, and on the way usual clusters of conversational weeds were exchanged, but Jimmy's mind was on other things. At the beach this morning Lisa had called his plan a silly dream, but what would she say now, when she saw the hundred ninety-four dollars in his pocket! Hawaii, here he comes!

"You can pull right in the driveway," said Joyce.

Her cottage was set back off the road, a doll house in a lake of green. Jimmy pulled the car up to her door.

"I was going to offer you that drink, but I wouldn't want you to be late for your date." Joyce was out of the car.

"Yeah, I'd really like to, but. . . ."

"Another time then," said Joyce, closing the car door.

"I'm afraid not. I'm leaving for Hawaii tomorrow," he said—modestly, he thought.

"Oh?" He was happy she was so surprised. "Faye didn't mention that."

"It's sort of a secret," said Jimmy.

"I'm very good at secrets," she said with a warm, mysterious wink.

"Anyway, it was nice to have met you, Mrs. Fickett."

"Nice to have met you too, Mr. Reardon," she crinkled.

There was a vague insistence coming from his lap—not that he was letting it do his thinking for him, but a free drink never hurt anyone, when it came right down to it.

"Well, maybe I will have one," he said.

JIMMY flicked his cigarette in the large pottery ashtray at his elbow and took another impatient sip of his vodka on the rocks. Anxious to see Lisa, he was almost sorry now that he'd accepted Joyce's invitation, but he was being polite.

He looked around the cottage, past the partitioned dining area to the terrace, back again to the red brick fireplace, and said to Joyce, who sat facing him in a high-backed upholstered armchair, "You've got a nice place here."

"Glad you like it," Joyce said, following his gaze as though she were new here, too. "Not my taste really, my ex-husband's."

"Oh," said Jimmy, now wondering if he was supposed to like it.

"He always thought of himself as the Great Dane type," she went on absently. "So everything's wood and dreary. I like brighter things, but I haven't got around to fixing it up yet."

"Looks nice though," said Jimmy, taking a big gulp of his drink to hurry things along.

She watched him pour the stuff down with something like awe. "I hope you outlive your stomach," she said.

He took a heavy breath to cool his throat. "Don't worry about my stomach—it's made of rustproof aluminum."

"Mine's the old-fashioned kind—cast iron," said Joyce after a small sip of scotch that made her lips sparkle. "But I think it's turning to tin. That's what happens when you get old."

"You're not old," said Jimmy, like he was supposed to.

Amused, "I'm older than you," she said.

There seemed to be a vague challenge in her voice, and in the instant their eyes held tight Jimmy suddenly realized he was alone in this house with a woman who was mentioning her age to him. Now why would she do that. . . .

"You aren't really expecting guests, are you?" said Jimmy. "I mean, you just made that up to get away from my folks."

She laughed evasively.

"And me," he added, "I guess I was pretty silly."

"You were cute," said Joyce.

There—she did it again! First wondering if he was old enough, and now saying he was cute. Something was lurking in that room, something pretty damn neat, and he was determined to bring it out. Dropping his eyes, he began to stare reflectively at the dark fireplace.

"I suppose it must have been difficult," he said after appropriate meditation, "breaking away from your family and friends to start a new life out here in the Midwest, setting yourself up in real estate. . . ."

"Not really, I'm having a ball," said Joyce.

"Still," he persisted, getting through to the inner woman, "I would think that after growing up in the womblike situation of a lighthouse, you might prefer a more quiet, Thoreau kind of existence."

"Oh, I don't know. . . ."

Slyly, Jimmy reversed himself. "I see—you're an adventuress."

"I make a good living," she said.

"The independent type, eh?" he said, with a worldly smile.

She shrugged.

He went abstract. "I think it's important to see the world as a place of bright colors, instead of the muted married-grays."

But she didn't get it or something, for she put her drink on the long coffee table and, sitting back, said "How does it feel, being out of school?"

"It's a step," said Jimmy, giving the question a dignity it didn't deserve.

"Faye tells me you worked for a photographer this summer. That must've been interesting."

"It was."

"Did you get to take any pictures?"

"I was Mr. Spaulding's associate—he owns the studio."

"How nice."

"Mostly I took still lifes for Marshall Field's."

"And now you're going to Hawaii."

"That's right," he said.

"And," she crinkled in a way a friend of his mother's might crinkle, "it's a secret."

"Yeah."

Now that she had turned him into a kid again, whatever it was that had been lurking around fizzled out like a flat Coke. And then she was saying, "I hope I'm not keeping you from your date."

"Better be going," he said, finishing the last of his vodka.

"Thanks very much for the lift," she said.

"That's okay," he answered. "Thanks for the drink. . . ." Even before he felt the warmth of her fingers pressed in his, the faint insistence it had given him in the car had grown to a brassy command. Jesus, Lisa was waiting, he'd had the old man's car out too long already, and Joyce was his mother's friend—he'd only make a goddamn fool of himself by giving in to it.

But he heard himself say, "You don't know what time it is, do you? I don't want to be too early."

She told him, and it was too early, so he wondered if he could have another drink, you know, for the road.

Two more vodkas on an empty stomach, his collar unbuttoned, his tongue loose, Jimmy felt he was making remarkable progress with what he was sure was going to be his first Older Woman.

He was talking about parental influence, making a few salient points here and there about neglect, the crying need for understanding, that sort of thing, so that she might see in herself a solution to Jimmy's desperate need for affection—and match that need with her own, because he knew instinctively that all women *need* more than anything else, or liked to think they do.

"I mean," he was saying now, "that the changes from a pastoral society to a primarily industrial culture have, you know, taken people away from their historic land roots. . . ."

He leaned in with intense eyes, open to ninety-four percent maximum.

". . . To give you an example, the way it affects fruit flies. Did you know that after a fruit fly goes up in orbit, it comes back with its, you know, reproductive system all screwed up? The baby flies barely hatch, and when they do, the whole thing is knocked off, more females than males, everything's gone wrong. If it goofs up flies that way, what do you think science does to people?"

"I don't know," said Joyce.

"Well, that's what I mean," said Jimmy, washing it down with another swig of vodka. "We probably won't know for generations, hundreds of years, even."

He was very aware that Joyce was pulling her dress down over her knees.

"I don't think we have any immediate problems," said Joyce. "Do you?"

"You kiddin'? With the world the way it is? The Bomb? I even wrote a poem about it, just a little one. Want to hear it?"

"All right," said Joyce, without too much enthusiasm.

"You got to understand it's not one of my best, because my best are long." He knew the poem by heart, but he looked to the ceiling as though wrestling with his memory. "Let's see. . . . It begins . . . 'They say that each and every man, is responsible for his destiny. My thoughts are willing to go that way—but what about the rest of me!' "

Joyce laughed. "Sort of Ogden Nash-ish, isn't it?"

"Sort of—I guess."

"Let's hear some more."

"I'd like to but that might take all night," he said with what he imagined was significance.

Abruptly, Joyce reached for her drink. "May I have one of your cigarettes?" she said, her face growing serious.

"Oh, sure." He fumbled with the pack. Jesus, maybe he shouldn't have made the remark about it taking all night.

Lighting her cigarette, he couldn't help seeing how her lips, red without lipstick, glistened in the light of the flame, and the soft way she held the cigarette in her lips. How smooth her neck was, and the tiny pit in the center of her collar where he could see her pulse. She was really pretty, with her catlike eyes and easy movement, and the skin on her arms didn't sag like Mrs. Peterson in civics, who used to smell lemony too.

Joyce had bigger boobs, too. Some women get bigger when they mature, and she was like that. When she leaned forward her jacket spread apart—she wore a light tweed suit that buttoned up the front—and he could see just a little of her underwear, the top of it where it turned to lace, and with his eyes he could feel the pale skin up there too. Suddenly he realized he was staring. He covered up by going on:

"I wrote one about the only solution to it all being personal contact between two people who can share a moment with one another, a piece of each other's eternity, sort of; want to hear it?"

He watched, fascinated, as Joyce exhaled, blowing the smoke out from her nose and mouth at the same time. Sexy as hell.

But she didn't answer, just sat with her legs slightly parted, pulling her skirt taut. He saw the tunnel and imagined how she was at the end of the darkness. Her eyes met his. She'd read his mind.

Now she was up, walking over to the bar, using silver prongs to pinch ice out of a bronze bowl, and seeming very preoccupied. Was it an invitation to leave?

None of it made sense. He thought he knew exactly what he wanted—Lisa, Hawaii. And yet somehow, for the *right now*, he wanted this woman, too—maybe even as much or more. Maybe Fred was right about what he said last night: what if his pecker was leading him around like a mule chasing a carrot!

Joyce stood with her back against the bar, holding her glass with both hands. She studied him for a moment with that same distant expression on her face and said, "Aren't you going to be late?"

"Thanks for reminding me," he said. "Mind if I use your phone?"

"In the kitchen—on the wall next to the refrigerator," said Joyce.

Avoiding her eyes, he walked not too steadily out of the room.

Lisa answered the phone.

"Hello?" she said anxiously.

"Hi, beautiful," said Jimmy.

"You're drunk," she said.

"Like hell!"

"Where are you?"

"Nowhere; I had to give a friend of my mother's a ride home."

"Do you know what time it is?"

"Boy, do I have a surprise for you! D'ya love me?"

"Jimmy, I've been waiting here almost an hour—in my formal! Mommy thinks we're going to the dance!"

"You sound great. Wait'll you see what I've got!"

"This isn't *funny!*"

"D'ya love me?"

"I don't intend to sit here all night!"

"Lisa, goddamn it, I'll be right there as soon as I take my father's car home."

"I wouldn't want Mommy to see you like that."

"Jesus, I said I'm sober!"

"Well, hurry up," she said.

"I will. . . . D'ya love me?"

Click.

Somehow it made him feel good, hearing Lisa so pissed off. Wrapping himself in quiet dignity, he left the kitchen to inform his mother's friend that he was leaving.

But he didn't get very far. . . .

In her stocking feet, Joyce was leaning over a stereo turntable built into a bookcase, and the gliding strings of David Rose or someone were warming the room. He watched her listen for a moment, then take her drink off the bookcase. That's when she saw Jimmy watching her.

"Oh," she said, as if she'd forgotten all about him. "Everything all right?"

He knew exactly what he wanted to do, to leave quickly and politely. Except he heard himself saying, "She wasn't even dressed yet."

Joyce nodded.

"There's still a little left in my drink—guess I ought to kill it—no use wasting the stuff," he said.

This time she gave no sign at all.

"You wouldn't like to dance, would you?" Jimmy realized with some embarrassment that it was he who had said it.

She looked at him. "Do you have time?"

"Won't get another chance. Be away a long time."

It seemed to be the right thing to say. She put her glass on the bookcase and walked into the dim light of the dining room.

"I hope I'm up to it," she said.

Funny, now that he'd practically forced her into it, he wasn't sure he could follow through himself. His legs were awfully weak as he stepped off the rich living room carpet onto the smooth dining room floor, and he couldn't even look at Joyce when he fit his arms around her and her lemony smell engulfed him. Strange, how tiny she seemed now, in her stocking feet and so close. Her tweed suit gave off heat like an electric blanket, and he wasn't that cool himself.

Actually, just dancing with Joyce was some accomplishment. Fred, for instance, could never pull it off. Jimmy was proud when he finally felt her woman's boobs heavy on his chest, and his cheek touching hers, although he was careful to keep the rest of himself away.

Suddenly, without a word, she pulled away and went back to her drink.

Confused, a little scared, Jimmy remained alone on the slick dining room floor. What if she were pissed off—his mother's friend!

"Did I do something wrong?" he said. Should he say something more, apologize for being so forward?

Except that might not be very bright—only draw attention to the fact that he was being forward. Best to just leave.

"Well, good night," he said.

Joyce turned to face him, her back to the stereo. "Jimmy," she said in a low voice.

"Yes?"

"Come here."

He went to her feeling kind of clumsy, and stood there waiting, his arms ten feet long.

She looked up at him, and he could feel a pounding in his ears, and her lips began to move and he thought she said something, which he later supposed she must've said, in light of the fact that only moments afterward, their clothes off, they were going through the neatest gyrations right there on the living room couch as she kept yelling the same word he thought she said in the first place over and over again, only then it was a "do you want to" question and now action-wise it was a command, a plea, a matter of life and death!

It was a mad ride to the sea on a wild bronco, but Jimmy stayed in the saddle to the end; in fact he made two round trips, and when she finally stopped bucking and let him off he was tired but full of a sense of having been someplace—How I Spent My Summer Vacation by James A. Reardon. . . .

Afterward, as the shower spray hit him, he really felt kind of in awe of himself. He was experiencing that great glow of after-sex masculinity that comes of having just spread that particular kind of cheer. He was just as glad it was over, though, when he thought about it. Lisa was going to be pissed off as hell. It must've been an hour since he spoke to her, and she was all dressed then. Man, wait till he told Fred about. . . .

He never had time to complete that thought, because suddenly he wasn't alone in the shower.

"You were taking so long," Joyce said. "Mind if I join you?"

It was the first time he'd actually ever taken a shower with a person of her sex, although he had taken showers with his brother when they were younger, which was really altogether different. Soaping each other was especially different. It was amazing how different soap felt when a woman's hands were sudsing you up, and how different it felt to be scrubbing an Older Woman's back and everything. And, of course, it knew the difference immediately and kept jingling its spurs impatiently, sort of, even though there had been three times that day, including Denise, that it had had its own head.

"Howdy," said Joyce as they galloped off again.

He was lying on her bed feeling guilty as hell now about Lisa when she came over from the dressing table where she'd been brushing her hair to sit beside him.

"Poor baby. Tired?"

Now that she mentioned it, he was, really. "No," he said.

Her hand inched up beneath the towel he'd modestly wrapped around himself. She didn't seem to notice what she was doing, and he was glad, because after all that, it would never go up. At least not for a few minutes, anyway.

"Lucky girl," she said.

"Who?"

Her hand found it and held on. "Your girl," she said.

Jesus, what a time. "Guess I better be going," he said.

"Going to write a poem about this?" she said.

"Want me to?"

"Long as you don't mention names."

She spread open the towel. Although Jimmy himself was totally exhausted, old it was doing fine.

"Just places and incidents," he said a bit thickly.

She didn't answer. He felt her boobs spread soft on his legs. Then her mouth felt hot. He looked straight up at the ceiling. Joyce was giving him another first. . . .

The phone shattered his ears.

"Sorry, darling," she said. "Can't not answer." She grabbed the phone.

"Hello . . . Faye?"

Holy shit.

"Well . . . no, but I'm sure he'll be right along. . . . Yes, of course, about ten minutes ago. I hope I didn't keep him. . . . Of course there's nothing to worry about. Yes, I'm sure. Good night, Faye." She hung up.

"I told her you were on your way," she said, "but I'm not going to let you go yet."

He couldn't exactly say he wanted to go under the circumstances.

She smiled at him mysteriously. "Want to try something?"

He nodded because if he were going to talk he might say no.

"You stand over there in front of the mirror—just stand there."

He waited where she put him and he watched her back away to the other end of the room, turning off lamps on the way so the only light was the moonlight coming through the windows, all the time holding his gaze. When she was against the opposite wall, her eyes wandered over his naked body like it was something to enjoy; Jesus, he hoped his nipples looked straight. Now her mouth was moving, every part of her seemed to have a life of its own. Kind of spooky. There they were, nothing on, staring at each other; he wanted to laugh, more out of embarrassment than humor, but he didn't. It was kind of neat, and an unusual experience to report to Fred on top of everything else, except that goddamn virgin sonofabitch'd never believe him!

"Touch yourself," she whispered.

"Beg pardon?" he said.

"Play with the little boy," she said.

"Oh."

For the sake of the spirit of the game, his hands obeyed. The effect on her was unbelievable. She stared hard at him and then began to explore herself. How the hell did she think all that up? Now she was at her boobs and her hair and leaning back. Watching her led him into a kind of fascination that made him lose his objectivity or something. Anyway, he lost himself. In a few moments a kind of mutual world enveloped them; they were in a heightened time of anticipation, straining toward each other, resisting, drawn, resisting, struggling against the pull.

"Jesus!" Jimmy shouted without meaning to.

"What? What do you want to do, Jimmy?"

That broke the spell. Suddenly she was just a naked woman and he was a jerk standing there playing with himself. Maybe people her age had to invent games like that to get their pots boiling or something. Dammit, what did she *think* he wanted to do?

"I want to screw you," he said, taking the direct route. That seemed to please her.

When it was done—again—he rolled over on the bed and closed his eyes. Joyce seemed to be sleeping.

He lay there for a long time, snatching his mind away from sleep. He was helped greatly by the image of Lisa waiting around in her formal.

Quietly shutting the door behind him with his foot, his clothes a bundle in his arms, Jimmy stopped at a murmur from Joyce.

"What?" he asked.

"Night . . . 'night, Mr. Reardon. . . ." she said sleepily.

"Good night, Mrs. Fickett," he answered with a smile.

Jimmy dressed in the living room, sitting on the sofa where earlier he'd triumphed with his first Older Woman. Everything was as they left it before the wild ride: the ashtrays littered with old cigarette butts, her gloves neatly folded on the brown upholstered armchair, glasses with the ice all melted, and a single record jacket on the floor in front of the stereo.

The room seemed all used up and tired, and he felt the same, but it was a good kind of used up. Jesus, Joyce had more energy than anybody he'd ever met in his life—she made Denise seem like a zombie, and Denise was only eighteen.

If he were staying in Weston they might have had great times together, Joyce and he, arguing and screaming at one another like Thomas Wolfe did with his Older Woman, finding strength and compassion and giving each other hope. But it was too late, he was

Hawaii-bound; they would have to be content with memories of showers and things.

He slid into the red-leather bucket seats of the old man's car and turned on the ignition. Enjoying the scrape of gravel on the tires and the power of Father's car he sped out of Joyce's driveway, making up his mind to risk using the car to pick up Lisa. He would bring it back home right after, and they could take the bus from his house to the Dead Pigeon to meet Fred and Denise. The old man might bust a gut, but the way he felt now, what the hell!

DEW seeped through his shoes as he crossed the lawn to Lisa's house. Mrs. Bentwright, dammit, answered his ring. Her presence blocked the doorway, and the light streaming from behind made her a shadowy monster with a halo of white hair.

"Why, Mr. Reardon," she said in such a way that he suddenly realized his tie was undone.

"Hi," he said, grappling with it. "Lisa ready?"

"She was ready—at eight o'clock when you were expected."

"Couldn't help it," he said, adding dramatically, "a friend of my mother's got attacked and I had to stay with her until she calmed down."

"Young Lochinvar!" Mrs. Bentwright said sarcastically, making no move to let him in.

What a goddamn cynic! "It was horrible," he went on, trying to look past her, inside.

"And I suppose that's how you got in that condition."

He knew she meant drunk but he chose to ignore it. "We were afraid the cops'd never get there," he said.

"Is that so? Well, I suggest you call your mother and tell her you're all right. She seemed awfully worried."

"My mother?"

"Yes, your mother called a while ago anxiously trying to locate you. Apparently she wasn't informed of her friend's predicament."

"That's how Mother is—always anxious." He tried to dismiss it with a laugh.

"At any rate, Mr. Reardon, I'm sorry, but my daughter couldn't wait."

"You mean she's not here!"

"You didn't expect her to sit around all night waiting, did you—her last night home? She got herself a respectable date."

"Where'd she go?"

"She'll write you from Hawaii, I'm sure."

"To the dance? She go to the dance?"

"Good night, Mr. Reardon." She slammed the door.

It was dark outside. He hadn't really noticed how dark it was before. And the stars were out. It would be autumn soon. Anyway, it smelled like autumn.

Shit! Lisa had a lot of guts!

He'd bring the car back home later. Right now it was more important to find Lisa and straighten things out. She had to be at the country club dance—she wouldn't go anywhere alone, and the kind of jerk she'd go out with was the kind of jerk who'd take her there.

He drove east into town, then north along the lake, passing regiments of streetlights until the road narrowed and melted into curves and the glare of approaching cars turned the frost on his windshield to haze.

Finally the lights of the club. The parking lot seemed crowded so he pulled off on the gravel beside the road. The Weston Country Club was phony Colonial Mansion: white-painted bricks and skinny square columns. Tonight, as on all gala nights, a red carpet crawled up the few steps leading to the entrance.

Jimmy didn't bother to walk around on the arched driveway, took the shorter route across the lawn, jumping over the hedges.

Two guys in red jackets stood near the doorway waiting to park cars. One of them recognized Jimmy.

"Reardon! What the hell are you doing here?"

"None of your goddamn business," said Jimmy.

"Hey, you gotta wear a tux to get in there!"

But Jimmy was already past the doors and into the thick-carpeted foyer with an oil painting of George Washington leading a charge, and chandeliers with electric candles hung low from the ceiling. He turned off down a hall to see a placard pointing to the "Summer's End Ball." A band was going: "Rumph, *Rumph*, ba, ba, ba, dooo, rumph, ba ba, *ba*."

Now that he was inside he lost his nerve. Better check himself out before going to the dance. He found two rooms, one marked "Lovers" and the other, "Lollipops." Jesus, you even had to make decisions about rest rooms! But he wished he'd never thought of it in the first place because as soon as he entered the "Lovers" room a colored man rose from his stool and began running water in the sink and folding towels and smiling more than efficiently. How the hell could anybody relieve his goddamn bladder with somebody staring over his shoulder and listening like that! Jimmy couldn't, so he faked it. But he knew the man was an expert, and, afterwards, he was embarrassed as he straightened his tie in the mirror, careful not to look at himself too long or too lovingly. His shirt had gotten stained along the way too, dammit!

Then Jimmy noticed a tray on the sill with half dollars and a few crumpled dollars bills which the attendant probably put there himself. Now the guy was watching him solicitously in the mirror. Jimmy smiled wanly and pulled one of Mrs. Spaulding's silver dollars out of his pocket as someone in a white dinner jacket came in and straightaway washed his hands. The colored man took the large coin from Jimmy and immediately deposited it somewhere beneath his tan jacket. "Thank you, sir," he said, then again, "Thank you very much." And Jimmy ceased to be for him as he started shoving the next towel in the newcomer's face while Jimmy waited for his change. Couldn't ask for it outright with that other jerk there. Jimmy cleared his throat and the attendant gave him a funny look. "Something else, sir?" Now the white dinner jacket was looking at him too. He wondered what Emily Post was for arguing with "Lovers" room attendants, but he said "No," and beating a hasty retreat, almost knocked down a creepy guy in a red dinner jacket outside.

"May I help you?" The man showed all thirty-two teeth.

"No thanks," said Jimmy, and he moved on quickly, feeling the man's eyes on him all the way down the hall.

A whole silver dollar shot, just like that. On a towel! Jesus, you could buy three for that.

A gray-haired gentleman with a carnation in his lapel stood at the entrance to the ballroom. "Good evening, sir," he said when Jimmy approached. "May I help you?"

The guy was looking right through Jimmy's buttoned jacket to the stain on his shirt. "No thanks. I'm looking for my girl."

"Your girl," said the man, as though he were translating Greek. "Maybe I can help. What's the name?"

"That's all right. I can find her."

"I'm sorry, sir, but the dance is restricted to members and their guests."

"Look," said Jimmy. "I've contributed quite a substantial sum to the maintenance of this dump already, and if I want to go inside and look for my girl I damn well better be allowed to! Get out of my way."

The man backed off but kept an eye on him.

Jimmy walked into the ballroom and stood at the edge of the jostling, churning mob, first looking toward the tables and then at the bobbing faces. He put his hands in his pockets and swaggered with what he supposed was authority, but it didn't help.

The ballroom had the same low chandeliers as the foyer, but they were strung with college pennants, and dimmed, so that most of the light came from the blue spotlight on the band. Some of the guys dancing had their jackets off, and the girls were all bouncy and fluffy in their formals. Everyone was tan and tawny. This was the young rich-race and they looked it. Jimmy felt pale, and he could feel his black suit shine and the spot on his shirt glow in the dark. He lit a cigarette defiantly and let it hang carelessly from the corner of his mouth before starting across the floor in search of Lisa, purposely hitting every other jerk with his elbow along the way. Some of the bobbing faces he recognized, but as he went farther into the throng, the faces and bodies merged into streaks of muted color, confusing him. Now why the hell would Lisa want to come to this goddamn place? He was beginning to get angry, which was good, because then he could holler at her before she hollered at him.

He made his way across the floor and stood scanning the crowd with his back to the tall windows hung with velvet. Damn her, where was she? He walked closer to the bandstand and the pounding grew louder. *Rumph, Rumph, ba, ba, ba.* No sign of her. He saw Suzie but he ducked before she saw him. That's all he needed now!

"Jimmy!"

It was Lisa behind him. She wore a tight green dress with a Japanese collar and her black hair was curled in a bun. She was startlingly beautiful even though her teeth were clenched.

"What are you doing here?" she said.

"What the hell are you doing here!" he shouted above the din. "I told you I'd be right over! Why didn't you wait!"

"Get out of here, Jimmy. You're drunk. I'm not going anywhere with you."

"Why not?" He yelled.

"Shut up! And don't you cause any trouble."

"You're the one causing trouble!"

Someone bumped him from behind and he almost lost his balance. The thunder of the band heightened his anger and confusion.

"Go away, Jimmy!" She was silhouetted against the blue light of the band and he could barely see her eyes, but he knew they were hard.

"Where's the respectable date you managed to scrounge up? I know all about that! Your mother couldn't wait to tell me—where is he? I'd like to see him!"

"Good night, Jimmy." She started away.

"Good night like hell! You're going with me!" He grabbed her arm.

"You stop that! I'm not going anyplace with you—let me go!"

"Why? Because I was a little late? A couple goddamn minutes?"

"Not minutes—hours!" She tore away and ran into the crowd, pushing her way through and into the hall.

"Dammit Lisa! Dammit!" he shouted. The man in the carnation backed away as he ran out the door in pursuit.

Lisa rounded the corner and disappeared into the "Lollipops" room.

He followed her in.

"Jimmy, you're insane! Get out of here!"

"Not until I talk to you."

"This is the ladies' room," she squealed. He reached for her arm. "Jimmy, please!" She was mortified.

The door opened and a familiar face appeared in the mirror on the wall. "Finally found a home, huh Jimmy?" It was Suzie, standing behind him.

Lisa was cowering against the table. "Tell him he can't stay here, Suzie!" she said.

But Suzie said, "Doesn't bother me," and proceeded into the inner chamber as a woman came out to look Jimmy in the face. He met her eye defiantly. She put a fist to her mouth.

"What do you want?" she said quietly, fearfully.

"I'm a goddamn lollipop!" he shouted. Suzie laughed.

"We'll see about that!" said the woman, rushing out.

Lisa raced after her.

"Hey, wait!" Jimmy called.

Outside, Lisa ran smack into a group of girls heading for the "Lollipops" room. She stopped when one of them said. "Hi." Jimmy halted on her heels.

"Hi," Lisa said, attempting coolness. "You know Jimmy Reardon, don't you?"

"*Do* I!" said a blue dress with little-girl boobs. Jimmy remembered vaguely she had no pubic hair, but he couldn't remember how, or why, he found out.

"I thought you were with Matthew Hollinder," another girl said to Lisa.

"She's with me," Jimmy said firmly.

"Matthew's looking all over for you," said a different girl.

"I'm going back to him right now," Lisa said, smiling hard. "See you later."

Jimmy pulled her away and she walked with him as though it had been planned that way. Good thing she was middle class enough not to make what her mommy would call a scene. But before they got to the dance, she turned on him.

"You get out of here right now or I'll call for help. I mean it, Jimmy!"

But a guy she knew passed by and she smiled and nodded at him as though everything were fine.

"I'm staying here," said Jimmy.

"No, you're not," said Lisa, throwing another smile to the carnation man, who was watching them with interest. "I don't ever want to see you ever again!" she added through a cheerful grin.

"Balls!" shouted Jimmy.

She smiled again at the carnation man.

"Don't you get vulgar either," she said under her breath as a brawny member of the rich-race came out of the ballroom toward them.

"Hey, Lisa, what're you doing?"

"Hi, Matthew," she said brightly. "I'd like you to meet Jimmy Reardon. Matthew Hollinder." She introduced them without looking at Jimmy, who hated the sonofabitch on sight.

The two boys nodded briefly to each other.

"Jimmy had just dropped by to say good-by to me before I leave," said Lisa.

"But I'm planning to rape her on my way out," Jimmy said simply.

"What?" The tall sonofabitch looked bewildered.

"He's got a rotten sense of humor," said Lisa, appeasing the sonofabitch. "You go back to the table, Matthew; I'll be right in."

"Are you going to be all right?" the sonofabitch asked Lisa.

"Don't worry," she told him.

"Worry," said Jimmy. The sonofabitch glowered and walked away.

"I hate you, Jimmy! I hate you!" Lisa said when he was gone.

"Give me a chance—I only want to talk to you, dammit!"

She made a move toward the ballroom; he caught her.

"If you go in there I'm gonna yell at the top of my lungs about how goddamn unfair you are, and I'm not kidding!" he threatened.

She stared at him a moment as if weighing that

possibility, then a slow moan escaped her lips and she darted past the ballroom towards the end of the hall and through the glass doors to flee into the darkness, Jimmy in close pursuit.

Soft squares of light from the windows lay on the lawn outside the club. Jimmy followed Lisa past the yellow glow and beyond the scattered white tables holding spires of collapsed unbrellas. They ran past the swimming pool and into the thin strip of trees separating the club's backyard from the golf course.

The moon roamed out from behind a bunch of clouds, and he saw her stop and fumble with her shoe, then disappear somewhere behind a tree.

"Wait up!" he shouted, tripping on a hidden sprinkler and sprawling on the grass.

"Dammit, wait!" He picked himself up and headed toward her only to change course at a rustling noise near the pool. He rushed at the faint outline of a figure.

"What the hell you doin', buddy!" said a man's voice when he got closer. He saw a girl wrestling with her bodice behind the bulk of the guy, and he took off back towards the tree.

But Lisa wasn't there either, and the bushes were thick. "Will you come out of there?" No answer. He ventured cautiously into the thicket. "Lisa?" Something moved. He stumbled and ripped his pants on a branch to the clinking of silver dollars. "Hell!" He quickened his pace and dove into a hedge, hearing twigs snap around him and scraping his face.

When he pulled himself out he looked up and there was Lisa right in front of him, catching her breath on a wrought iron bench next to a bird bath in a clearing beside the golf course.

When she saw him she jumped up and started again.

"Wait! Please wait!" He caught her.

"Let go!" She fought.

"Not until you listen to me," said the out-of-breath hunter as his prey dug an elbow into his stomach. His stomach felt weird.

"I despise you!" she said.

"I don't care, but I'm not letting you go until you relax and. . . ."

Elbow in his ribs again.

"Dammit." He pinned her arms. "Cut it out!"

Now she stood rigid and didn't say anything. He waited a moment.

"Are you all right now?" he asked.

Still quiet.

"If I let go, promise not to run?" No answer, but he took the chance.

He shouldn't have.

"Lisa quit that!" Exhausted as he was, he managed to catch her again. "Give me a chance! That's all I want, a chance to explain, for crissakes!"

He held her arms and she kicked him once, hard.

"Oh!" he screamed. "My leg!" He hopped a bit on one foot, then slid to the ground with one long, terrible moan. "My wound! It's bleeding again!"

"Serves you right," she said, but she wasn't running.

"It was your heel," he groaned.

"It's your own fault."

He groaned again. "They only sewed it up this morning. The stitches!" It was so convincing he himself was beginning to worry. "Oooo. . . ." He stretched out on his back. Cautiously, she leaned over.

"If this is one of your gags. . . ."

"Jesus, you're really something!" he moaned.

She reached out as if to touch him, then drew back. "I didn't realize. . . ."

"It's all right."

"Let me see. Maybe I can do something." She ventured toward his leg and sat beside him. "Now I feel terrible," she said.

"Terrible enough to forgive me?" He pulled her down to him.

"I'm always forgiving you."

"Please?" He rolled on top of her and kissed her gently.

She smiled, coldly. "Be careful."

"Of what?"

"Your leg."

"It doesn't make any difference now." He was gallant.

"You! You liar! There's nothing wrong with your leg! You're disgusting. Get off me!"

"Not till you listen to the truth about why I was late."

"I'll scream!"

"No you won't!"

She screamed. He put his hand over her mouth. "Now quit it!" She tried to shout through his fingers, he pressed his hand tighter. "Are you gonna scream?" The eyes staring up were almost luminous. She shook her head. "All right." He took his hand away.

But she started to scream again, so he clapped his hand back. "Look." He tried reason. "I would've explained all this before because it's so goddamn simple if you'd only listen!" He waited a while. "Now just give me a second." When he took his hand off this time, she was quiet.

"All right, the simple truth is—"

"Don't tell me. I won't listen to any more of your lies. Ever since I've known you you've been late for something."

"You wouldn't believe me even if I told the truth!"

"Why don't you make that experiment and see?"

"Okay . . . I ran out of gas."

She laughed without amusement.

"See what I mean? Okay, dammit, I left my mother's friend's house right after I called you and ran out of gas on the way to pick you up—didn't even bother to take the car home first so I wouldn't be late! Three miles I had to walk!"

"You make me want to vomit!"

"I'm telling you the honest truth! My old man's probably calling the police right now about his goddamn car. Jesus, I break my neck and what happens? Your mother tells me you went with someone else! How am I supposed to feel?"

"I don't care how you feel."

"That's no lie."

"And I wouldn't have gone with Matthew if you showed up on time."

"You couldn't wait a decent few minutes!"

"Three hours! I waited three whole hours!"

"So big deal, three hours!"

"And I thought this was going to be a night we'd always remember. I had such plans. . . ."

"What kind of plans?"

"For us. All today I thought . . . about us, and I . . . wanted us. . . ." Rushing on, "I wanted you to make love to me tonight and all you did was embarrass me in front of everybody!"

"I told you I was sorry!"

Tears welled in her eyes. "Oh God, you're so stupid!"

"You just refuse to understand, don't you!"

She began to cry softly. "That isn't what I meant."

"What're you crying about?"

"Go away and leave me alone. I wish you hadn't come here—I wish I never had to see you again." She was shivering. "All the time I waited for you I thought about how it would be tonight, and you've ruined everything."

"We can still have a good time; I'll make it up to you, I promise."

"No, because it's not the same. It's not the same anymore."

"Yes it is, you'll see."

"Jimmy, I was going to let you make love to me—all the way."

"Lisa. . . ." He was too touched to be surprised. Planting little kisses in the opening of her Japanese collar: "Lisa. . . ." He kissed her eyes and the tip of her nose. "I love you, Lisa. I love you."

"Jimmy?" Her voice wavered.

"Yes?"

"Jimmy . . . now?"

He felt himself sore and limp against her. Now? After what he'd been through! "Right after the dance, I'll be outside waiting. You can ditch that guy and—"

"Now, Jimmy."

"Right now, you mean?"

"Right now."

"But Lisa, someone's liable to come strolling along any minute."

"I don't care."

"But what would happen if you started to. . . . I mean, some virgins bleed."

"Do you have to talk about that?"

"Well, Jesus, I'm only being practical."

"It's funny you were never practical like that before!"

"But it never came up before—this particular thing, I mean."

Suddenly she was in control. "Will you please remove yourself?"

"Huh?"

"Please get off me?"

"But I was only telling you. . . ."

"You don't have to tell me anything. I understand all about it now!"

"What do you understand?"

She pushed him away and sat up. "Are you sitting on my shoe?" she said bitterly.

"Yes, and I'm going to stay that way until you stop crying and explain what the hell you're so upset about."

"I'll go without it," she said firmly, and started to limp away.

"All right, here it is," he said, handing it to her. "Now will you tell me what's wrong?"

"Nothing's wrong. Everything's perfectly fine. I just never want to see you again, that's all."

"Why?" he screamed.

Struggling with the shoe, she bounced around trying to put it on without having to sit down. "It's quite obvious," she gasped, finally accomplishing the task. "You can't make love to me now because you've just been with one of your—your diseased tramps!" She tested the heel in the ground and flew toward the club.

He ran along beside her. "Lisa! You're jumping to conclusions. You can't convict someone on circumstantial evidence, for crissakes!"

"You've got your life to lead and so have I. So have I!" She sure sounded determined.

"Look, if you really want to hear the truth. . . ."

She wasn't interested in anything but what was on her mind: "I don't care about your truth! But you might be interested to know that my date—Matthew Hollinder—I've never even kissed him, but tonight, tonight I'm going to give him a *big* surprise."

He stopped in his tracks. "What kind of surprise?"

"Figure it out," she said acidly. "You're the expert." And she opened the doors and hurried down the hall toward the ballroom, where Jimmy caught and held her.

"You mean you're—you and Hollinder?"

"Good-by, Jimmy," she said triumphantly, and she meant it.

She left him standing there and disappeared inside the crowded ballroom. *Rumph, ba. . . .*

He leaned against the wall, his eyes glazed. The goddamn thing just had to fizzle out at the most important moment of his life! Six months, six months of patience and top level planning, of loving and believing and coaxing and wooing, and now this! This power failure, this blackout, and for what? For helping out that poor frustrated woman. Was there no justice!

He began to walk slowly toward the foyer with the painting of George Washington, then glanced into the dim blue haze of the ballroom. Lisa was in there somewhere with that sonofabitch.

"Let's go, son," said a voice. An arm clamped gently on him, and he was being pushed.

"Hey!" Jimmy said indignantly. "What is this?"

"We'd rather not have any trouble with you," repeated the voice, and the grip tightened. It was the man with the carnation.

"Wait a minute!" Jimmy tried to break loose. "Where are we going?"

"Outside. And please lower your voice."

The creep in the red jacket with thirty-two teeth joined them. He wasn't smiling.

"Just walk with us," continued the carnation man. The Teeth held the other arm, and they walked Jimmy through the foyer toward the steps outside.

"I was visiting my girl! You can't kick me out for that!"

Their removal of Jimmy was expert, and attracted almost no attention. Even Jimmy hardly knew what happened.

At the top of the short stairway, they stopped. "Did you drive?" said Carnation.

"Why?" said Jimmy.

"Where did you park?" Carnation said firmly, keeping his grip.

"Andrew!" A female voice called from the top of the stairs, behind them. "What the hell are you doing with my fiancé?"

It was Suzie Middleburg, stuffed into a lace and satin gown and sporting an expertly sloppy hairdo.

"Miss Middleburg!" said Teeth respectfully.

"Is that your girl?" Carnation asked Jimmy.

"I'm not talking," Jimmy said.

"How dare you," said Suzie, bounding down the stairs. "How dare you!"

"I'm sorry, Miss Middleburg, we didn't know." Carnation apologized. The men let go of Jimmy.

"Did they hurt you, darling?" Suzie pursed her lips in ultra-concern.

"No offense, Miss Middleburg," said Teeth. "But do you suppose you could keep your fiancé away from the ladies' room?"

Suzie sighed dramatically, patting Jimmy's cheek. "But I get lonely without him."

She led Jimmy up the driveway as tooth and flower retreated to the dance.

"You know," she said when they were alone, "you ought to take up anarchy. You've got a flair for it."

"Shit," he said, not playing.

"What happened? Fight with Lisa?"

He sure as hell didn't want to talk about it to Diarrhea Mouth, but he needed her company. "Suzie, are you with someone?"

She shrugged. "Not unless you count the Judge and Little Miss Muffett."

"That's good. I feel like a vodka."

"This an invitation?"

"To the best place you know."

"I'll take you to our leader," she said.

"I can drive, I've got my father's car."

"Sure you can handle it?"

"What do you mean? I drive a hundred percent better when I'm stoned."

She took his arm. "Till death do us part," she sighed.

JIMMY was lost in a holocaust of self-recrimination and scattered blame for his lost opportunity as they raced downtown along Lake Shore Drive. About halfway there, Suzie, fluff and all, jumped into the back seat, explaining that she might need the extra second to review her life. It didn't change the tone of his driving.

"Our leader" turned out to be a short Italian named Fernando, owner of Fernando's and the animated host to Chicago's most prominent citizens. Suzie had told Jimmy that the tune of his three-syllabled *'Evening,* immediately determined a patron's place on the social ladder, and if he added an *Ah* to the greeting, his name was probably italicized in the *Blue Book* or somewhere.

Suzie rated not only a Puccini-like *'Evening* and an *Ah!* but a pat on the cheek, which impressed the hell out of Jimmy.

"So goot to see you, Miss Middleburg," said Fernando, with his arm around Suzie's waist, leading her past the cloak room. Jimmy followed a few steps behind. "May we serve you dinner or cocktails?"

"Cocktails," said Jimmy in a fine, deep voice.

"Of course," smiled Fernando. "Table or bar?" He spoke to Jimmy, bowing slightly.

"Bar, I think," said Jimmy, in splendid control.

"Certainly." Fernando slid back a stool for Suzie.

The bar was small and only had six stools. Although the bartender stood in front of Jimmy and Suzie, Fernando summoned him as though he were blocks away. "Alex?" he said, an authoritative finger in the air.

"My young friend would like something to drink." To Suzie: "What is your pleasure?"

"Triple vodka," said Jimmy, answering out of turn and realizing it too late.

"Triple vodka," Fernando repeated to the bartender. "And you, Miss Middleburg?"

"Bourbon—neat," said Suzie.

"And bourbon," said Fernando. "And would you like yours on the rocks?" he asked Jimmy, making a life-and-death question out of it.

"On the rocks," repeated Jimmy.

"On the rocks," Fernando said as if the bartender were deaf. Boy! This was the million-dollar treatment. Looking around, Jimmy saw that the restaurant was narrow and sparsely filled. They were alone at the bar, but two couples and a pair of women sat behind them at cocktail tables. At the other end of the room another twosome sat finishing a meal, their legs nearly touching under the table.

"So!" Fernando was saying to Suzie. "How have you been?"

"Lousy," said Suzie.

"How terrible you are!" Fernando laughed.

"Sorry, sir," the bartender said to Jimmy, "but I'll need some identification."

"Oh, sure." Jimmy was suddenly aware of the ice clinking in the glasses behind him, of the rustle of Suzie's skirt, and of his face, which must have been the color of blood. Fernando looked sadly at the bartender while Jimmy pretended to have lost his wallet. He might look six-three, though, because he was on a stool. He opened his jacket and the stain became neon, so he quickly buttoned that.

"I can vouch for him," Suzie said through a loudspeaker. "He's thirty-two."

Fernando leaned into Suzie's ear. "I'm so sorry," he said, "but the police are so strict about those things. . . ." He shrugged profoundly. "What can I do?"

"Don't ask him for it," advised Suzie.

"How terrible you are!" Fernando clapped his hands.

"Here," Jimmy said, for better or worse. He couldn't stall any longer. He lit a cigarette and let it hang from the corner of his mouth, deftly blowing out the match. Sublimely unconcerned.

"Is this your young man?" Fernando asked Suzie while the bartender memorized Jimmy's I.D.

"One of them," said Suzie. "Sort of captain of the team."

"Wonderful!" shrieked Fernando.

Without warning, Fernando patted Jimmy's back, and he nearly jumped off the stool. "You must be careful," he whispered to Jimmy. "She's dangerous." The man had no breath, like a dentist, and he was getting on Jimmy's nerves.

"Yeah," said Jimmy, trying to remember the address on the I.D.

About six hours later, the bartender returned the card. "Thank you," he said, and turned away to make drinks while Fernando said, "Now I leave you two to yourselves, and if you need me, I'm here." He disappeared somewhere behind them.

The bartender put the drinks before them and Jimmy reached eloquently to the inside of his jacket. He'd knock the guy's eyes out with his beautiful wad, but the bartender stopped him.

"It is already settled," he said. "These are Fernando's pleasure."

"I should have ordered a double," said Suzie.

"Here, give him one on me," Jimmy the International Playboy said, separating a dollar bill and throwing it on the counter, after making sure it wasn't one of Mrs. Spaulding's two-dollar bills.

"Fernando doesn't drink," said the bartender, in almost a hushed tone, as if that were amongst the nobler achievements.

"Keep it for yourself then." Jimmy waved the buck away as though it were Kleenex.

"Thank you, sir," beamed the bartender.

Suzie eyed the bankroll. "Been robbing vending machines in ladies' rest rooms?" she asked.

"Murdered a rich friend," said Jimmy.

"Just for fun?"

"I'm taking a little trip."

"Joliet's very nice this time of year."

"So I hear. That's why I'm going to Hawaii." He

finished the drink, and the bartender magically refilled it.

"Hawaii? That's in Lisa's direction, isn't it?" Suzie was on a scent.

He opened his eyes innocently. "Is it?"

"Going to share the same hut?"

He stirred his drink thoughtfully and didn't answer. Jesus, Diarrhea Mouth.

"Place sure isn't crowded," he observed, changing the subject.

"Never is till after midnight when the expense-account Johns get here. I like it best then, but the Judge comes for the bores."

Jimmy caught the narrow gray eyes of a silky-haired blonde seated at a table behind Suzie and held on until Suzie glanced over her shoulder to see what was distracting him.

"Don't let her get to you—it's nothing personal," said Suzie, blowing smoke toward the bottles. "She's just a whore who digs young boys."

"Really?" Jimmy was impressed.

"And him," Suzie went on, referring to the colorless middle-aged man across from the blonde, "he's a big executive, probably a bank president, with a wife and two kids. Only he doesn't like to sleep home anymore because he's getting old and doesn't want his wife to know he's losing it. That's why he's out with the blonde; he doesn't care if she knows he's incapable. . . ."

She had to bring that up!

"You can tell his condition by the way he keeps hitting his drink with his pinky," Suzie added.

Jimmy frowned at his own pinky.

"She's expensive," Suzie, the expert, went on. "Probably the hundred-dollar type. Keeps a twenty-year-old boy in an apartment on the Gold Coast who makes extra money by sleeping with old men who also have two children and a wife. What you call the balance of nature."

As she continued, Jimmy tuned off. He tried to drink without even lifting the glass from the counter. One thing he was determined not to think about was the sonofabitch at the dance, and what Lisa might be doing with him right now, or even if she wasn't, what she said she'd do, which was almost as bad. He tried to divert his thoughts by counting the bottles in the wine rack. Three were missing. He loosened his shirt button and went deep into the glass, swirling with the ice.

Suzie was still fixed on her banker. "He takes hormone pills," she said, "but they don't help."

He wished she'd shut up on that subject!

Jimmy smiled at the bartender who filled his glass again, and Suzie found a new mark: "And are you ready for those two chicks behind us? My psychiatrist would give me a finder's fee for them. The younger one probably seduced the older one." Suzie daintily downed her drink and got quick attention from the bartender.

"Wait till I get to Hawaii. Gonna bust that place wide open, and I don't give a good goddamn, y'know? By myself, too. All by my goddamn self."

"She really thinks she's hot stuff, the one with the short hair," said Suzie.

"And she can have the sonofabitch," mumbled Jimmy. "He probably doesn't know what to do anyway, dumb bastard. And I won't even talk to her on the plane tomorrow. Six months she'll be sorry she couldn't wait until after the goddamn dance."

". . . Pretty soon everybody'll be like worms," Suzie went on. "Won't even need another person. Hot and cold water in the same spout."

Jimmy suddenly heard her. "What?"

"Those two behind us."

He swung around. "You mean those ladies?"

"Don't say it too loud, they'll hit you."

"Look like mother and daughter to me," said Jimmy, now watching them through the mirror.

"Because you're a square."

"And you're hip."

"That's right."

"How come you know so much about it, anyhow?"

"Because I had a nanny once who was a lesbian.

Wore men's shoes and a monocle and said she was Swiss."

"How does that make her a lesbian?"

"She wasn't really Swiss at all. She was German. And she looked just like Hitler, except she had a blonde moustache."

"Will you come off it, Suzie? If I listened to you about everything I couldn't even trust my own mother."

Suzie tossed him a weird smile, and he shivered. He was glad when she went on, her voice pulsing with intrigue. "I think Nanny was a member of the SS in Germany and worked in a women's prison camp. She walked with a goose step."

"Really?"

"You could hear her all over the place, stomping around. And she used to eat sausage with a knife."

"Does that make her a lesbian?"

"It was the way she attacked it!" She leaned in confidentially. "Those two behind us, when they think nobody's looking they walk with a goose step. I'm positive!"

What he should do is tell Suzie to stop eating off other people's vines and start growing her own, but he couldn't. "Anyhow," he said, "keep your lesbians to yourself because I'm not interested or attracted or anything." He clanked his glass on the bar.

"Of course you aren't," said Suzie, almost too smoothly. "That's one of the things I know about you—among other things."

In the mirror he watched Suzie's number-two topic get up from their table. When he saw one of the women pick a speck of lint from the other's dress, he got pissed off because it made him think Suzie might be right, though he knew damn well she wasn't.

Suzie watched from her throne as the women left the restaurant, then she took an easy breath and spoke contentedly to her reflection in the mirror.

"D-e-f-i-n-i-t-e-l-y," she said.

"I'm going to the can," said Jimmy.

He weaved his way through the tables, suddenly realized he didn't know where he was going. He turned to go back and ask the bartender, but Suzie was waiting with a pointed finger. Jesus. She nodded toward the back of the room. As he passed the banker and the whore, he decided the girl didn't really look like a whore. Her eyes were clear and blue, and she giggled like a little girl, not like a whore at all. And the banker seemed a damn nice guy.

He found the rooms, marked "Brokers" and "Mistresses," and took another quick look at the banker before he went into "Brokers." He wondered why the hormone pills didn't work.

He almost ran back out when he saw the towels piled up and the tray filled with money. He wasn't going to go through what happened at the country club again! But no guardian seemed to be around, so he placed himself before the urinal.

What he should do is get back there and beat the hell out of him. But that wouldn't do any good because the sonofabitch was too big. And stupid. Probably wouldn't even feel anything, like a fish. Anyway, it was Lisa's fault. And right now he probably has his hands all over her, even if he doesn't know what to do about it. That's the trouble with those football bastards—seasonal, like grub worms. Only reason Lisa went with the jerk at all was because Jimmy was late. So he got the leftovers. No brains, is why, and most of those guys are virgins anyway. Talk big, get nowhere, man. Lisa never even kissed him good night.

But that didn't mean she might not do something else. Jesus!

And what if Jimmy could never do it again after tonight. Some people get that way. It never happened to him before, never. But it was mental. Maybe he should see a psychiatrist; he might be ruined for life.

It wasn't until Jimmy leaned over the sink to use the free towels that the hand appeared. A shaking hand, and it held a bar of soap, and it belonged to a very old man who shook too. He smiled pathetically at Jimmy. " 'Evening, sir," he said. Jimmy wanted to hit the bastard with his own soap, but thought better of it. This time he was going to win.

"Hello," said Jimmy, nonchalantly taking the soap and running the water, yet careful the stain on his shirt wasn't showing. He washed his hands thoroughly, taking his time, receiving the towel proffered him. Might as well wash his face, too. "Pardon me," he said to the tottering attendant. "Have you another towel? For my face?"

"Yes, sir," the man said, producing it.

"Thank you," said Jimmy in a clipped way. He dried his face, then scrutinized his hair. "Uh, oh," he said. "Hair tonic. Have you got any?"

"Yes, sir," the man said, getting it.

"Thank you," said Jimmy. "I need a comb, too."

"Coming up." He opened a drawer and removed a new one from cellophane.

Lord and Master Jimmy was jubilant. "There," he said when he finished. "Now I'm all set."

"Yes, sir," repeated the shell of a man. His head shook uncontrollably.

"Except for one thing," added Jimmy. "Think I need a shine—no, not a shine. Could you just dust off my shoes?"

"Gladly, sir," said the man, separating a clean towel and getting down on his knees. Jimmy didn't want to make him do that, though, so he sat on a stool to make it a little easier.

"You missed a little spot," he said.

"Sorry, sir."

The man finished and crumbled a few steps backward. "That's fine," said Jimmy.

"Thank you, sir," said the man, waiting.

"Think nothing of it," Jimmy pulled the wad from his coat pocket as if by mistake, then replaced it and went to the loose change in his pocket. The attendant showed no reaction, however.

"Now," said Jimmy, shaking the loose change in his pocket, "what's the cost of the comb?"

"No charge, sir."

"None at all?" Jimmy feigned surprise. "That's very generous." He pulled some change from his pocket and toyed for a moment with two silver dollars, glancing up to catch the goddamn-greedy-privacy-invading-mercenary's reaction. But there was no reaction.

"Well, then," Jimmy said expansively, "here you are."

When he placed that nickel in the arthritic hand he not only felt he'd bought his freedom, but that, in one single gesture had made up for all those countless millions who had been victimized by the bandits who lurk in comfort stations all over the world.

"Thank you very much, sir," the punished man said with dignity. He didn't seem at all defeated or anything, and suddenly Jimmy was anxious to get out of there.

He rushed back through the tables and took his place at the bar. A new drink was awaiting him and, glancing around, he downed half of it at once.

The whore was plucking the banker's chin, and her boobs seemed about to pop out. Jimmy watched her closely, tried to imagine what she'd look like naked, which wasn't difficult, and to think of her in Joyce's bedroom, whispering the same things Joyce whispered, and standing that way. He struggled as hard as he could to put her in that room and place himself beside her. Then he waited for a stir. But nothing happened. He thought even harder. Nothing, dammit!

"I know for a fact there aren't four left out of our whole graduation class," Suzie said all of a sudden.

"Four what?"

"Girls who have not been deflowered, as they used to say in great-grandma's time," Suzie said. "I can tell just by the way a girl wears her lipstick or says hello whether she has or not."

"Prove it," said Jimmy.

"Ask me one." Suzie dared him.

"Okay—Denise Hunter," he ventured.

She shook her head, and the way she looked at him made him wish he hadn't asked. Except how could Suzie know anything?

"You sure?" he said, pouring ice on the trail.

She nodded. "And I know the boy who did it. It was last summer at a splash party at the Bentwrights'."

"Lisa's house!"

"Before you knew her. Anyway, Denise went into one of the rooms and, whammo, the petals fell. Just like practically every other girl in the senior class. Just since the beginning of summer," she slyly observed, "I've counted enough fallen flowers to decorate the Rose Bowl."

Lisa was in the senior class, but he refused to ask.

"Who did it to Denise?"

"Is this a personal, or a clinical inquiry?"

"I'm curious, that's all." He'd never asked Denise who was first, and she hadn't told him. Now it pissed him off that she hadn't. And he didn't like Suzie's jokes, either.

But he wasn't prepared for: "On the record, it was Matthew Hollinder."

When Jimmy regained himself, he said hoarsely, "You sure?"

"Not only Denise," smiled Suzie. "He plowed most of last year's crop single-handedly."

Jimmy squeezed his glass till his knuckles turned white. Then, in a near-whisper, "You said . . . there were four virgins?"

"Just about."

"Who?"

"Lolly Newgold. . . ."

She was right about the first one. Lolly was as sexy as a milkshake.

". . . Alice Poulton, and Marianne Storres," finished Suzie.

"That's three. You only named three!"

"And me," said Suzie.

He couldn't control it. "That all?"

"Unless someone's been holding out on me."

"What do you think about Lisa?"

"Lisa?"

"Is Lisa one!"

"A virgin, you mean?"

"No—a herring, a herring I mean, dammit!" He got another look from the bartender.

Suzie pretended to be pensive. "I've always wondered about Lisa. 'Course you should know. . . ."

"I now damn well she is."

"Well then, there you are. . . ."

"You're goddamn right I'm there! There I am!"

He knew damn well he didn't have to worry about Lisa, but that didn't stop him from worrying. "One thing I know, she doesn't go for the star-athlete type." He sounded sure.

"You mean Matthew," Suzie said helpfully. "You don't have to worry about him—he's probably driving her nuts right now with how he got the National Science Scholarship and won that Atlantic Poetry Contest. All he talks about is things like that."

"Poetry contest?"

"But he's not bad looking, that's what saves him."

"Y'mean he writes poetry?"

"Oh, sure—but most women like his short stories better."

Thc sonofabitch!

Suzie scraped onward: "He doesn't even want to be a writer, says it's too easy. He's going to teach history on the university level or run for political office—guess that's why he chose Yale. I wouldn't be surprised if he became President of the United. . . ."

Her voice grew distant and faded altogether. Yale. The sonofabitch was going through Yale writing short stories and poetry with his left hand while playing football and knocking off all the goddamn flowers on the way to the goalpost!

Suzie nudged him. "Hey, wake up!"

She waved her head toward the back of the restaurant. "There goes old Saint Nick and his favorite pair of stockings."

The banker and whore rose and left their table, heading toward the door. Jimmy and Suzie watched as the pair neared the bar. Fernando interrupted their journey.

"Mister Blake! You are leaving so soon? I wanted to talk to you!" Fernando bowed slightly to the stockings.

"Afraid so," said Mr. Blake. "We've got to leave early to pick up Mrs. Blake at the airport."

"Well," Fernando sighed with appropriate disappointment, "if you must. . . . But," he brightened, "I see you soon, now."

"You betcha," said Mr. Blake, leading stockings up to the door.

"And have a nice time," Fernando said after them. "You too, Miss Blake. Such a pretty girl, your daughter!"

A triumphant Jimmy turned to Suzie. "Ha!" he said. "So she's a whore, huh? And he can't make it with his wife, huh? That's his daughter! Jesus, how wrong can you be?" He enjoyed a hearty laugh at her expense. "Jesus!"

But Suzie didn't seem defeated at all. "Can't win 'em all," she shrugged.

Jimmy felt much better. He summoned the bartender: "Art, may I have the check, please?"

"Hold it!" Suzie took the check out of the bartender's hand. "I'll sign for it." She waved the check in the air. "This is my only means of communicating with the Judge, and I refuse to lose my means of communication."

She was shouting, and Jimmy felt every eye on Gigolo Reardon. "Let me pay it." He tried to grab it away."

"Quit that!" said Suzie. "I'm buying and shut up!" She swept the pen over the check in a grand flourish.

"Now why the hell did you do that?" whispered Jimmy. "They'll think I'm a goddamn cheapskate!"

"There is no *they*," thundered Suzie. "And besides, how else can I get even with the Judge for not letting me cash checks? You want to deprive me of salvation?"

"Okay," said Jimmy, embarrassed. "Okay, okay. I'll be right back."

"What, again!" she shouted.

Boy.

In the "Brokers' " room he startled the tottering attendant by placing a whole dollar bill in the trembling hand. Hell, someone had to take his money.

"Everything resolved now?" Suzie asked when he returned to the bar.

"Uh huh," said Jimmy, helping her from the stool and bumping into Fernando at the same time.

"So sorry," said Fernando. "I wanted to spend some time with you before you left! Why are you sneaking off like this?" Fernando pinched Suzie's cheek.

"Hey," interrupted Jimmy. "Do you happen to know those two ladies who sat behind us? At the table?" He glanced triumphantly at Suzie.

"There?" Fernando pointed to the vacant table.

"Yeah," said Jimmy. "Those two. Mother and daughter, right?"

"Lesbians," Fernando whispered.

"Dum-te-dum," said Suzie.

AFTER leaving Fernando's and "Brokers" and "Mistresses," Suzie Middleburg and Jimmy Reardon drank, analyzed and argued their way through "Dukes" and "Duchesses," "Hamlets" and "Ophelias," and "Squaws" and "Braves," leaving in their wake 1 grandfather who dug his twenty-year-old granddaughter, 6 nymphomaniacs, 4 queers, 1 mother-killing dwarf, 2 drug addicts, scattered alcoholics, and an occasional lesbian. Also, one twenty-five-cent bathroom attendant.

By the time they finally made their way back to the car in the icy bleakness of after-midnight, Jimmy was very, very drunk. And thoroughly convinced that *it* would never, never go back up again for the rest of his life. He couldn't stop thinking about it, and the more he thought about it, the more impossible it became, and the more he tried to stop thinking about it, the more he thought about it, and that's how it went. The goddamn thing was dead, and so was Jimmy. And Lisa was dancing somewhere with that sonofabitch. And Suzie wouldn't even tell Jimmy the name of her psychiatrist because he wouldn't specify his illness and besides, she wasn't sure she could trust her psychiatrist with young boys.

Jesus.

Adding to the bleakness of it all, Suzie was deliberately driving him up the wall with sneaky remarks about Denise Hunter.

"But anyway . . ." Suzie was saying as they drove out of the Loop toward the South Side because Jimmy wanted to show Suzie where things really move, around 63rd and Cottage Grove.

"But anyway what?" said Jimmy.

Suzie pretended to be preoccupied. "Just, 'but anyway. . . .' " she said and dropped the subject to stare out the window. "Such a hopeless neighborhood—must be a depressed area. 'Course, I like depressed areas better than all the other kinds. . . ."

"Why?"

"Take away people's money and food and jobs and everything, and what've you got? Brotherhood, that's what. Lots and lots of good old . . ."

"All right. All right! See if I give a damn!" If that's how she wanted it, that's how she was going to get it. See if he'd ask her one more thing about anything.

". . . brotherhood," Suzie said, blissfully unconcerned about Jimmy's unconcern. "Reminds me of poor old Fred," she sighed, still watching out the window. "Pooor old Fred."

Since Jimmy wasn't giving a damn, he began to sing. Loud. "Drink to me on-ly wi-ith thine eyyy-yes and I—I'll not ask, for wine. . . ."

"Poooooooor old Fred."

"Goddamn it! Quit that!"

Suzie played hurt. "Why'd you stop singing? I had my heart absolutely set on coming in on the second chorus, and you stopped."

He tried hard, and managed to calm himself into an almost-sweet tone. "All right, I'm gonna tell you what the bargain is. The bargain is, I want you to tell me about Fred."

"Fred?" Suzie was bewildered.

"I mean Denise!"

"Oh, F-r-e-d!"

"So help me God I'm gonna. . . ." He slammed his fist on the steering wheel.

"Well, now," Suzie began briskly, "if the topic under discussion is *our* Fred, as it is my understanding that it is, and also because. . . ."

Jimmy was honest-to-god ready to cry.

"But say we just assume, then, for discussional purposes, I am willing to go along with a conversation about Fred. What . . ." She folded her arms and looked business-like and turned to Jimmy. ". . . just what is it you've got to say about Fred?"

Jimmy moaned and banged his hand on the steering wheel some more.

"I can tell by your attitude that you really don't want to talk about Fred at all," said Suzie. "Which is all right, because I really don't care about Fred anyhow." She took a breath and added: "Who I do care about is Denise. Would you like to talk about Denise?" she asked pleasantly.

Jimmy clenched his teeth. "Nope."

"Well," blew Suzie, "it seems that on a certain time on a certain day, which appears to be Saturday for discussional purposes, a certain boy visits a certain girl who lives in a certain house on a lake. A big house. Like me to go on?"

"Perfectly up to you," Jimmy shrugged. "I'm bored already."

"Then there is this certain boy, who has this certain best friend—whose name I can't remember—who also goes with this girl who lives in a house on a lake, a big house."

"Doesn't prove a thing!" said Jimmy, forgetting his boredom.

"Of course not," said Suzie. "It's silly. Just because I have this girl friend who lives next door to a certain D. Hunter and spends all her silly time looking at those silly sailboats on the lake through her very good Italian binoculars. Just because that silly girl happens to use those binoculars every Saturday afternoon, just because of that, who could possibly prove a thing! I didn't even want to bring it up in the first place."

She was trapping him. He never saw a girl with binoculars. "Still doesn't prove anything," he said.

"That's what I said." She stared out the window for awhile. Then: "Errol Flynn sure played the hell out of Robin Hood, didn't he?" she said.

Jesus.

"Suzie," Jimmy said meekly, "will you do me a favor? For old buddies' sake?"

"Anything, lover."

"Will you not tell Fred? He'd be pretty pissed off

and besides, I was only doing it with Denise for his own good. Hell, I didn't even want to do it. It was for Fred's sake, poor old Fred."

"All right," said Suzie. "And we won't tell Fred the other thing, either."

Uh oh. "What other thing?"

"A particular other thing."

Sometimes you just gotta give up pride. "Please tell me?"

"Do you think I can just toss away a particular thing you can't get anywhere else? I can't give up a particular thing unless it's for another particular thing. Now, if you had a particular thing. . . ."

"All right," said Jimmy. "What do you want to know?"

"I don't know what I want to know; if I did I wouldn't ask."

"But I don't have a particular thing!"

"Dum-te-dum."

Jimmy stared fearfully out at the dark street and the shabby apartment buildings. What the hell could he tell her! Then he remembered.

"Okay," he relented."I've got something."

"Good?"

"It'll kill me to reveal it," he said.

"That's what I want."

"Okay, sadist—but first tell me what you've got."

She looked at him all aglow. "We know who sees Denise on Saturdays," she said, "but who comes on *Sundays?*"

Sundays! "Who?"

"Not every Sunday—just when Denise's folks go away for the weekend."

"Who, damn it!"

"A kid named Matthew Hollinder."

The goddamn sonofabitch!

Jimmy slammed on the brakes, sending Suzie to the dashboard and stalling the engine.

"What are you doing?" shrieked Suzie, terrified.

"I'm going back to the dance," said Jimmy. Lisa! That guy was a sex maniac. No telling what he might do. . . .

But now the car wouldn't start. Jimmy pressed the accelerator to the floor; still nothing happened.

He fumbled with the starter, but no response.

"We're outta gas," observed Suzie.

And they were. They were really outta gas! He rested his head on the steering wheel, waiting for tears, but they didn't come.

Except for the light streaming out of scattered bars, and a flashing "Eat" sign across the street, the place seemed dark and deserted. And there was no gas station in sight.

"Gotta go get gas. And you better come, too," he said.

"Not me. I'm staying put."

"I don't think that's such a good idea—not in this neighborhood."

"I can't move in these heels. Don't worry, I'll lock myself in the car."

It was final. He opened the door a broken man. No power. No gas. . . .

"Hey, wait, best buddy—what about that particular thing?" said Suzie.

No choice now. He'd have to sacrifice his whole reputation for Fred's sake. Might as well, nothing left anyway.

"What is it?" screamed Suzie.

He gathered his forces. "Well . . . you remember that venereal disease I told you about?"

"The clap? Everyone in school knew that."

"Yeah, only it wasn't the clap at all."

Suzie was spellbound. "Something worse?"

Jimmy drew a sad breath. "It was only a couple of lousy crabs."

Anybody would think there'd be hundreds of gas stations right near downtown Chicago, but there weren't. After pushing the car to the curb with super-alcoholic strength, Jimmy had to walk a very crooked mile for a can of gas.

And when he finally got back to the car, Suzie was gone.

Frantic, Jimmy stepped back into the street.

"Suzie! Suzie Middleburg! Goddamn it, Suzie, get back here!" he shouted to the forbidding buildings.

A light flicked on, a shining tooth in the bleakness.

"Shut up down there!" someone shouted.

Through the window underneath the flashing "Eat" sign he saw a few non-operative patrons bent over coffee mugs, but no Suzie.

He ran along the street, stopping to follow concrete steps down to strange hallways with bare bulbs and brass mailboxes. Backing out, he tripped over the outstretched leg of an old wino.

A dog appeared behind him; no ordinary dog, it was of the Baskerville variety. Jimmy cringed against the railing.

"All right, Crumpets," said a voice that turned out to be a cop's. "Hey, you the one making all the noise?" he asked Jimmy.

"Noise?"

"What're you doing around here?"

"Walking."

"Well make sure you keep outta trouble, kid. This ain't no public park."

"Yes, sir." The cop moved away and Jimmy tuned up again.

"Suzie Middleburg! Miss Suzie Middleburg!"

"Told you to shut up, dammit." It was the window again.

Sploosh! A water-filled bag burst at Jimmy's feet, throwing water on his pants. Too startled to speak, he looked up at the windows.

"Now beat it!" finished the voice, slamming the window.

A headline flew into Jimmy's head: "Eminent Jurist's Daughter Slain. . . ."

In the car again, he checked the back seat for Suzie's body. But the body wasn't there.

". . . Debutante Suzie Middleburg Slaughtered on Joy Ride With Little-Known Weston Youth. James A. Reardon Sentenced For Criminal Neglect and Manslaughter. . . ."

"Suzie!" he pleaded at the curb.

A man in an outsized overcoat stumbled by.

". . . Famed Jurist's Beloved Daughter Strangled With Lace Gown, Then Raped And Beaten By Man in Tattered Overcoat . . . Weston Youth Held On Kidnapping Charges. . . ."

"Suzie Middleburg!"

In a bar he read a printed sign: "Cherrystone Bourbon—25¢." Again he saw the man in the outsized overcoat, who now stood amongst a row of faceless men on stools.

Out of breath, Jimmy dashed over to the thick-jowled bartender. "Hey, you seen a girl in a big white dress?" He showed the girl's proportions with his hands.

The bartender eyed him warily. "What?"

"I'm looking for Suzie," Jimmy explained patiently. "She's wearing this big white dress with lace on it."

"Move along kid. She's not in here."

"You know where she might go to get a drink?"

"I said out, kid! You don't want me to lose my license, do ya?" It wasn't a question, the way he put it.

"But I've got to find her," persisted Jimmy.

The bartender bounded around the counter and Jimmy retreated back to the street.

In a new direction, a door opened from the street to a dark passageway. There was a staircase, and to the side of it hung a black curtain through which came a weird sing-song of voices. Charging in, Jimmy was shocked to find himself the target of a hundred pairs of almond-shaped eyes—all men—Chinese men.

White as a cue ball on one of the green felt billiard tables, Jimmy blinked at the smoke and the stillness and backed up slowly. Then bolting out the room he screamed, "They're after me!" and there he was again on the pavement, and two shabby men dressed in shredded gabardine jackets were listening attentively.

"There's a goddamn opium den in there!" he shouted. "Right behind the door!"

The jackets turned to each other and laughed.

"What's the matter, kid, you get shook up?" asked the tallest one. He had red hair and freckles and seemed boyish except for his eyes. They were old, wrinkled eyes.

"Chinese Benevolent Society," said the other jacket. He was unshaven and seemed older than his companion. He smoked a pipe.

"Benevolent, hell!" said Jimmy. "Not the way they looked at me!"

"Don't worry about it," said Red. "They were probably more scared than you were. Anyway, what you doin' in this neighborhood? Playin' hookey?"

"No . . ." began Jimmy.

"Or you out after a little ass?" said Pipe.

"I'm lookin' for this girl; she's wearing a white lace formal and her name's Suzie Mid—"

"Come on, kid," said Friendly Red, taking Jimmy's arm. "We got just what you're after."

So that's what they were! "But I'm not after that!" Jimmy broke away. "I told you. . . ."

The duet exchanged a knowing smile.

"What's the matter?" Jimmy didn't like the way they looked at him.

"You shoulda' told us," said Red. "We got all kinds—big, small, white, black, girls . . . boys. . . ."

"I gotta find Suzie." He felt their eyes on his back as he hurried up the street.

"We'll be here when you're ready," the one with the pipe said after him.

But Jimmy was already gone, following a new street to where what looked like green mist was floating out of a store window, in which a blunt sign read "Saltair Lounge—No One Admitted Under 21."

Inside a creepy-looking bartender was talking to a woman with fluorescent blonde hair whom he kept calling "Angel."

"Hey, Alex?" Jimmy addressed the bartender. "You see a girl in a white formal come here? Name of Suzie?"

"Sure," said Angel.

"When?" asked Jimmy.

Angel lifted a heavy head and her eyes seemed to focus generally in Jimmy's direction. She mouthed a while, and finally managed: "Go 'way."

"It's very important," Jimmy pleaded, and turned to appeal to the bartender, but he had disappeared.

"You go *'way,*" shouted Angel. "Go away!"

Jimmy moved down another stool.

Angel's attention was held by her reflection in the mirror: "White formal—s'what I wore. Nearly made the runner-ups—Miss Rheingold, 1955 . . . nearly. Twenty bucks an hour! Coulda' been tops, wasn't for that Greek bastard!"

Jimmy was glad when she went back to her beer, but it wasn't long before her lips were floundering again.

"C'm'here," she said. "Come here!" she screamed, and Jimmy, scared, took his former stool. Her teeth were black and broken and the skin on her neck was puffy and wrinkled. But she wasn't so bad when her mouth was closed, and he wondered for an instant whether he could get it back up, and if she'd take him home to her apartment and her brass bed, but decided against the whole thing when she opened her mouth again. "Still could, y'know," she coursed onward. "They still want me . . . need to get rid . . . few pounds, all it is . . . few-pounds . . . then I'm gonna work for the *Vogue,* the *Vogue* magazine. . . . Damn Greek bastard. Took everything I had. Fuck him. I'll show him! Just knock off a few inches, that's all. . . ."

"They need models," said Jimmy. "I know, I'm a photographer myself." He reached for his wad. Maybe she'd talk about Suzie if he bought her a drink. "Bartender!" he summoned. "One for the lady, please!"

The bartender came out of the men's room and, without looking up, placed beers before Angel and Jimmy.

Angel was in the midst of smearing lipstick almost to her nose when she noticed the beer and Jimmy proudly returning the money to his pocket.

"Hey, you!" She focused on him generally. "Some whore? . . . Think I'm some whore?" She shrieked. "Get out! You bastard!" even louder, trying to hit him with her purse, which landed behind the bar.

Jimmy stumbled off the stool, forgetting about the change from his two-dollar bill. "Sonofabitch! Fuckin' bastard!"

Two men who weren't there earlier sat at the bar

laughing. One smoked a pipe. But Jimmy couldn't bother to place them. Anyway, he was on another block now, peering over a red curtain strung across a storefront, struggling to see over the curtain and into the light, but managing only a glimpse of the flaking ceiling.

An outline of a hand was painted clumsily on the window. "Madam Cornwallis—Palm Reading—Character Analysis—Your Future—Passport Pictures."

It was futile trying to see inside, so he turned back to the street: "SUZIE!"

A woman appeared from a hallway, smiling, motioning to him, bobbing up and down. "You wish to learn future?"

Jimmy tried to ignore her, but she took his arm. "Come," she said pleasantly. "I tell you all about future."

He was still explaining how he couldn't take the time when he found himself blinking in the light of a gray, blue, and yellow room, the various layers of paint flaking into a sullen rainbow. Mostly the room was yellow.

"I'm looking for this girl," he explained.

"Come. Sit."

She shoved him down on a spring-burst sofa with a sleeping baby at one end. An ancient potbellied stove sputtered from a nearby corner. Children were sprawled on the floor, many of them. Some were crawling.

"I was just . . ." Jimmy began.

"Very cheap. I tell your fortune very cheap."

Before he could answer, she was staring at him gravely, taking his hand, spreading it flat, mumbling something, placing her hand over his, then taking hers away, then looking up at him wide-eyed.

"What is it?" he asked with concern.

"Mmmmm . . ." she frowned mysteriously.

She was very, very pregnant, and he was careful not to bump her. She wore a man's shirt, buttoned only at the center, and he could see her billowing boobs laced with tiny blue veins, and tipped with gigantic nipples. As she ran a tickling finger over his hand, she seemed to grow even more worried, and he found himself staring closely at the criss-crosses on his palm.

"Mmmm . . ." she said. "I see, I see you live long time, have much happiness. Heart line very good. You very warm and generous person." She looked into his eyes. "Right?" she asked.

"Guess so," said Jimmy. He wasn't going to brag about it.

"And very smart. Much brains," she added. "Right?"

"Sometimes," Jimmy said modestly.

"And this time, this line here, it means you planning to take a trip, right?" Her red eyes looked to him again.

Jimmy was truly amazed. "Yeah—to Hawaii. How'd you know that?"

She giggled. "I know!"

A little girl in a torn sweater crawled up next to him. "Get away, Elicia!" said the woman, pushing the girl to the floor and returning to Jimmy's palm. The girl came back anyway.

"I see it is an island. With dancing girls. One of the dancing girls like you much. . . . Right?"

"Is the girl's name Lisa?"

The little girl pulled his hand away. "Stop!" said the woman, shoving the girl. The woman stood up. "Just one moment. I tell you her name." She walked to a drawing on the wall. It was a hand, charted like a map. She looked closely at the lines and printed explanations.

"I think her name Lisa," the woman said when she returned.

"Jesus! That's right!" said Jimmy.

"And this . . . this is. . . ." She stopped tracing for a moment, consulted the chart again. "That is right," she said, replacing her finger in his hand.

"This one is your love line. I can see you are very, very lucky in your love . . . or . . ." she pondered. "Very *un*lucky. It is not clear. Hmmm. . . ." She went back to the chart. The little girl came back with another little girl, and they began to bounce on Jimmy trying to look at his palm and making him uncomfortable.

"How's it look?" asked Jimmy.

"Hmmm," answered the woman.

A door opened at the back of the room, and a fat man emerged in a dirty undershirt. He walked to the small refrigerator, took a quart of milk and put the container to his lips, glancing wearily at Jimmy and the woman, who was still reading the chart.

"Ah!" the woman said finally. "It looks good. You have been lucky in love, right?"

"Well, not really."

"No?" The woman was upset.

"Yeah," Jimmy gave in. She looked so unhappy to be wrong. "Yeah, I guess I have."

"Good!" said the woman, taking his hand. "Now we go on. This line mean. . . ." She seemed puzzled. "So sorry," she apologized, "but my sister, you see, she usually tells the fortune." The woman looked up. The man in the dirty undershirt was standing over her shoulder, milk running down his chin. She bent into Jimmy, who was covered by children. "My sister do this usually, but she go to movies," she whispered.

"That's all right," said Jimmy.

"I know too," she said. "But not so good as her." She laughed, a bit embarrassed, grinning at the man over her shoulder, then went back to Jimmy's palm. "I can tell you will have lots of money."

"Really?" said Jimmy.

"Very much money," the woman nodded.

"Not so," the man said wearily, his sleepy eyes on the outstretched palm.

The woman gave him a sharp glance. "I say yes."

The man shrugged.

"I think so too," said Jimmy, coughing under the burden of the kids, one of whom was jumping on his sore part.

"Thank you," the woman told Jimmy gratefully. She turned and spat at the man's feet.

"Pig," said the man.

The woman ignored him. "And this line, it tell me you laugh very much."

The man bent over the hand. "That line mean he have six children," he corrected.

"Really?" said Jimmy, who couldn't figure out which line was in question.

The woman yanked the hand and looked deep into Jimmy's eyes. "Don't listen to him! You have very much laughter!" she said.

"Six children!" argued the man.

"Laughter!"

"Children!"

And one of the little girls put her finger in Jimmy's eye, making it water.

The woman pointed angrily at the chart. "You look!" she told the man.

"You look," said the man, going to the chart. "See?" he gloated. "Six children!"

"Ah!" The woman spat angrily, but went to the chart.

The woman studied closer while Jimmy got bit by one of the other little girls.

"Bullshit!" said the woman.

"You can't even read English!"

"I know hand by memory!"

The man stomped across the room, fought with one of the kids for Jimmy's hand, ripped it into the air, and stuck his fingernail into the palm. "Six children!" he shouted.

The woman jerked the hand away, spat at the man and told Jimmy, "You not listen to that man!"

Under the weight of the sprawling, groping children, Jimmy stared dumbly at the screaming man in the dirty undershirt and the spitting woman in the yellow-flaking room with the gray chart of the giant hand and suddenly all of it was distant and apart from him.

He ran past the Saltair Lounge onto a more familiar street.

In front of the Happy Hour he bumped into the man in the outsized overcoat, sending him to the pavement. Apologizing, he helped the man up and was rewarded by a shower of swear words; Jimmy was amazed at the old bastard's ingratitude.

Now he walked more carefully. He'd have to get back and call the police. No Suzie. He didn't mean to get her lost, he *loved* Suzie! She was the only one he really loved, and that was the truth. *She'd* never have turned him away for some sonofabitch. Poor Suzie. Poor, poor Suzie.

"Eat," the sign flashed again.

Two figures leaned against a railing.

"Hey, buddy, you lookin' for a chick in a white dress?"

"Yeah! You guys seen her!"

Then he has splashed against the wall with a glaring bulb blinding his eyes. He was in a hallway, and the rough hands of Red dug into his pockets while Pipe pinned him to the wall, a switchblade knife at his throat.

"He hasn't got it!" Red said to his companion.

Jimmy tried to scream; Pipe covered his mouth.

"You better cooperate, kid, or I'll cut a smile in your throat you won't be able to laugh out of."

Jimmy plunged his hand into the inside pocket of his jacket. The money wasn't there, and he tried his trouser pockets, panicked that the knife wouldn't wait. It wasn't there either! Even Mrs. Spaulding's silver dollars were gone!

"Y' stashed it," said Pipe. "Where?"

"The shoes!" said Red.

Red removed the shoes as Jimmy went through his pockets for the fifth time. "What could've happened to it?" he asked.

"Not in his shoes," Red told Pipe.

"It's got to be someplace!" Jimmy was almost crying. "I had it in my hands just a minute ago!"

"Someone got there first," Red surmised.

Pipe withdrew his knife from Jimmy's throat and looked at him contemptuously. "You little bastard!"

Jimmy began to get pissed off. "Am I supposed to apologize for not having the money for you to rob?"

Pipe smacked him across the face, and before Jimmy could think he was flailing out with his fists at the two of them. Then a window opened somewhere and a voice was calling for the police and Jimmy found himself running and the two erstwhile stickup men were gone.

Inching along, peering down steps and into gulleys, retracing his path as well as he could, he searched for his lost salvation at the Happy Hour and the Saltair Lounge, but no one knew anything about any money. As for Madam Cornwallis and family, it was unbelievable, but they were gone, and so was the damn storefront, hand and all. . . .

"Watch it!"

Bales were tossed at his feet. Morning editions of the *Tribune* barely missed his toes, and he was mocked by the leering groan of a truck as it sped away.

And then he was under the flashing "Eat" sign again and there was the car.

Wait! Someone was in it!

"Hey, Ulysses, where the hell you been!"

It was Suzie.

WITH Suzie sweeping along at his heels, daintily pinching her long dress with both hands to shield it from the grime, Jimmy took the steps to the eighth precinct two at a time.

He arrived out of breath in the brightly lit room smelling of old wax to find a line of tawdry people awaiting the cursory glance of a bored desk sergeant. In one corner, behind a partition, two cops laughed over something in a magazine.

Sobriety incarnate, Jimmy leaned over the partition.

"Excuse me, officers," he said.

Ignoring him, the cops went on laughing. One of them had no eyebrows, and the other, who sat behind a desk, was looking up into the first cop's face as they shared a joke.

"Hey, you guys," said Suzie, speaking their language.

The first cop glanced in her direction, pointed to the desk sergeant and went back to the magazine.

"Hey, Jimmy," Suzie said loudly, "you sure the bomb was planted in this station? I never got it straight."

Jimmy wasn't that anxious for attention. "Quit that," he whispered.

"What was that?" asked the first cop.

Suzie was innocent. "I was just commenting to my friend on the indifferent attitudes of professional law enforcers when they encounter a state of emergency, that's all."

"What emergency?" the second cop asked without interest.

"I've been robbed!" Jimmy blurted.

The second cop waved him away. "The desk sergeant'll take care of you." He was through discussing it.

"What is your name, officer?" said Suzie in her best rich-race voice.

Jimmy tried to pull her away.

"Better yet, what is the number of your badge," Suzie persisted.

"You after trouble, young lady?" the second cop inquired.

"Are you, officer?" Suzie retorted.

Jimmy was getting nervous. "Come on!" He yanked at her but she was riveted to the floor.

The first cop walked to her. "What's your name, miss?"

Suzie leaned in close to him. "Number 713," she read from his badge.

"Jesus!" whispered Jimmy.

"I asked your name, miss," the cop repeated.

Suzie bared her teeth in what might pass for a smile in tigresses. "Suzanne Elizabeth Middleburg, beloved, favorite, and only daughter of Arthur A. Middleburg, otherwise known as Chief Justice Arthur A. Middleburg, who happens to be deeply concerned about his daughter and his daughter's friends!" She leaned in to the badge again. "It *is* 713, isn't it?"

713 looked from Jimmy to Suzie and back again. The other cop rose from his desk. "Just a minute, Arthur," he told 713, "I'll handle this."

Suzie memorized his badge, too. "672, huh?"

"What's your problem?" said 672.

"Someone stole my money," said Jimmy anxiously, "and—"

"Have you been drinking?" 672 interrupted.

"He has," piped Suzie. "At my house."

"Where'd you lose it?" 713 asked Jimmy.

"I'm not sure, exactly, because I didn't have it when those two guys beat me up after I got out of the palm-lady's place. So I might've lost it there because of all the kids crawling all over me."

672 winced. "Start with the two guys. You say they beat you up?"

"Well, not exactly—they were only looking for the money. It was right after I got out of the palm-reading place. She didn't know how to read 'em right because her sister or somebody usually did, so she got in a hassle with some raunchy man over whether I'd have a lot of kids or not. So I left, and then I. . . ."

713 and 672 exchanged weary glances. "Okay, okay, one thing at a time," said 672. "So these two guys accosted you. Where?"

"In a doorway across from the 'Eat' place. That's where the dog was, only he wasn't there when they got me."

"Ever see these guys before? Can you give us a description?"

"One has red hair and the other one smokes a pipe. I met 'em the first time in front of the opium den and they tried to fix me up, but I couldn't because I was looking for—"

"Opium den?"

"That's right," Jimmy explained patiently. "An opium den, a Chinese opium den."

713 blinked. He did have some eyelashes, red ones.

"Now wait a second," 672 broke in. "Let's go back to the guys who beat you up. Did they get your money?"

"No, I told you that already."

"Then you lost it before that."

"I can't remember!"

"Where did all this take place?"

"Across from the 'Eat' sign!" Jimmy was getting impatient.

"I mean the street, kid! The name of the street!"

"How should I know? I stopped there when we ran out of gas. But I could take you there—it's about three blocks away from the El tracks, I remember that. But I'm not sure of anything else because I lost Suzie and that's what was on my mind. To find her, I mean."

"You're Suzie, I suppose," said 672.

"As in Arthur A. Middleburg," assented Suzie.

"And where were you all this time?"

"In the john across the street."

"The john," repeated 672.

"The *lady's* john," asserted Suzie.

"That's why I couldn't find her," said Jimmy.

"Naturally," said 672.

"How much money did you lose, kid?" said 713.

"Two hundred dollars, almost," said Jimmy.

"Two hundred?" 672 was surprised.

"Dollars," Jimmy supplied.

"What were you doing with all that money?" 713 asked suspiciously.

"I'm on my way to Hawaii."

"To Hawaii," said 713 with a cop-glance at 672.

"Sonny . . ." 672 leaned in like a buddy to Jimmy. "Confidentially, just between you and me, how much've you had to drink?"

"A beer," said Jimmy. "Maybe two." And then as a cloud of doubt passed over 672's face: "I guess probably it was around three."

"Three."

"Give or take one or two."

"And you, miss?"

"I'm saying nothing that might tend to incriminate myself," said Suzie.

Some time later an exhausted 713 pulled his squad car to a halt in front of the Saltair Lounge. His forehead was sore from nervously removing and replacing his cap, and he was alone with Jimmy and Suzie since 672 had absolutely flatly refused to take further chances with his sanity

"Now you're sure this is the place," said 713. A lesser man might have wept. They'd been to nineteen others that looked like the place.

"Absolutely," said Jimmy.

"Because if it isn't, I'm taking you back to the station, and I don't give a damn whose father is who!"

The three of them went in the padded door, found the place empty.

"Hey!" shouted 713.

No answer.

"It's not even two o'clock," said Jimmy. "They have to be open." He pointed to a vacant stool. "See, that's where the *Vogue* model was before she threw the purse at me."

"Sorry," said the bartender, emerging from the back. "I was getting some ice."

"Hi!" Jimmy greeted him enthusiastically.

The bartender frowned.

"You ever seen this kid before?" asked 713.

"Never serve minors," the bartender said mechanically.

"Yeah, yeah, I know," said 713. "But has he been in here tonight?"

"You remember me!" said Jimmy. "I sat right there next to Angel!"

"He's nuts," the bartender said. "Never saw him before. Now if you'll all excuse me, I've got to check my cash."

"The kid says he lost two hundred dollars in here," said 713.

"I said maybe," corrected Jimmy.

"Sure," said the bartender, "and maybe the moon is made out of goat cheese."

After the Saltair Lounge they found the opium den, which turned out to be an empty billiard parlor hung with streamers and Chinese lanterns and a sign in English proclaiming a hand-laundry association had met there that night.

Red and Pipe had apparently closed up shop, and the store with the giant hand had left the city—soothsayer, undershirt, kids, and all.

When they finally found him, the Happy Hour bartender, less humorous but more firm than the other one, said he'd swear on his newborn infant's life that Jimmy was lying.

"You mean you're giving up just like that?" Jimmy said to 713 when they finally returned to the station.

"I'll write out a report," he said hoarsely, "and then I may resign from the force."

"Chicken," said Suzie.

After one of Suzie's credit cards paid off at a gas station, they headed towards Weston. It was a quiet ride. And when Jimmy pulled up under the El station to park in front of the Dead Pigeon, Suzie made no move to leave the car.

"Let's go!" he commanded.

"That place is decadent and obscene, and I refuse to

be corrupted by all that avant-garde stuff. Besides, I don't like coffee anyway." Suzie wasn't going to budge.

"You think I'm gonna leave you here alone and let what happened downtown happen all over again!"

"It won't." She folded her arms and looked with dignity out the window at the rows of cars. "I've already been once. I don't have to go again."

"If you won't walk, I'll throw you over my back like a bag of potatoes and carry you in," he threatened, in no mood for her shenanigans.

But when he tried to pull her out she clung to the steering wheel and gasped, "My dress!"

"What's wrong with your goddamn dress!" he demanded.

"It'll look ridiculous in that classless society!"

"This is a hell of a time to act like a girl!" Jimmy shouted. "I've got to find Fred to help me get my money back; that's more important than how you're dressed!"

He took her arm, lifting her roughly from the car.

The ground shook and a train chortled overhead as they entered the Dead Pigeon.

All the wooden tables were filled, and waitresses in long hair and sweaters rushed about wiping hands on aprons. A fragile, pretty girl with close-cropped hair was hunched over a guitar soulfully singing about a ". . . Scarlet ribbon in her hair . . ." as Suzie sought anonymity in a poster-plastered niche. Jimmy hurried through the candle-lit dimness in search of Fred.

"Hey, Todd, you see Fred Roberts?" He addressed the owner of the coffee shop at the helm of a spitting expresso machine.

The machine gasped with a burst of steam, and Todd looked up to grin at a thin girl with wispy hair before he answered Jimmy. "Yeah, man, he was in earlier with some chick."

The girl ignored Todd and smiled instead to Jimmy as she passed by. She was blonde and he recognized the stainless-steel braces but couldn't remember from where.

"Don't bug the chick, man," Todd growled. "She's taken."

Every girl in the place was "taken" if you listened to him, but it was common knowledge that he always went home alone. Some people said he was impotent. Jesus, Jimmy felt a rush of horror at their kinship.

"Told you not to come in here all boozed up anyway," Todd was saying above another burst from the machine. "Got a hang-up with the fuzz now about the noise."

"I'm not lookin' for trouble with the fuzz, man," Jimmy got in the groove. "I'm after Fred."

"Cat's been callin' you ever ten minutes, but don't hang around here. Wait for him at a table someplace and quit buggin' me."

Jimmy found Suzie leaning against the post listening to the short-haired girl singing her mournful song. They were both crying as though they shared the same sorrow.

". . . All the stores were closed and shuttered, all the streets were bare . . . not one ribbon for her hair. . . . Through the night my heart was aching, just before the dawn was breaking. . . ."

"Jimmy!"

He spun around to face a very excited Fred Roberts.

"Where the hell you been! I called Lisa and she wasn't home, and neither was Suzie, and you didn't show up here."

Voices began to murmur "Quiet!"

"Come on outside," said Jimmy. "I got to talk to you!"

Outside, they stopped under the swinging sign.

"Jesus," said Jimmy, "am I glad you got here! You gotta come downtown with me right away."

"Jimmy," Fred interrupted with popping eyes, "my old man said if I left the house he'd circumsize me all over again, but I had to talk to you! The whole town's looking for you!"

"What for?"

Fred's eyes blinked behind his glasses. "Car theft!"

A patrol car passed by. "Look out!" Fred yanked his friend back into the doorway.

"What car theft?"

"Your mother's been calling my house all night

about your stealing a car and taking it to Hawaii or something, and my mother has the police radio up full volume!"

"Your mother's nuts—I just borrowed my father's car. I'm gonna bring it back as soon as we find my money!"

"What money?"

"My two hundred dollars, jerk!"

"What two hundred dollars?"

Jimmy was exasperated. "Dammmit, I'll tell you the details later! Let's go!"

He rushed back into the Dead Pigeon to find Suzie while Fred stayed outside on the sidewalk, his smile growing to a giggle. Jimmy heard him and came back. "What the hell're you laughing at?"

"Fools and their money are bound to part, but you can't even wait for the inevitable—you have to volunteer!" He began to laugh again and added, "Some whore probably got it!"

"Jesus! I lose my whole future and you get hysterical. What the hell kind of guy is that?"

"Jimmy," Fred said, suddenly sounding tired, "I don't want to laugh, but this is so typical of you. It's nothing new. Why'd you have to take two hundred dollars with you? Who were you trying to impress this time?"

After all Jimmy did for Fred, his best friend turned out to be a genuine prick.

"I just happened to have it on me!"

"Oh sure, sure . . ." said patronizing Fred. "You just happened to have two hundred dollars on you, and you just happened to get drunk."

"Okay, so I got drunk! What the hell would you do, huh? If your girl got pissed off at you on some half-assed circumstantial evidence and started hanging around that sonofabitch Matthew Hollinder! What would you do!"

Fred grew alert and gave a short whistle. "Matthew Hollinder?"

"What's that supposed to mean?" Jimmy asked cautiously.

"Matthew Hollinder never leaves a girl hanging," Fred said with respect.

"You seem to think that's a goddamn virtue!" shouted Jimmy.

"Well, Jesus, don't you?" said Fred. "He never misses!" He laughed heartily.

"He's a menace to this whole goddamn society! And I think you're a sonofabitch to think it's funny! How would you like it if it was Denise instead of Lisa?"

"I wouldn't go out and get drunk and lose my money over it," said a smug Fred.

"You wouldn't, huh? No—you'd just run down to the basement and try to commit suicide!"

Fred matched his friend's anger with calmness. "Denise is not Lisa," he said securely.

"Yeah? Well, I wouldn't be go goddamn giddy about Matthew Hollinder if I were you! He doesn't rest—even on Sundays!"

Fred stopped smiling. "Would you care to amplify that statement?"

But Jimmy thought better of it. "Okay, you win. Let's forget it and get the hell downtown." He turned to the doorway.

"Why are you so anxious to go downtown?"

"Because I want to get my money back!"

Fred moved in closer. "You know something."

Jimmy was getting annoyed. "Look, you and I both know that Denise is a very nice girl and very reliable and she wouldn't ever do anything—she's waiting for you."

"Who said she might do anything?"

"Jesus, nobody! How can you believe every speck of gossip you hear?"

"What did you hear, Jimmy?"

"Nothing, goddamn it!"

"I happen to know that Denise goes to a special ballet class on Sunday afternoon! And it can't be Sunday morning because she doesn't get up until noon—and I see her every night including Sunday! So she can't be seeing Matthew Hollinder on Sundays; does that clear it up?"

"That's what I've been saying, you jerk!"

But Fred was still smarting. "You sure it wasn't Saturdays you heard about?"

Jesus.

"I never see her on Saturday afternoons—just at night," pondered Fred.

"Will you stop being so suspicious!" protested Jimmy. "It's practically psychopathic, the way you're looking for a way to hurt yourself. A goddamn masochist! Destroy yourself on your own time, will you? Right now there's a real problem: My money!"

Suddenly: "You laid her! I can tell by your goddamn face! You laid Denise!"

"See what kind of a friend you are! You'd believe it about me, but you won't believe it about Matthew Hollinder!"

"You mean that's true too?" Fred asked in a small voice.

"Sure!" Suzie blew out the door. "There're two days in a weekend, aren't there?"

"Shut up!" said Jimmy.

Fred looked incredulously from one to the other. No one said anything. Then Jimmy placed a consoling arm around his friend. "I guess I should've told you a long time ago what kind of a girl she was, Fred, but I just couldn't hurt you."

Shoving Jimmy away, "You lousy bastard! I ought to cut your pecker off!"

"Please!" protested Suzie. "I'm a maiden lady!"

Whatever else Fred had to say was lost in a quick groan as he raced under the El tracks to his car.

SUZIE thought it best to return to the dance because her father had probably noticed that she'd gone by now, and in another hour or so, he'd be wondering where. And Jimmy agreed; no telling when she might decide to go to the bathroom again, and he had to get back downtown to look for his money. Without Fred.

She was still talking about Fred's problem when they neared the country club's curved driveway.

". . . You think you had nothing better to do on your Saturday afternoons than sit around in front of Denise's old television set!"

"Think Fred'll ever talk to me again?" said Jimmy.

"*Talk* to you?" she sounded outraged. "Some day he'll thank you. I'd certainly appreciate it if my best girl friend slept around with my boy friend just to help me out. How many people are there these days you can count on?"

"Very amusing," said Jimmy.

"You should be immortalized!" She deepened her voice. "I only regret that I have but one life to give for—"

"Drop it!"

"They should build a monument in Lincoln Park." She made a salute. "To Jimmy Reardon for courage and valor beyond the call. . . . You're really gorgeous. After being around you, I'm even beginning to like the Judge's child bride!"

"What am I supposed to do now? *Un*-screw her?"

Suzie ignored him.

"Anyway, if Fred was up to the job, Denise wouldn't have called in outside help!"

He pulled to a short stop at the edge of the club's lawn.

Suzie sighed. "You know," she said, clasping her hands over her heart, "I may even start to call Little Miss Muffet *Mother* from now on. . . ."

Jimmy watched in silence as she moved godlike from the car to sweep regally over the grass, then up the red-carpeted stairway to disappear beyond the foyer with the oil painting of George Washington.

He was pretty damned pissed off by her triumphant march. If Suzie thought she'd finally found someone to feel superior to she could go to hell! He was just a goddamn victim of circumstances, for crissakes!

But it was stupid to get worked up about Suzie's newfound salvation while two hundred dollars was floating around somewhere on the South Side. He started up the motor as a group of laughing girls emerged from the foyer. He saw that the girl in the blue dress who had no pubic hair was among them, and so was Carnation, nodding his head like a windup toy. The petty little bastard in the red jacket was running to get the group's car. Maybe the dance was breaking up. Jesus, soon Lisa would be leaving with the sonofabitch—if they hadn't left already!

Switching off the motor, he looked toward the ballroom. Dim blue light glowed through the trees, and there were plenty of cars around, so maybe it was still going on. What if Lisa knew about how he was beaten and robbed and how he fought against overwhelming odds to hang on to the money that would bring him to Hawaii? What if she saw the pitiful state he was in? She sure as hell wouldn't go with the sonofabitch over Jimmy's limp, bruised body!

He turned on the car's inside lights and checked himself in the rearview mirror. He was a pitiful sight, all right, with his sore cheekbones and the hair matted across his forehead.

But it lacked something. He left the car and flopped around in the dusty roadbed, opening his jacket and pulling out his shirttail. Then he rubbed his hands in the dirt and smeared it on his face, careful to avoid the bruises, which had to show, and anyway there was the risk of infection.

The result was so pitiful it almost made him cry himself. If Lisa didn't faint when she saw him, the very least she'd do would be to get hysterical.

. . . Lisa would be at the other end of the ballroom, dancing with the sonofabitch to the soft music in the dream-blue light. The couples near the doorway would be the first to see him, and the shock would turn them rigid, like statues. Then, magically, the pitiful sight would spread from couple to couple, bringing stone silence. . . .

Jimmy ripped his shirttails and took out one shoelace. Nothing more pitiful than clomping shoes.

. . . And while the entire ballroom waited expectantly, eyes, hearts, and minds glued to the pitiful figure stumbling near the doorway—even part of the band—Lisa and the stupid sonofabitch would still be dancing, hardly suspecting the awesome sight about to greet them. Finally the band would grow discordant and quit altogether. And it would take that long for the sonofabitch to realize something was wrong. That's when Lisa would see him. . . .

The effect was complete, though it would've been nice to have a little blood. Of course, he could be bleeding internally. That thought comforted him as he began the short trip across the lawn.

He ran in close to the wall to keep himself away from the light and the parking attendant; he couldn't afford to run into Carnation or Teeth again, either.

Inside, a British-sounding voice boomed out at him. It seemed pretty goddamn ridiculous to have after-dinner speeches at two o'clock in the morning! Well, what the hell. Jimmy straightened to his full height and ducked into the ballroom, clomping his shoes loudly.

But even if he'd been stark-naked and blowing a tuba, nobody would've noticed because every face in the whole goddamn place was fixed solidly on the blue-spotlighted bandstand where, strutting like a goddamn bronze peacock, looking six-foot-eight, thundering and lifting his arm in flight, and sounding like a goddamn Oxford graduate, was that goddamn sonofabitch Matthew Hollinder! Reading poetry!

Jimmy nearly buckled under.

"As Ariel, cruelly tasked
By fortune's ill demand was
Yet set free . . ."

The words came tolling, reaching out over the hushed crowd and resounding back to where Jimmy stood crusty and torn near the doorway.

The masterful voice rose and fell, and women, chins in hand, gazed soulfully from their tables at the handsome figure spouting the biggest bunch of bullshit Jimmy had ever heard.

". . The Tempest boldly met
To capture wings again
In Shelley's . . ."

It wasn't hard to pick out Lisa from the group of couples clustered about the bandstand. She stared up at Hollinder as though she were ready to rush up and wash his goddamn feet! And Jesus, so did Suzie!

". . . Yearning breast; and through his
Song renew herself as
Truth will live . . ."

Truth! What the hell does he know about truth! The truth is, he's waiting to renew Lisa right after the dance! She never liked Jimmy's goddamn poetry that much!

". . . When passed from soul to soul.
So too must every man
Search out his . . ."

With his shoe thudding conspicuously on the ballroom floor, but attracting no attention whatsoever, Jimmy moved closer to the stage. How the hell could people keep a straight face during all that pompous shit!

Hollinder paused and lowered his voice and the crowd hovered expectantly. Even Jimmy stopped clomping.

". . Breast and therein live as
Goodness lives, in fertile
Wombs of principle. . . ."

On the last word Hollinder raised his chin, then let it drop slightly to show a shining smile that radiated to every part of the hall, into vases and under carpets even. Suzie shouted "Hooray!" and Hollinder peered down from Olympus to Lisa. He laughed and jumped from the bandstand with an agile, corny leap. The crowd let out a roar of approval and closed around him. Everyone seemed to want to touch the sonofabitch, to share his glory as he modestly made his way through the crowd, dragging Lisa with him.

Not knowing quite how he got there, Jimmy was suddenly aware of the boards springing beneath his weight and blinding blue spotlight as he clomped across the bandstand to the microphone.

He tried to squint through the piercing light and look down at the crowd, but all he saw were vague forms and he couldn't hear a thing.

"I have come back!" he heard himself shout, and the words echoed back to him through the loudspeaker.

"I have come back—
From a pit of pimps and
Whores."

He had their attention now. "Ladies and gentlemen, I am making this up on the spot," he said, "so if you'll just bear with me." Nervously, he started to tuck in the ripped shirttail, but he wasn't sure whether or not his zipper had come undone so he left the tail hanging the way it was, and instead wiped a blade of grass from his eyes and licked his lips. Someone, a girl, giggled.

"I have raced the turtle and
  The hare.
I have come back!
I have come back!
Need I wash behind the
  Ear?"

". . . The ear . . ." echoed back from the loudspeaker, and it sounded pretty damn good as Jimmy followed it with:

"Is there logic in
  A tear?
Who has rolled my stone away?
Shall I come back
  Another day?"

His range of sight was increasing, and now he could see through the crowd to where Lisa stood pale beside the sonofabitch, who probably couldn't understand one goddamn word of what a real poet had to say. Jimmy sure as hell was in top form.

"I have come back!
I have come back—
To dance on a broken
  Toe . . .
The old ass, alas,
  In a sling—
No corny words to fling.
It is Ulysses home to roost
'though, perchance, a
  Little juiced . . ."

Groups of people began to break away and walk slowly toward the door because all that truth was too much for them. He couldn't see Suzie, so she was probably back at her table.

The girl with the covered mouth shook her head and left with her date, and Carnation talked animatedly to a very nervous Teeth. "But he's Miss Middleburg's fiancé!" said one of them.

"I have come back!
I have come back—
To look out upon this
Appalling pall—
And naught there is to say
My friends,
Save: Fuck you all,
You all. . . ."

"That's enough!" said Teeth. "We've got to find Miss Middleburg!"

Jimmy spoke desperately to Lisa:

"In my beer you dropped your
Cigarette.
Don't you have the least
Regret?"

At this point Lisa should've been tearing up to the bandstand and throwing her arms around him and sobbing and begging Jimmy's forgiveness, but Lisa was off schedule. She looked to the floor, and Hollinder seemed uncomfortable. "Just a drunk kid," said someone.

And then came the loud, definitive statement issued from somewhere near the tables: "I never saw him before in my whole life!"

It was Benedict Arnold Suzie Middleburg!

"Come down from there young man!" someone shouted, and Carnation came out of the darkness beyond the blinding lights. Teeth was on his heels, and they leapt up onto the bandstand.

"I have come back! I have come back!" was Jimmy's gallant finish.

". . . Come back . . ." finished the echo as Jimmy was dragged down off the stage and across the floor, sandwiched between Carnation and Teeth.

For the second time they led him through the foyer, past the oil painting of George Washington, and down the red-carpeted steps.

The petty-bastard parking attendant applauded as they passed by.

"Fuck you, too!" said Jimmy.

"Now, where's your car?" inquired Teeth.

"I'll get there by myself," said Jimmy.

"That won't be necessary," said Carnation, pulling Jimmy off the steps and around the curved driveway just in time to see Lisa and Hollinder slide by in a white convertible.

"Hey, wait! I have to tell you something!" Jimmy cried after the car, but it turned its red tail on him and dipped off.

Carnation and Teeth made sure Jimmy found his car and stood guard while he drove away, wildly honking his horn.

Then the lights of the country club were fading behind him and the road was turning into curves as he sped after the white convertible.

He had to increase his speed until the old man's car heaved at the smallest bump, but soon he had narrowed the distance between them.

Alongside Hollinder's convertible. "Hey, you sonofabitch!" Jimmy shouted out the window. "Pull over!"

Lisa stared out the car, motioning Jimmy away, while Hollinder stepped hard on the gas and pulled in front, but Jimmy was not to be outdistanced. He stuck on the sonofabitch's tail until all at once the rear lights of the convertible turned a brighter red, and the car stopped on a dime, leaving Jimmy barely enough room to squeal his car to a standstill inches from the other's bumper.

The goddamn reckless idiot almost made Jimmy wreck his father's car!

Jimmy rushed from the car with a powerful slam of the door.

"What're you, crazy?"

Hollinder came out to face him, left his door open. "All right, Reardon," he said.

Lisa ran around from her side of the car, shielding her eyes from Jimmy's headlights. "Please don't! Matt!" she said.

"I don't think I'll have to," said Hollinder.

Jimmy clenched his fists. "You don't?!"

"Why don't you take your little kiddie car home to

mamma?" Hollinder said gently. "Before I kick the shit out of you."

"Lisa, y'hear that? He's lookin' for it!" said Jimmy.

"Don't do it, Matt—you'll only get yourself in trouble!" She was about to cry.

And suddenly Jimmy was swinging out at the bronze face and Lisa was screaming. Then his chin and his stomach exploded at the same time and he was flat on his back looking up at millions of cheerful, winking stars.

Hollinder stepped over Jimmy's limp, bruised body to where Lisa stood and led her back to his white convertible.

Jimmy heard the motor start. He sat up as the car clicked into gear. Jesus, Lisa wasn't even looking back at him!

"Hey!" Jimmy shouted after the rapidly disappearing car. "Aren't you even gonna kiss me good-by?"

THERE were other islands. Haiti, for instance. Voodoo maybe, and natives who speak French. And even if they don't have good teeth like someone said, every year there'd be a fresh crop of thirteen-year-old girls.

Because he didn't realize how far he'd gone, Jimmy was startled to find his car alone on the great concrete arc merging Lake Shore Drive with the four-o'clock-quiet streets of the Loop.

Defeat is not something to be scorned. By accepting it, probably the very fibers of his being were being strengthened. Maybe he wouldn't feel it right away, but before long he'd begin to recognize the growth in himself. Jesus, he might have changed already!

Even the old man would perceive his new stature. Unafraid and with arms open wide, Jimmy would bound up the stairs and burst through the door to meet with full force the old man's anger. He'd tried, he'd pitted himself against all the odds and now here he stood, broken. But he was greater in defeat than most men were in victory! Can't you see that, Father?

Like hell you can. The old man would hang him just because he hadn't shaved! Nope, it was definitely impossible to surrender honorably to his father. But he had to surrender to someone, and soon, because he couldn't drive around the Loop the rest of his life, that's for sure. Napoleon was lucky because he had the Czar or somebody to surrender to, but who did Jimmy have?

Really a hell of a situation. Mythical, almost. As part of a myth he could spend the rest of eternity running around asking people if they were honorable enough for him to turn himself in to. And poets would write about him and ballads would be sung and he'd be part of required reading in English IV.

Allowing himself to enjoy the unlimited prospects of mythdom, he drove west to the El tracks and began to weave absentmindedly down the street which ran through a colonnade of riveted steel pillars. And because he was concentrating so hard, he barely missed smashing into the orange, buglike street-cleaning truck that was churning up dust and spraying water as it drawled along the curb.

But the danger was quickly passed and soon forgotten as he drove along, casually glancing at storefronts and admiring the yellow and red scratches etched by the neon signs. It made him feel good to know that "Gordil H. Federson, Pharmacist," had been around since 1870, and that those dusty cardboard boxes in the tall windows of that warehouse supplied the fingernail cutlery for most of the United States and maybe the whole world. All of it was very calm and very ordinary, but it made the wind less biting.

Suddenly his headlights picked up something looming ghostlike up ahead, growing larger as he approached. He stiffened and tried to stop, but then it was right in front of him and there wasn't time. For an instant his eyes met the wild, leering gaze of a stubble-faced drunk with a drooling mouth who came within inches of his life as Jimmy swerved sharply and went around him.

Through his rearview mirror he watched the drunk fade away, furiously waving a brown paper bag at the car. The incident was over so fast he wasn't sure if he'd been scared or not, but it was creepy just the same and he was glad when the figure disappeared. Yet even then he couldn't shake the haunting image of those eyes.

They seemed to be suspended before him, staring, just staring. To break the spell he looked around him at the tired gray buildings and the blaring neon signs which now, instead of comforting him, seemed to leer out at the car as if they were calling him up dark stairways and mysterious alleys.

The more he thought about it, the worse it got. It

was ridiculous! He was scaring the hell out of himself for no reason at all!

He'd almost talked himself out of the eyes and the neon when he began to feel the gnawing sensation that someone or something was stretched out on the back seat of the car.

It would have been very simple to look around and check. All he had to do was move his head a bit and peer down behind him. But he couldn't do it. He tried reason. Obviously if anyone were crouched back there, they would have clubbed him or stabbed him or slashed his throat long ago. And certainly he would have heard it breathing or scraping its foot or something. But still he couldn't bring himself to turn and reassure himself. He was even afraid to look in the rearview mirror!

Then he heard the low, insistent noise coming from behind, and he hunched into the steering wheel. Jesus, there really *was* something there! Frantic now, and mustering all the courage and willpower he possessed, he painfully raised his neck and craned cautiously over the seat to come face-to-face with the leering, grinning, drooling, horrible thing.

But the seat was totally empty except for the remains of an old *Life* magazine. The relief poured from him in one long sigh. Yet the sound was still there and growing louder. Like thunder now. Didn't seem to be coming from the seat but from the sky! Then with mounting panic, he recognized his old enemy, the El.

It came rushing at him from behind, rumbling overhead, thundering out of its icy tunnel in a fury of flying gum wrappers and old cigarette butts.

The ground began to tremble and the car windows rattled and he slammed the accelerator to the floor.

But just as the car lifted in response to the pressure of his foot, a traffic light changed in front of him and he hit the brakes to send the car skidding along the newly-washed street.

The grease-black pillar seemed to lift itself away from the curb and race up to him, turning thicker and blacker in the beam of the headlights, and he remembered at the moment of impact that this car was the old man's soul.

The crash threw him against the steering wheel and the El laughed overhead—laughed and laughed into the distance until its sound was drowned out by the noise of the motor, which seemed to be vomiting steel. He sat there, bewildered, staring in shock at the pillar illuminated by the one headlight left shining.

He hardly dared to breathe because this was it—from the way his heart flopped around, he had to be having an attack. But he forgot all about that problem when he looked through a web of cracks in the windshield to see steam rising from the hood.

Oh Jesus wow! The thing his father loved and cherished and polished all the time and deprived everybody to buy so he could look good when he when to the office!

Abruptly, the terrible sound of the motor stopped. It couldn't conk out on him like that!

But that was the end of the car and the end of everything, because when he turned the key his father's shiny new automobile expired with a whimper, a tiny, helpless clunk.

He left the car and edged around to the pillar. It was sickening. The headlight was sprayed all over the street, the bumper was bent back to the tire, and there was only a hint of the hood's once graceful lines. Jimmy touched the remnant of a fender with his index finger, hesitantly, as though testing a dead body.

It didn't have to be as bad as it looked. He didn't know very much about cars, but it was only common sense that just because the radiator was a little dented and the fender was crumpled—which was only useless tinsel anyway—that didn't mean the car was wrecked altogether. He'd seen plenty of cars riding around without hoods and fenders—some people even liked them better that way! He stepped out of a pool of oil caused by a drip somewhere in the engine.

It really wouldn't be so bad with just a little body work. He might even be able to do it himself, if he had a wrench and a sledgehammer.

The lights of an oncoming car engulfed him. He'd

forgotten about the cops! Now he was going to be arrested for drunken driving!

Throwing himself to the ground, he rolled beneath the car as a set of wheels eased to a stop an arm's length away. Jimmy refused to look.

"You all right?"

He buried his face deeper in his sleeve.

A door creaked open. "You hurt?"

The voice seemed too old for a cop's. Risking a quick glance, Jimmy looked up to see the shaking running board of an ancient truck, and one shoe with a split sole descending to the ground. "I'm okay," he shouted, and began to slide toward the quivering truck. But his shoulders were wedged between car and ground, and he couldn't budge.

The split sole was joined by its mate. "You sure?" persisted the voice.

"I was just checking under here," explained Jimmy, still struggling to get out.

The shoes lifted out of sight and the truck groaned into gear. "Well, don't worry," the kindly voice went on, "I'm going past the police station, I'll send you some help." The motor rattled and the running board shook and the wheels eased away.

"Hey, wait!" Jimmy fought toward the departing truck and with a rip of his sleeve managed to break free in time to see it round the corner. They'd trace the car to his father, and the old man would pick his heart out with a tweezer.

Leaning against the car door, Jimmy watched scraps of paper pinwheeling in the wind. Maybe a hurricane would come and sweep them both away, him and the car, and a hundred-thousand years from now an archeologist would pass this way and find a trace of oil, and wonder who had left it, and what kind of person he was. The archeologist would never know that this particular pool of oil was all they ever found of Jimmy Reardon, who disappeared from earth before the dawn of Sunday morning.

But at least if a hurricane did come, it might get rid of the case against him. Get rid of the car. And then the cops couldn't arrest him and the old man would think the car was taken from him by an act of God instead of an act of Jimmy's.

And that's it! Get rid of the evidence before the police come!

He spotted a phone booth half a block down, in front of the Chicago Hard Goods Company, and raced toward it. The booth was old and green and dimly lighted, and after fifteen rings that took two months apiece, the information operator answered.

"Information," sounded the tin voice.

"Hello, could you give me the number of a place that tows cars? A wrecking place?" Jimmy asked.

"Surely sir. Which company did you wish, sir."

"Any company!"

"You'll have to be specific, sir," chided the voice.

"I'd love to be specific, operator, but I don't know a specific company!" He was controlling himself.

"Have you looked under Automobile Towing in the yellow pages of your directory, sir?" patronized the voice.

"I don't have any yellow pages," he screamed, "I'm in a telephone booth and there are no yellow pages!"

"I'm sorry, sir, but I'm afraid I can't help you unless you give me a specific—"

"But this is an emergency!"

"Oh, I am sorry, sir." The voice was apologetic and Jimmy sighed. "If you dial 'O' for operator she'll put your call through to the proper authorities."

His cannibal father was waiting with knife and fork in hand and she wanted him to be specific! He slammed the phone down and looked out at the windows above the Chicago Hard Goods Company. Maybe there was a night watchman or someone who'd let him borrow their yellow pages.

But the building seemed stingy and bleak, and there was no sign of life. He was about to try the other side of the street when the sign again drew his attention. "The Chicago Hard Goods. . . ." There had to be a Chicago Towing Company—there was a Chicago everything else!

The booth seemed more cheerful now, and the operator answered sooner.

"Hello, can you give me the number of the Chicago Towing Company?"

"I'll check for you, sir," said a voice no better than the other one. "I have three listings under that name. Which one did you wish, sir?"

"The first one!"

"Thank you, sir. That number is 456-7177," she said, and her voice sounded beautiful.

He was happily about to redeposit his dime when he was startled by a face outside the booth. A girl stood smiling at him through the window, her hands plunged deep in the pockets of a yellow corduroy raincoat. What the hell was a girl doing out at this hour? He slid back the accordion door to tell her he'd be just a minute and to get a better look at this new development.

She was something, all right. She didn't seem very old, but he couldn't tell exactly because some parts of her didn't seem real. Her hair was set in about eight carefully determined and altogether different directions, and the whole pile was squashed down by a rhinestone hairnet so that it resembled a gold wig. The thin smile was drawn on her face with lipstick, and her light blue eyes were surrounded with lashes that almost hit her forehead when she blinked.

She raised the toe of one of her high-heeled alligator shoes and nodded toward the phone. "It's all right, take your time."

"It's kind of an important call, won't take long," he said, and slid back the door.

She was pretty, kind of, and he stole another look at her while moving his dime to the slot. But he missed the slot when he saw she was staring back at him, and the dime fell to the floor. Since Cary Grant Reardon would never bend over for a mere dime while under the gaze of a pretty girl, he frisked his pockets for another. But all he could muster was a quarter and three pennies. Jesus, he'd dropped his only dime!

"I'm sorry to keep you waiting," he said, opening the door with wavering nonchalance, "but I seem to have dropped my dime."

She shrugged.

"So I'll just look around," he explained, kneeling to

the pavement and sifting his fingers through the dirt on the floor of the booth. "It should only take a minute."

"Sure, go ahead," she said cheerfully, and seemed amused.

Coughing in the dust, Jimmy frantically searched every corner of the booth with no success.

"Your cuff. Did you look in your cuff?" suggested the girl.

He sort of wished she'd keep her goddamn suggestions to herself since it was her fault he'd dropped it in the first place, and besides, it was embarrassing. And he wouldn't have admitted it was in his cuff even if it was—which it wasn't.

"Hey, wait just a minute!" She bent over and came up with the dime held triumphantly in her fingers. "Lookie what I found!"

He held out his hand. "You're pretty good," he said, not quite able to hide a trace of resentment.

She smiled and drew the dime to her breast. "Finders keepers?"

Oh shit, he didn't have time to play around!

"Look at him!" she laughed, and stuck out the coin. "Here, I was only kidding."

With her watching from outside, he couldn't remember the number, and by the time he got through information again and reached the sonofabitch at the Chicago Towing Company, he almost wished he hadn't bothered.

"Okay, okay, so where do you want it brought to?" the bored voice was asking.

"I don't care," said Jimmy, "so long as you take it away."

"You don't care," came the sarcastic echo. "Would you like us to dump it in the fuckin' river?"

He glanced at the faintly smiling girl pinching her bottom lip and lowered his voice. "Couldn't you just get it and keep it at your place until I make up my mind?"

"Sure. At the regular storage rate," gloated the voice.

"How much is that?"

"Two-fifty per day."

"How much would it cost to fix?"

"How the hell should I know! I ain't seen the car yet!"

"All right, come and get it—but right away, it's an emergency!"

"I'll send a man down as soon as I can."

"But you've got to come right now!"

"Look, sonny, we get there when we can. You want us to haul the fuckin' vehicle or don't you want us to haul the fuckin' vehicle? It's up to you."

"Okay, but please try to hurry, just try, will you?" Click. The bastard!

Now he had to call his mother and tell her he was safe and get her to bring down enough money for him to find a place to stay until payday, when he could begin to get the car fixed. He sure as hell wasn't going back home to become a target for the old man's frustrations, if he could help it. The only thing was, he didn't have another dime.

He slid open the door. "I hate to bother you again, but you don't happen to have change for a quarter, do you?"

"I might. But if you'll excuse the curiosity, how do you come to have so many people to call at four o'clock in the A.M.?" There seemed to be a note of admiration in her voice.

He winked rakishly. "Business."

"Yeah? What kind of occupation you in?"

"I don't mean occupation business. I mean personal business."

She seemed to be satisfied with that, and reached into a transparent plastic purse embroidered with geese and ducks. Jimmy could see green Kleenex and cosmetic cases as she daintily picked out some change.

"Here," she said, handing him the coins. "And hurry up, please. I'm beginning to get the chills."

"You can go first if you want," he offered gallantly.

She shrugged and slipped into the booth without a word. He saw her full breasts lift slightly when she reached up for the receiver. It was pretty unusual, meeting a girl like that right on the street. Jesus, what if she was a whore? She had enough stuff on her face for a whore, that was for sure. Maybe he could get it back up with her; maybe he'd been rehabilitated after all this time. He looked more closely at her boobs and tried to imagine what they'd be like bare. He tried hard, but nothing happened. It seemed even deader than before.

She probably wasn't a whore anyway. Even with all that stuff on her face, she couldn't have been too old. Maybe she was calling her father or someone.

She hung up and stepped from the booth. "You can use it now."

Glad to be rid of this smiling reminder of his funtional disorder, he cheerfully bid good-by to girl and boobs. "Thanks for the change," he said. "And it was nice to have met you."

"Pleased to have met you, too," she said.

Carefully depositing the dime, he dialed home. The phone was seized almost before it rang.

"Hello!"

Startled by the sudden harshness of the old man's voice, Jimmy dropped the phone and jumped back, fearfully watching the instrument swing by its cord.

"Jimmy? Is that you?" The booming voice filled the booth. "Answer me, goddamn it! Where the hell are you?"

Holding the receiver away from him as though it were alive, he slowly returned the phone to its hook, and suddenly became aware of the girl still staring through the window.

"I got an electric shock," he opened the door to explain. "They don't make telephones the way they used to."

She laughed.

"And I hate to tell you this, but I don't think the busses are running right now. I mean, you'd better try the El."

"I'm not waiting for the bus," she said.

He closed the door. Whatever she was waiting for, why the hell didn't she wait someplace else and stop making him nervous!

Avoiding her eyes, he stared sullenly at the eighteen

cents remaining. No matter how he sliced it, it added up to just one more call. He'd like to take a chance on his mother again, but the old man would be expecting another try, the bastard. And it was his fault from the beginning! If he hadn't refused to give him the money for college—and then stuck in McKinley—Jimmy never would've thought about Hawaii, he never would have got the money; he never would have *lost* the money because there wouldn't have been any money to lose! And not only that, if the old man hadn't been so upset about the visit from Joyce, Jimmy's mother wouldn't have to compensate for Father's bad manners by insisting that Jimmy drive Joyce home. And then Jimmy wouldn't have done anything with Joyce, and Lisa wouldn't be with Hollinder, and the car wouldn't be folded up against the goddamn El pillar!

Hell, Jimmy was practically an innocent bystander, but it really didn't make him feel better. He was still tired and still needed a place to sleep. He could stay with Fred, if his friend weren't so pissed off about Denise. Or maybe Suzie, except her father would never allow it. And Denise was out of the question—now that Jimmy had cancelled his time on Saturday afternoons, she probably couldn't even remember his name. And Lisa? Jesus, Lisa. . . .

Weighing everything, Fred was the only possibility. Best friends might squabble about things like girls, but in matters of mortality, they stuck together. Anyway, Fred was the only one with a car.

"Mmm?" answered a barely-alive voice.

"Hello? May I please speak to Fred?"

"Mmmm," stated the voice, and Jimmy heard the phone drop and someone ask who it was and someone say how the hell should I know. Jesus, what if they hung up on him! Jimmy's heart beat exactly thirty-two times before he heard Fred's mumbled " 'lo?"

"Hello, Fred? This is Jimmy."

"Who?"

"Jimmy! I'm sorry about what happened with Denise, but I got in this accident downtown and I need someplace to stay until I get the car fixed up and I was hoping maybe—"

Click.

"Hey, wait a minute! Fred? Fred!" And that was his last dime!

Without warning, the sirens burst in his ears. They were right outside the phone booth! Shoving the girl aside, he got to the corner just as two fire engines surged by. A couple of lousy fire engines!

He turned back to the sound of loud-clicking heels as the girl ran up to him. "So that's why you been makin' all them calls! The police're after you!"

He retreated to the curb. "No! I just thought maybe the whole place was on fire!"

"You stole something," she said flatly.

"I did not!"

"What was it? Money!"

He had to tell her something to keep her quiet. She was making more noise than the fire engines. "Okay," he relented, "I wrecked my father's car."

She stepped off the curb and peered down the street. "Hey," she said with awe, "you really did, didn't you." She looked back at him respectfully. "You didn't kill somebody, did you?"

"No, I only wrecked the car."

She seemed disappointed. "Oh."

"But I was drunk when I did it," he added to raise her spirits.

Suddenly she began to laugh. "You college kids! I know that crowd. What are you, a freshman?"

"Sophomore." The lie came easily.

"Yeah? Where at?"

"Harvard."

"Really? What a coincidence. My family went to Harvard, too."

"Your father?"

"Sure, and my mother, too. They're very educated people. Only we don't get along." She tightened her collar. "I don't live with them now." She nodded toward the street. "I just live around the block. Where you from, anyway. Not around here, I bet."

"I'm from Weston, that's on the north—"

"I know where it is," she broke in. "Pretty sharp neighborhood. Lots of wealth, I mean."

Growing uncomfortable under the weight of her stare, he changed the subject with, "You work nights?"

"What's that supposed to mean!"

She sure got excited easy. "I thought maybe you just got off the night shift in a factory or something."

"A factory!" She patted the rhinestone hair net. "Do I look like factory help?"

Jesus, then she was a whore after all. Remembering that whores must be treated as ladies, he chose his words with care. "I didn't mean to offend you, miss," he said.

She turned an indignant profile to him.

Before the girl went through her whole routine, he'd better make it clear that he was worth a total of eight cents. "And I'm sorry to have to tell you this, but I really don't have very much money," he gently informed her.

"You what?"

"I only have eight cents."

"Who cares?"

"You mean that's enough?"

"Enough for what? What're you talking about?"

A patrol car appeared, gliding to a halt beside the telephone booth. "Please!" Jimmy grabbed her hand. "It's the cops! Pretend you're with me!"

"I will not!"

"You've got to!"

"Hey, what's goin' on there?" asked the cop.

"Nothing, officer," said Jimmy. "We were just taking a walk."

Tearing her hand away from Jimmy, the girl told the cop, "It's all right, Chuck. I knew him in school."

A dumbfounded Jimmy asked meekly, "You know that guy?"

"He happens to be my fiancé," the girl announced from lofty heights. "For who I have been waiting."

"Oh, Jesus, I'm sorry!"

"You should be," she said, and then began to laugh. "But it's okay. I guess you got a lot of problems."

"Sharon, dammit!" said the cop.

"Hold your horses," she told him, and whispered to

Jimmy, "Don't you worry about your father's car. I won't tell my friend, I promise."

"Thanks," said Jimmy.

Bobbing on her alligator heels, the girl went clacking towards the car. Now he'd be alone with eight cents and no place to sleep. If he had one more nickel—but what for? So he could call home? He'd never get through to his mother unless the bastard was eating Fig Newtons or sitting in the john.

Hey, the old man always went to the bathroom when he woke up! Especially if he woke up excited!

Only trouble was, Jimmy'd called a few minutes ago, permitting plenty of time for the john, except that before he went to the john, Father would probably give Mother hell! All the stuff about "He's your goddamn son, Faye!" which would postpone things. And if so, Father should be heading for the john just about now!

"Hey, wait!"

He caught the girl as her hairnet went sparkling into the squad car. "You don't have an extra nickel, do you? For the phone?" It was embarrassing, but it had to be done.

She unsnapped the ducks-and-geese purse to take out green Kleenex and tarnished cosmetic case, then looked sorrowfully at Jimmy.

"Sorry. . . ."

So now he would go begging in the streets for a nickel while his two hundred dollars floated merrily about town and the old man flushed the john.

"Wait a minute," the girl leaned into the car.

Jimmy didn't hear what she told the cop, but after a hushed, sharp exchange, her fiancé reached in his pocket and then the girl was handing Jimmy a nickel.

"I really appreciate this," he said. "And someday I'll pay you back."

She smiled and without moving her lips whispered, "It's Sharon Kline and I'm in the book."

The cop mumbled something about he don't look like no college kid to me, and then the motor started and the girl shouted to Jimmy, "Happy Harvard!"

Jimmy watched the patrol car move into the street

and for one agonizing second he thought it was turning toward the wreckage, but it turned the other way. Yeah, happy Harvard.

Clutching the nickels in his palm, he hurried back to the phone booth where the light seemed even dimmer than before. The cold glow of morning was just beginning to color the sky as he deposited his last chance and began to dial home. But before he could get connected he remembered an old trick. Pressing the coin return, he got his money back and called the operator. Maybe he could save the dime for another call in case he was wrong about the old man's timing.

"Operator," came the standard voice.

"Hello, I've been having some terrible problems with this phone," Jimmy said firmly.

"What seems to be the trouble, sir?"

"I've been dialing 279-1843 and I keep getting the wrong number."

"I'm sorry, sir. I'll try that number for you."

The nickels clinked back into the return cup and, with satisfaction, Jimmy listened to the operator dial. Abruptly, his triumph ended.

"Jimmy goddamn it! Where the hell are you?"

He hung up. It was now clear that Father would sit by the phone until his bladder burst, which made trying to reach Mother hopeless.

Suddenly the shrill sound of the ringing phone filled the booth. Jesus! What if the old man found out where he was! No, that was ridiculous; Jimmy had to keep control of himself. Proving his strength under fire, but disguising his voice just the same, he cautiously lifted the receiver.

"Hello?"

"Hello, sir. You seem to have been disconnected."

"That's all right."

"I'll be glad to try your number again."

"No, no, that won't be necessary," he said quickly. "I'll place the call later."

"Yes, sir." Click.

Anyway, he still had his nickels. What he had to do was parlay them into someplace to stay. Fred was out, the stubborn sonofabitch. And Suzie still had the Judge, although that would never keep her home if Jimmy could produce another juicy story. He'd already used up the one about the disease, but he hadn't told her about Joyce. Hell, all he'd have to do is hint about something concerning an older woman and Suzie'd bounce downtown on a pogo stick if she had to. That was a possibility, all right. Still, something else was nibbling at the outer regions of his confusion.

He let it in, and it was Joyce. Why had he been so stupid, overlooking the obvious! Joyce had a car, Joyce had a whole houseful of room, and Jimmy sure as hell got along with her! And by now she'd had her beauty sleep, but Jesus! What if she wanted to go again? He'd just have to handle her.

"May I have the number of Joyce Fickett? In Weston, please?"

He heard the flipping of pages and the almost-immediate reply, "That number is 279-8009." This operator made up for all the evils of her race.

"Thank you, miss," he said fervently, and hung up to dial "O."

"Hello, operator," said cheated-citizen Reardon, "I've been having one helluva time with this damn phone!"

"I'm sorry, sir. What seems to be the trouble?"

"I keep dialing 279-8009, and I keep getting the wrong number, and that's twice now!" Might as well make something on the deal.

"Thank you, sir. What number are you calling from?"

"456-8754."

"And your address?"

"My address?"

"Yes sir."

"1228 Apolean Way, Weston, Illinois."

"Thank you, sir. Your money will be returned to you by mail within two weeks."

Oh shit, what was she trying to pull! "You mean I'm supposed to stand around here in the cold for two weeks? What the hell kind of an outfit are you running anyway!"

"I'm sorry, sir. I'll try your number now."

"Wait a minute! How do you expect me to get home

at five o'clock in the morning? That damn phone took my bus money!"

"Do you wish me to get your number, sir?" She sounded about to unplug him.

"279-8009," Jimmy said quickly.

R-i-n-g . . . r-i-n-g . . . r-i-n-g. . . . There were seven before he heard the misty groan of Joyce Fickett.

"Hello, Joyce?" breezed the down-on-his-luck, devil-may-care, man-about-town, his tone telling her that nothing really bothered him very much, but he needed her.

"Who'sis," said Joyce, vaguely conscious.

"This is Mr. Reardon!"

"Mr. Reardon," she parroted.

"Mr. Reardon, remember?" He forced something like a casual giggle.

"Al?" she wheezed. "Al, honey, what time is it?"

"Not Al, *Jimmy!* This is Jimmy Reardon!"

"Oh, Jimmy baby, I'm sorry. I thought it was your father."

Your father? His Father? Al! Al Reardon!

"Jimmy?" Her voice was suddenly awake. "Jimmy, are you still there? Jimmy!"

He hung up. His father, his moral, upright, coffee-slurping, status-seeking, putting-in-overtime, hard-day-at-the-office, early-rising, early-bedding, and make-your-own-way-in-life father had been screwing Joyce Fickett! That balding man with responsibility, with three children and a devoted wife and time payments and a secure job—was an extramarital joy-boy! Corrupt and decadent and not even good looking!

All that time, all those years Jimmy thought the old man cared more about work and money than his family, but it wasn't true! The old man cared more about Joyce Fickett! It was a deadly blow to a young man about to go out and face the world with a semblance of dignity, with strong resolution and a faith in the basic goodness of mankind. What dignity, what purpose could Jimmy have now? How could he rise above his meager birthright? How could he break away from the corruption all around him? No wonder he was having so much trouble—his goddamn old man was an adulterer! It was hereditary!

But he mustn't think only of himself at a time like this, after all, there were others involved: his mother, his poor long-suffering mother, who must have endured ten thousand small humiliations at the hands of that bastard. How unfair it was! And his sweet little sister, Rosie, still only a kid but already the old man's influence was apparent on her—the poor, grasping, money-grubbing miser. And his little brother, not even an adolescent yet, a mere boy, hardworking and industrious—what chance would Toby have? What identity could he have with a man like that? They were doomed, all of them, unless someone could cure this leprous growth, unless someone could set right those wrongs, unless. . . .

Calmly he deposited his nickels. There was no longer any need to go through the operator. The phone at home was seized as before.

Jimmy listened carefully. He did not want to miss what might be his old man's last imperial outburst.

"Talk, you little sonofabitch! You talk to me or I'll break your goddamn ass!"

The request was perfectly okay by Jimmy.

"Joyce Fickett, Father," he said.

WITH dawn's classic splendor climbing up behind them, Jimmy and his father stood side by side on the wooden El platform. On a nearby bench sat a colored matron with a shopping bag between her thick legs, and next to her slept an unshaven man with the morning paper folded in his lap. All of them were going home.

Jimmy peered down the tracks for a glimpse of the train, but there was none in sight. He was sober when the cops found the car, and after telling them how he'd been run off the road by this jerk in a white convertible, they let him off with a ticket for negligent driving, which Father had agreed to pay.

Now the old man stared solemnly into the cluttered horizon of tarred rooftops and television antennae. The carcass of his automobile was on its way to the garage, and the sonofabitch from the Chicago Towing company said that in a few expensive days, it would be fixed good as new, almost. And the old man had agreed to pay for that, too.

The name of Joyce Fickett had not been heard from either of them since the old man showed up.

At first Jimmy hadn't known how to feel. He'd been pissed off, that's for sure, but after the initial shock wore off and he began to consider the implications of Father's act, anger gave way to confusion. After all, middle-aged men didn't go around screwing their wives' friends without some kind of reason . . . or did they?

They did in Weston, but how could the old man have gotten so community-oriented in such a short time, when it takes most people years to adapt themselves to environmental changes, especially when their habits are set. Unless, of course, Father had been a lecher for years.

Yet if the old man had a history of being a lecher, would he have become involved with a friend of the family and increased his chances of being found out? Knowing the security risk, an experienced man would have avoided the entanglement.

That left other motives. Like the need for sexual reassurance. It was normal for older men to doubt themselves, and Father might have used Joyce to compensate for some kind of virility anxiety.

Or maybe Father was neglected at home, maybe he just didn't get enough love. Maybe when Father bellowed about soggy hot dogs he was really saying: "Look at me, I'm a human being and I need to be loved!" That meant Father wasn't actually a sonofabitch, just a desperate man in search of affection and concern. When he thought about it, Jimmy hadn't been much of a son, and perhaps Father turned out this way because Jimmy had neglected some of his responsibilities.

All of this had gone through Jimmy's mind, and now, as he stole a glance at the sparse area in the back of the old man's head, he knew he must find a way to help this silent, anxious person who was crying out for understanding and love.

Unexpectedly, Father spoke. "You know, I've been thinking. It might not be such a bad idea, your going to Hawaii."

The sonofabitch! The goddamn lecher wanted to get rid of him! Refusing to answer, Jimmy returned his gaze to the tracks. A train was growing in the distance.

"Even though you didn't show much consideration for your mother with that note you left."

Consideration for Mother! Where does he get the guts!

"You're not a baby anymore. Might be the best thing, getting out on your own like that." The voice was quiet, allowing the approaching rumble to overcome it. "Planning on leaving this morning, weren't you?"

"I was," Jimmy told him, watching the train loom big.

"I might be able to swing a sport coat if you need one."

"Thanks anyway," Jimmy shouted above the din, "but I'm not going. I think I'll stick it out in Weston for a while."

If the old man had said anything more, Jimmy wouldn't have heard. He was listening to the screech as the train roared past, and he was rigid, waiting for the fear to come. But this time it never came.

Then he looked down to see his hand clutching the old man's. He used to hold Father's hand like that when he was a kid and they took the train downtown, when everything was safe. But that was a long time ago, and now, glancing at his father's face, Jimmy found a look there that must have been as silly-surprised as his own.

Their hands broke apart and Jimmy led the way to a seat in the rear of the car. He was about to slide in and take the window seat when he hesitated and allowed the old man to get in first.

Father had a smile on his face as he accepted the gesture, and for some reason it made Jimmy smile too. It was sort of funny when you thought about it: here they were, a couple of father and son attitudes as far apart as they were familiar, poking and prodding at one another, but never touching—and now all at once they were men together. There was another difference too. As father and son attitudes, Father ate out of the big bowl and made all the big noises, but now. . . .

Although they had fallen into the same bed, one of them was just sowing a wild oat, while the other was reaping grounds for divorce, consummating a transgression, sort of, which had to be kept secret, and would be, Jimmy vowed—as long as they got equal-size bowls and were entitled to equal-size noises from now on. Of course they would still play at being attitudes as far as the family was concerned. But as far as father and son were concerned . . . well . . . it seemed that Jimmy and his old man had finally gotten to the same place at the same time.

He felt his father's shoulder against his as the train jostled them together, and it warmed him.